TED TAYLER

TAME THE STORM

BOOKS

By Ted Tayler

The Freeman Files

Red Herring Season
Gathering Clouds
Still Standing

Vinci Books

vinci-books.com

Published by Vinci Books Ltd in 2025

1

Copyright © Ted Tayler 2022

A CIP catalogue record for this book is available from the British Library.
Paperback ISBN: 9781036705039

Chapter One

_____

Monday, 14 December 2015

"QUIET TONIGHT, DAVE," said Emily.

Dave Awdry, the landlord of The Volunteer pub, glanced at the clock at the end of the bar.

"Not long before Christmas, Emily," he replied. "They'll be saving their pennies for the holiday period. You'll be glad of an evening like this by the time we reach the New Year."

Emily Chivers looked around the deserted bar, gauging whether anyone was likely to order another drink before Dave called time. She wasn't looking forward to the walk home. Temperatures had dropped over the past week, and the forecast was for another hard frost. Despite being a fit and healthy twenty-year-old, Emily felt the cold. Her mother reckoned it was a cross the Chivers family had to bear.

"Some people swan around in skimpy outfits no matter the weather," her mother would say. "How they don't catch their death beats me. As soon as the nights draw in, I wear a thick jumper inside the house, and I'm never without my winter coat if I venture outside. You should do the same, sweetheart. You can't be too careful."

Emily shivered despite the extra clothing and the space heater behind the bar.

"Any more for any more?" called Dave, hoping to get upstairs to a warm bed alongside Karen, his wife.

Since Emily turned eighteen, she worked for Dave and Karen at The Volunteer and fitted three weekday evenings into her busy social calendar. That allowed Karen to have Monday and Thursday evenings off. Dave took a break on Wednesday night. So far, the pub they took over in 2010 didn't earn enough money to allow them to have a day off together.

The only reply Dave got to his question was silence. His hand hovered under the bell. Nobody would come through the door this late in the day. He groaned when he heard someone pushing back a chair on the hardwood floor.

Emily had spotted movement in the dark corner of the room and was already pouring a pint of bitter for Clive Palmer in a fresh glass.

Dave Awdry watched as Palmer handed the young barmaid the exact money, thanked her politely, and returned to his chair.

Palmer wasn't popular in the village. Dave could remember when he'd arrived in the village just under a year ago. Since then, nobody could accuse Palmer of being a trouble-maker. He wasn't a heavy drinker nor a violent man. In fact, one of the first things Dave had noticed was how well-spoken he was. But the rumours had gathered pace a month or two later.

Purton was a large village just four miles northwest of Swindon. It was only a matter of time before that major town's urban sprawl consigned Purton to history. Ringsbury, at the southwestern end of the village, was a fortified Iron Age camp before the time of Christ. The Romans had settled here, and villagers unearthed many relics in their gardens over the years.

Thirty years ago, they uncovered a Romano-British cemetery when they upgraded the Grade II-listed Northview Hospital. The first written record of the village was in Saxon times at the end of the eighth century AD, about the King of Mercia's dealings with the Benedictine Abbey at Malmesbury. There was confusion over the various ways of spelling 'the Pear Tree' village, but Purton came out tops and stuck.

No, Dave Awdry thought, things *should* stay as they were. There were undoubtedly arguments and disputes over the centuries, notably during the English Civil War. The cannonballs dug up in the pub car park were proof positive a battle had occurred somewhere close by. But, all said and done, it would have been better if Clive Palmer had chosen somewhere other than this quiet spot of Wiltshire to live.

You can't keep a secret for long, though, not today, and the truth came out in time. Clive Palmer had served an eighteen-month sentence in HMP The Verne, near Portland in Dorset. The prison had closed recently, but it hadn't taken a genius to discover the place housed sex offenders. That was good enough for the majority in the village for Clive to be dubbed Palmer the Paedo from that day forward.

Dave and Karen had never been ones to rush to judgement, and they weren't alone. After all, Rob Dolman had given the man a job at his haulage firm. Several of Dolman's drivers used the pub, and it was only natural for Clive Palmer to mix with them.

Nobody had an issue until the rumours started flying. Clive Palmer had always been polite and friendly, but he increasingly drank alone as word spread throughout the village. However, it didn't appear to bother him.

Take tonight, for instance, Dave thought, as he rang the bell for time. Palmer had arrived at half-past eight and had sat quietly in the corner, sipping one pint after another. In five minutes, he'd leave the bar and walk two hundred yards along the High Street to the field where he parked his caravan.

Clive would be fit for work in the morning and back in The Volunteer at eight o'clock for the weekly Quiz Night. Dave and Karen had insisted on teams of four when they first introduced the idea, but with dwindling numbers, they had to allow a little latitude these days. So Clive Palmer entered on his own, and Karen checked his answers as nobody at the other tables was willing.

Karen pointed out anomalies with his answer sheet the first time this happened. But Dave never asked Clive why he crossed out several correct answers or left gaps. Things were hard enough for the bloke. It would have been even worse if Clive had won first prize every Tuesday night.

Clive Palmer never mentioned his life before he'd gone to prison, and nobody asked about the circumstances. Someone in the village had learned Palmer's offence involved a fifteen-year-old girl from Wandsworth. There was an ex-wife somewhere in a nearby London borough and two children. Palmer would have been in his early forties when the attack took place if, indeed, it was an attack. The gossip-mongers weren't interested in the finer points of the case.

Palmer was a paedophile, plain and simple. He was on the Sex Offender's Register, and the police knew where he lived. This was just as well because in the seven months since the truth surfaced, there had been several incidents where uniformed officers had needed to get involved.

After a quiet night in the pub, Palmer had returned home to find someone had smeared excrement over the windows of his caravan. The police blamed youngsters who couldn't spell the word they'd heard their parents mention in conversation.

In October, a thirteen-year-old girl claimed she was followed while walking home from the youth centre. Her parents at once pointed the finger at Clive Palmer and reported the incident to the police. When interviewed, he said he was in The Volunteer that Tuesday night. Twenty people could give him an alibi.

Dave and Karen had told the Police Community Support Officer who came to check that Palmer was in the bar from eight o'clock until closing that night. The officer said nobody else would confirm Palmer wasn't in the pub but merely said they didn't remember seeing him. Karen had fished the scoresheets out of the wastepaper basket in the office and showed the PCSO the quiz sheet she had checked.

"Who else do you think that could be?" Karen had asked. "Nobody talks to him except to make a snide remark. Is there another 'Clive P' in the village? I check his answers every week because no one else will. I'll swear on a stack of bibles he was sitting in the corner on Tuesday night, no matter what the others might like you to believe."

The dust settled within a few days, and things returned to what had become the norm. Most of the villagers shunned Clive and verbally abused him at every opportunity. Yet, Rob Dolman continued to employ him.

"Why not?" Dolman had told Dave Awdry when he

dropped in for a pint after work one evening. "Clive is reliable and hard-working, and I've never received a single complaint from a client. Quite the opposite. Several have called me to say they wished my other drivers were as helpful and polite. Perhaps it helps that most of my business is with customers in neighbouring counties, or on the far side of Wiltshire, towards Salisbury, but I haven't got a reason to sack him. If I did, Clive would have me in court for unfair dismissal, and I couldn't argue."

"Goodnight all,"

Dave heard the comment as he emptied clean pint pots from the glass washer. He glanced over his shoulder to see Clive Palmer making his way towards the door.

Emily waited until the inner door had closed and then went to lock and bolt the main entrance.

"You can get off home now, Emily," said Dave. "I'll put away these last few glasses."

"I'll give Clive a minute to get clear," she replied. "Did you hear the latest?"

"Karen and I don't listen to gossip," said Dave.

"I heard a whisper from one mother on our street last week. She was watching her daughters on the climbing frames in the playground off Church Street that afternoon. Since they learned about Clive Palmer's past, most mums go with their little ones. If they can't get there themselves, they ask a friend to keep an eye out."

"Was Clive Palmer not working that afternoon?" asked Dave. "That seems odd. What happened?"

"One of the younger children, five years old, ran across to her mother. She was chatting with her friends and had lost sight of her daughter. First, she thought the little girl had just tripped and fallen, grazing her knees, but the girl told her she was frightened. A man had picked her up and brushed the dirt from her legs when she slipped and fell."

"That could be innocent enough," said Dave. "The sort of thing any caring father might do, but you risk getting accused of all sorts these days. So it's best to leave any care and attention to the parents. Even if they're not keeping a close eye on what's happening."

"I suppose so," said Emily. "Clive would have been working though, wouldn't he? And the playground is at the opposite end of the village from where he works and lives. So if he *was* there, there could only have been one reason."

"Stop that, Emily," said Dave. "Don't add more fuel to the rumour mill."

"I've heard they're going to force Palmer to leave the village," said Emily. "He's attacked a young girl once. That sort never changes. I'm praying that I'm too old for him. I've got mace in my handbag if anyone tries their luck."

"If circumstances were different, I'd give you a lift home, Emily," said Dave.

"When do you get your licence back?" asked Emily.

"Eight months, three weeks and a day," said Dave. "Karen will kill me if I get done for speeding again."

"I'll be okay," said Emily, adding more layers before venturing outside. "Tell Karen I'll see her on Wednesday night."

Dave followed Emily through the bar and watched as she crossed the road to start her ten-minute walk home. The streets were empty. Anyone with any sense was indoors on a frosty night such as this. Dave locked and bolted the door and switched off the ground-floor lights.

As he climbed the stairs to their accommodation, he wondered whether Karen would still be awake. When he heard her gentle snoring as he closed the flat door behind him, he consoled himself with the thought that their bed would be warmer than the one Clive Palmer was getting into.

Tuesday, 15 December 2015

"MORNING, BOSS," said Ken Webb. "A fresh start, isn't it? So where am I off to today?"

Rob Dolman stood beside the radiator in his office and blew on his hands.

"Peter Wright beat you in this morning, Ken. He got first dibs. I've sent him to collect goods from that injection moulding firm near Chilcompton. Then, after he's dropped off in Swindon, he can fit in a couple of jobs in town. I've marked them on the board."

"You know how much I enjoy making that trip, boss," said Ken. "Ah well, it serves me right. It was tough getting out of a warm bed today. So what's next on the schedule?"

"Cheney Manor, Europa, Callenders, or Clearwater. Take your pick from those industrial estates. The sooner you get on the road, the better."

"Cheney Manor is closest," said Ken, checking the details on the board behind Rob's desk. "I can cover that and Callenders by the end of the day and get the gear where it needs to go. My hours aren't near the limit, but I can't manage any other journeys on this board. So Palmer will have to handle those. No sign of your man yet this morning?"

"No," said Rob Dolman, looking at the office clock. "It's not like him to be late, and he's not taken a sick day since he started working here."

"Maybe he's done a runner, boss," said Ken Webb. "I heard he was seen touching up a five-year-old in the playground last week. Several of the younger fathers are planning a late-night visit to his caravan. Not a baying mob with baseball bats and Molotov cocktails, but scary enough to force Palmer to leave the village."

"I heard the gossip, Ken, but there was no way Clive Palmer was involved. He didn't return to the depot until five to five that afternoon. He left Dorset Autospares in Downton at half-past three. You couldn't make that fifty-mile trip any quicker. So no way was he in that playground off Church Street between three and half-past."

"Did you check on him then, boss?" asked Ken.

"Not a bit of it," said Rob. "That was where he made a delivery, all signed for, no problems reported from Downton. I trust him."

"Why do you stick up for him, boss? He served time for underage sex. Nobody wants him in the village."

"I've run this haulage firm since my late twenties," said Dolman. "After I left school with no qualifications, I flitted from job to job and never settled on anything. There were times when I could have taken the wrong path, like my brother-in-law, Andy Redman."

"Andy's your brother-in-law? I never realised."

"Andy's been in and out of trouble since he was ten. Why my sister, Pat, thought she could persuade him to stay on the straight and narrow beats me. Every time he comes out of prison, he struggles to find someone to give him a break. It's a vicious circle. Andy tries to make a go of it. Either he's on the dole for weeks, and one of his cronies offers him the chance of easy money. Or business drops off at the firm that took him on, and he's first out because of his record."

"Why didn't you offer Andy a job, boss?" asked Ken.

"Pat wouldn't hear of it," said Rob. "She realises Andy's a hopeless case. She doesn't want this firm's reputation tainted."

"So why was Palmer different?"

"I don't know, Ken," said Rob. "When I interviewed him, he had a clean licence, spoke well, and was keen as mustard. Clive admitted he'd spent time in Portland but swore that nothing similar would ever happen again. So I gave him a break."

"Even when the rest of the village learned the truth?"

"The truth can be a funny thing, Ken," said Rob Dolman. "You get a different version of it with every newspaper you read or TV news channel you watch. Each paints a version of the truth that suits their purpose. Clive Palmer didn't go into details, so I don't know exactly what got him into trouble with the law, but I've had no complaints since he's been here. He's still got a clean licence. He's always polite and cooperative to customers, and his time-keeping has been exemplary until this morning. I was struggling with new paperwork from HMRC last week. Clive stayed behind for thirty minutes to help me make sense of it. He's a clever bloke, you know. I had been thinking of advertising for a logistics manager to take the pressure off me. My wife would appreciate me getting home earlier in the evening. Clive could handle that role; he's developed a good understanding of the haulage business despite only working here for ten months."

"I'd better get moving," said Ken. "How will you cover these other trips if Palmer's done a midnight flit? Peter Wright can't do them."

"Don't worry about that, Ken," said Rob. "You just

finish the items on your sheet. I'll walk over to the High Street and see where he's got to."

"Okay, boss. With luck, the heater won't pack up in the van today. See you later."

Rob Dolman took another look at the clock.

No doubt the client at Cheney Manor would be on the phone in a few minutes, wondering when the van would arrive. Ah well. They'd have to wait for Ken to get a move on. There wouldn't be anyone staffing the office for the next twenty minutes.

Rob donned his coat, scarf, and gloves and headed out of the Portakabin. A brisk walk to the High Street lay ahead. Although he'd never visited Clive Palmer's caravan, he knew his employee had persuaded a local farmer to let him park on waste ground behind a long, prefabricated storage building. So the caravan was hidden from view from the street. But, of course, that hadn't stopped those tearaways from finding it and daubing it with muck. But out of sight, out of mind. Clive hadn't mentioned any further cause for a sleepless night since.

There were no signs of life when Rob reached the end of the long barn and spotted the caravan under the trees. He'd already called Clive on his mobile before leaving the office. But, unfortunately, it had gone straight to voicemail. Rob tried once more as he stepped warily across the frozen ground.

The farmer had scattered several hundred cobblestones along the first thirty yards to give his vehicles extra grip when heavy rain turned the grassy stretch into brown sludge. Each stone was slippery enough to bring a man down or twist an ankle in this frosty weather.

Rob finally made it to a safe gravelled surface by the caravan. He could hear Clive's mobile ringing inside. A loud knock on the door didn't get a response. Rob tried the door, but it was locked. He tried to peer inside, but the glass was covered in frost, and the curtains were drawn.

"Something the matter, Mr Dolman?"

"Morning, Mr Oatley," said Rob, recognising the farmer who owned the land. "Clive Palmer hasn't turned up for work. I can hear his mobile phone. It's unlike him to let me down."

"He's not well-liked," said John Oatley. "I'm not sure I made the right decision letting him park his van here, but he pays his rent on the dot every month. I must wait ninety days for my other customers to pay what they owe. Should we call the police, do you think?"

Rob Dolman shivered, and it wasn't the frosty morning that caused it.

"Many people wanted Clive gone from the village," he said.

"Best call them to be on the safe side," said John Oatley.

Rob took one last look towards the caravan and dialled 999.

Chapter Two

THE EMERGENCY CALL came through to the detective squad room at Gablecross at eight thirty-eight. DS Jake Latimer had just arrived in the office.

A little over six months ago, Jack Sanders had been the Senior Investigating Officer on a case involving the murder of one of Swindon's prolific criminals, Grant Burnside. A sniper shot the gang leader at the Cheney Manor Industrial Estate, and despite their best efforts, they hadn't located the killer.

Jake had worked on the initial phases of the investigation and was still adding titbits to their stack of evidence and witness statements. It was boring, but it paid the bills. Jack Sanders was scheduled for retirement before the murder case and was now on garden leave. Theo Hickerton, Jake's old boss, had blotted his copybook on an earlier case and was licking his wounds in the Traffic Section, which left Jake like a ship without a rudder.

Life would have been dull if it hadn't been for Janina,

the Lithuanian girl he'd met at a massage parlour during his duties. Jake answered the phone.

"DS Latimer. How may I be of assistance?"

"Good morning. My name's Rob Dolman, and I am from Purton. One of my employees didn't turn up for work at eight this morning. I'm stood outside his caravan with his landlord, John Oatley, just off the High Street. We're concerned he may have come to harm."

"What is your employee's name, Mr Dolman?" asked Jake.

"Clive Palmer," replied Rob.

Alarm bells rang in Jake's head.

"I'll get someone to you in thirty minutes, Rob. Don't touch a thing."

Jake ended the call and looked across the squad room.

"Mark. What have you and your gaffer got on today?"

"Nothing that won't wait, Jake," came the reply. "What have you got for us?"

"You won't know until you get to Purton High Street," said Jake. "A guy called Clive Palmer is inside his caravan, condition unknown."

"Palmer? He's on the list, isn't he?" said Mark. "Things have been quiet out there for a while. I hoped they would stay that way. Leave it with us. We'll drive out to Purton and check."

Jake Latimer watched Mark Harvey head for DI Ben Moore's desk, and then he returned to his filing. It was warmer here than in a field in the countryside, ten miles away. Batman and Robin were welcome to it.

"Remind me again, Mark," said Ben Moore when they reached the car park. He jumped into the passenger seat of his sergeant's Ford Kuga. "Why does the name Clive Palmer sound familiar?"

"He's a registered sex offender, guv," said Mark. "Palmer served eighteen months in Portland, and instead of returning to his home in London, he picked Purton's name out of a hat. It's fair to say the locals haven't accepted him as one of their own. There have been a couple of minor incidents where uniforms needed to get involved. But, despite accusations he was up to his old tricks, they proved to be unfounded. Until today, Palmer appears to have been a good boy, holding down a job with Dolman's, the haulage people. You must have seen their vans in town."

"British racing green, with gold lettering?" said Ben Moore. "Yes, they're a familiar sight. Put your foot down, Mark. Have you found the heater on this beast yet? My feet are freezing."

John Oatley had suggested to Rob Dolman they shouldn't stand on the frozen ground for another thirty minutes, waiting for the police to arrive. John was in his late sixties, and although farmers were used to being outside in all winds and weathers, discretion can be the better part of valour.

The pair had moved inside a smaller building opposite the long barn to watch for activity inside the caravan and spot the new arrivals.

"Do you ever take a walk across here late at night, John?" asked Rob.

"I'm in bed by ten," replied John, "and usually awake before the alarm at five. I paid a late-night visit twice after the police got called out, but the kids never returned. We've had security lighting and cameras installed on the sensitive areas of the farm for several years. I've never considered putting anything in this corner of the property. There's nothing worth stealing."

"So someone could have been lying in wait for Palmer when he arrived home from The Volunteer."

"Is that where he drinks?" asked John. "Would he be an enthusiastic drinker? Perhaps he's still unconscious from a heavy night. We should tell the police to check with Dave Awdry."

At a quarter past nine, they heard the crackle of tyres on cobblestones and frozen earth and walked outside. The farmer and the haulage firm owner walked to greet the men getting out of the Ford Kuga.

"You must be the detectives we're expecting," said Rob.

"Yes, sir. DI Ben Moore from Gablecross," said Ben. "My colleague is DS Mark Harvey. Which of you gentlemen called us?"

"That was me, Rob Dolman. John Oatley here owns the farm. Clive Palmer has parked his caravan under the trees for the past ten months. Clive didn't turn up for work at eight, so I walked across from the depot to check he was okay."

"Any reason to assume he wouldn't be okay?" asked Mark Harvey.

"You know the history," said Rob. "Plenty of people in the village wanted him to move on. But, so far, nobody has gone further than name-calling and muck-spreading."

"Wait here, and we'll look," said Ben Moore. "Mark, have you got any kit in your boot?"

"Yes, guv," Mark replied.

"A large screwdriver will be enough to snap the lock on that door," said John Oatley. "I can get one from the barn behind me if you have got nothing."

"Thank you, Mr Oatley," said Mark. "I'll get the kit and gloves on, guv, just in case, and try to get inside without damaging any fingerprints on the door handle."

Mark Harvey delved into the boot of his car, dressed in blue protective clothing, donned his gloves, and accepted a screwdriver and hammer from the farmer. Rob Dolman watched as the two detectives approached the caravan.

"Rather them than me," said John Oatley. "Even if Palmer just fell and hit his head when he got home drunk last night."

Mark Harvey worked the flathead screwdriver under the top left-hand edge of the caravan door. He didn't need the hammer; he could slide the screwdriver between the door and the doorframe towards the handle and apply pressure to the lock. It popped immediately, and Mark swung the door open and stepped inside.

"You'd better call for the full team, guv," he called to Ben Moore. "It's a bloody mess."

"Did you bring a second set of clothes, Mark?" called Ben.

"I always carry a spare, guv," said Mark. "The over-shoes might be a tight fit, but you don't want to come here as you are."

Ben Moore called Gablecross HQ, and a police surgeon, forensic team, and six uniformed officers were soon racing towards Purton.

John Oatley and Rob Dolman looked at one another.

Ben Moore got dressed and joined his colleague inside the caravan.

Clive Palmer's body lay face-down on the floor in a large pool of blood. Someone had stabbed him at least six times in the neck, upper arms and back.

"I don't detect any signs of a break-in, guv," said Mark. "Nothing appears to have been disturbed. No signs of a struggle, either."

"I agree," said Ben. "So, what are we thinking? Palmer

got home, opened up, stepped inside, and a vigilante emerged from the shadows beside the van, attacking him without giving him a chance to defend himself?"

"There's no sign of significant blunt-force trauma to the back of the head, guv. The attacker could have stabbed Palmer, yes, but he should have offered resistance before succumbing to blood loss. No, it would make more sense that Palmer knew his attacker and invited them inside. That doesn't make much sense, knowing what we know about Palmer. The man had few friends in the village or people prepared to talk to him. Two of them are standing outside. Also, we need to check where Palmer was last night. Oh, I don't reckon the door was locked, guv. It was just stuck."

"Okay, I'll talk to Oatley and Dolman," said Ben. "We'll close the caravan door for now to preserve the scene. Watch your feet when you move back, and try to avoid the blood. Reverse your car into the entrance to the yard to stop anyone entering until the cavalry arrives. I'll check with Oatley to learn whether anyone will come this way from beyond these peripheral farm buildings. Then we'll start making a list of everyone who had a grievance against Palmer."

Mark Harvey carefully stepped away from Clive Palmer's body and brandished his notebook and pen.

Ben Moore shook his head.

"Don't say it, Mark. You're going to need a bigger notebook."

"I suppose we should be thankful Purton only has a population of four thousand, guv."

The detectives returned outside, and while Ben Moore closed the caravan door, Mark Harvey crossed the yard to his car.

"He's dead then?" asked Rob Dolman.

"I'm afraid so, sir," said Ben. "I've sent for a crime team to attend the scene. It appears Clive Palmer has been murdered."

"I must get back to the office," said Rob. "Customers will be expecting one of our vans for a collection or a delivery. I'm a driver short. So, I'll have to do it myself and advertise for a replacement. What a mess."

You haven't been inside the caravan, thought Ben Moore.

"I need the two of you to stay here for a while longer, I'm afraid," he said. "Our colleagues will arrive in twenty minutes, so while we're waiting, tell me your whereabouts yesterday evening. Standard procedure, for elimination purposes, you understand."

"Mr Dolman tells me Palmer used The Volunteer pub, two hundred yards up the road," said John Oatley. "He could have gotten back here after eleven if he had been there last night. I was in bed by ten and didn't stir until ten to five. Then, after I'd showered, eaten breakfast, and put on my overcoat and wellington boots, I went outside and checked my two farmhands hadn't taken a duvet day. As I returned to the farmhouse, I spotted Mr Dolman standing ten yards from the caravan using his mobile phone."

"What about before ten last night?" asked Ben. "Can anyone confirm where you were?"

"I lost my wife ten years ago," said John Oatley, "Breast cancer. I finished work at around six, made a meal, and watched television for two hours before bed. Never saw a soul after five in the afternoon until I spoke to Mr Dolman."

"Can I ask where you were last night, Mr Dolman?"

"At home, with my wife and children," said Rob. "I left the office at six and didn't step outside the door until a quarter to eight this morning when I walked to the depot.

We live a few hundred yards from the yard. It has its advantages, although the wife would disagree. After I sent my other two drivers out, I walked over to see what had happened to Clive. I was calling Clive when Mr Oatley spotted me. I can show you my phone if you wish to check."

"That won't be necessary, sir," said Ben. "Mr Palmer's mobile phone is inside the caravan. So we can check the log for missed calls. Perhaps that phone will help us find who came here late last night and murdered him."

Mark Harvey had returned from his car.

"Anything you want me to do, guv?" he asked.

"What time does the pub open?" asked Ben Moore.

"No idea, guv. Half-past ten or eleven, I guess."

"Dave Awdry lives over the shop," said Rob Dolman. "Dave or his wife Karen will be on the premises, I'm sure."

"Right, get yourself over to The Volunteer then, Mark. Check whether Palmer was in there last night. Was he with anyone? Did he leave alone? Think on your feet and get as much background as possible. Try to get the names of staff and customers from last night too. Was there an argument or altercation?"

"Got it, guv," said Mark. He trotted off towards the entrance.

"Hang on," shouted Ben Moore. "Give me your keys, or I won't be able to let the others into the yard."

Mark Harvey stopped and trotted back.

"DS Harvey," called John Oatley. "Can I have my tools back, please?"

"Sorry, sir," said Mark. "I dropped them in the car's boot along with my soiled protective clothing. I can get them cleaned and return them later if that's agreeable?"

"It will have to be," said John. "Do you still need me, DI Moore? Just like Mr Dolman here, I have a business to run.

"Will you or either of your people need to drive through this yard today? The forensic team will need to work here for the rest of the day, at least."

"I'll have a word," said John. "We'll use the other exits for the foreseeable future. I'm sure you'll give me the all-clear."

"Certainly, sir," said Ben. "We've got both of your details, and given the circumstances, you two are the least likely people to want Clive Palmer dead. Sorry for the inconvenience, Mr Dolman, but can you use another exit to get back to your depot?"

"I can give him a lift in the Land Rover," said John Oatley. "It's only a five-minute walk from here."

"Thanks," said Rob Dolman. He checked his phone. Thirteen missed calls. Unlucky for some.

DI Ben Moore was alone in the yard as the farmer and the haulier disappeared behind the farm buildings. Ben thought he could hear the approaching sirens of the forensic crew and his reinforcements.

Meanwhile, Mark Harvey stood at the back door of The Volunteer. He'd searched high and low for a bell at the front with no luck. He rang the bell for a second time. A buxom blonde woman opened the door. She didn't look pleased to see him.

"Keep your hair on. We don't open until eleven, and you don't look like a drinks rep. So where's the fire?"

"Detective Sergeant Harvey, from Gablecross Police Station. I need to speak to the landlord."

"Our licences are up-to-date, and we've not had any trouble. So why on earth do you want to interview my husband? Dave! Have you been driving while disqualified, you idiot?"

Mark winced as his ears took a battering. He wondered

how much damage her husband's ears had suffered over the years. A harassed-looking man peered over the shoulder of his wife.

"Come in," said Dave Awdry. "I'm finishing the bottling-up and getting ready to open. We can talk in the main bar. We've got coffee brewing. Fancy a cuppa?"

"I won't say no," said Mark Harvey. "Something hot and strong will be most welcome."

"I won't ask if you want a tot of something extra to help warm you," said Dave. "This isn't a courtesy call. So how can we help?"

Karen Awdry had followed the two men through to the bar and started preparing three mugs of coffee.

"Milk and sugar?" she asked.

"Just milk, thanks," said Mark. "Your husband has done nothing he shouldn't have as far as we know, Mrs Awdry. It's one of your customers we're interested in."

"That can only be one person," said Dave. "Is this a follow-up to the rumour about the incident at the playground?"

"I'm unaware of any incident reported at Gablecross in the past month. However, I read the last report concerning a teenage girl who thought someone had followed her home from the youth centre. Unfortunately, we still haven't identi-fied the person responsible."

"We're talking about Clive Palmer, though, aren't we?" asked Karen.

"I told Karen this morning that Emily Chivers, our barmaid, heard a man at the playground had frightened a little girl," said Dave Awdry. "He comforted her after a fall from the climbing frame in the playground. She'd grazed her knees. Clive works for Rob Dolman and doesn't finish until half past five. So he couldn't have been in the village around three o'clock that afternoon. The child's mother had collected her from school and taken her to the playground for a go on the swings before returning home."

"Did you see Clive Palmer last night?" asked Mark.

"Yes, Clive was in the bar," said Dave. "He got here at half-past eight. He sat in the corner after I served him his first beer.

"I wasn't working last night," said Karen, handing Mark a mug of steaming hot coffee. "I was upstairs in our apartment watching TV, but that's Clive's corner. He sits with his back to the door, hoping nobody will bother him."

"Do your customers bother him?" asked Mark.

"It depends on what you mean," said Dave. "I wouldn't stand for anyone doing or saying anything extreme. The people who use this pub know Clive drinks here. If they want to avoid him because of how they perceive his character, then other places in the village are open. Whether any remarks that get passed in his hearing bother him, well, I have my doubts. Clive broke the law, served his sentence, paid his debt to society as they say, and now he's trying to make a fresh start here."

"You were happy to have Clive Palmer drink here from the outset, were you?" asked Mark.

"In this trade, you learn to size up a new face when they come through the door. Karen's the same. We can spot a trouble-maker in seconds. When Clive first ordered a drink here, we didn't know who he was or where he came from. He spoke well, was polite, and was a decent bloke as far as we could tell."

"When the truth came out, it didn't make you sorry you'd welcomed Palmer with open arms?"

"Woah, hang on," said Karen. "Clive's a good customer, and we can't afford to turn custom away. We treat our customers alike. Nobody gets preferential treatment, and we speak as we find. He's never given us cause to regret our decision."

"Agreed," said Dave. "Several people who used to be regulars in The Volunteer have moved on since they discovered Clive spent time in prison. That was their prerogative, but they went down in our estimation after the crude comments they made in here. We were happy to see the back of them. Most of those people took the story they heard from Tom Angell at face value. If that had been the whole truth, I can't see Rob Dolman giving Clive a job in the first place. As for John Oatley, he didn't tell him to sling his hook once the rumours surfaced. Even after Tom made sure everyone in the village knew the story he'd heard, John still let Clive keep his caravan on his land."

Mark made a note of Tom Angell's name. He was worth a follow-up.

"You mentioned a barmaid," said Mark. "Will she be in later?"

"Emily doesn't work Tuesdays," said Karen. "It's our Quiz Night, so Dave and I run things together. She'll be in tomorrow lunchtime."

"Wednesday is my day off," explained Dave.

"I assume Clive Palmer wasn't your only customer last night," said Mark. "Could you tell me who was here?

"It was quiet last night," said Dave. "If you gave me thirty minutes, I could come up with a rough list of names. Emily could put a surname to several I don't know so well."

"You could check through last night's till roll, Dave," suggested Karen. "Most customers stick to the same drinks, and couples often order the same round. The men might drink pints of lager, but one wife will be on vodka and the other on gin. So you're only searching for two dozen names, if that, aren't you?"

"We were quiet," said Dave.

"Look, why do you need this detail?" asked Karen. "What's this about?"

"Did you hear any sirens when you answered the door to me earlier, Mrs Awdry?" asked Mark.

Karen shrugged her shoulders.

"The sound of sirens has become so familiar I ignore it."

"Rob Dolman called us this morning because Clive Palmer was late for work," said Mark. "Did anyone pick an argument with Palmer last night while he was in the pub?"

"No," said Dave. "Clive was the last to leave. That's not unusual. He gives everyone else time to clear off before heading home himself. I didn't hear raised voices outside after he left. Emily locked the main door behind him, so I'm sure she would have said if she'd seen or heard anything. I let her out maybe ten minutes later, and everything was quiet on the High Street."

"Did someone have a go at Clive last night?" asked Karen. "Was it those kids again?"

"I'm afraid it's gone way beyond name-calling and spreading excrement, Mrs Awdry. My boss and I responded to Rob Dolman's urgent phone message. We found Clive Palmer's body inside the caravan. The police surgeon will be with him now. My guess is Palmer died within an hour or two of leaving your pub."

"Oh, the poor man," said Karen. "Are you sure it wasn't an accident or natural causes?"

"Clive was too level-headed to take his own life," said Dave, "no matter how much name-calling he had to stand. Emily told me last night that the young fathers on her estate intended to force Clive to leave the village. Perhaps they scared him so much that he had a heart attack."

DS Mark Harvey shook his head.

"More than one person may have been there last night," he said. "But the inside of the caravan didn't suggest more than one person attacked Palmer. Who knew him well enough to get invited inside at that late hour?"

"Rob Dolman and John Oatley were the only two people to give Clive the time of day, apart from us," said Karen. "Although Clive didn't drink with us every night of the week. He wasn't welcome in the other pubs. I suppose he could have gone into Swindon or further afield."

"When he first moved to Purton and started driving for Dolman, he used to meet the other drivers here," said Dave. "Peter Wright and Ken Webb have been with Rob Dolman for years. They were among the first to switch their allegiance after Tom Angell's tongue started wagging."

"We're forgetting where Clive might have had more chance of making friends," said Karen. "Rob Dolman sends his vans across Wiltshire and the neighbouring counties."

"The opposite is also true, love," said Dave. "There's a Tom Angell in every town and village. Clive could have met people with connections to Wandsworth, where the offence occurred. People who thought an eighteen-month sentence was insufficient."

DS Mark Harvey noted the potential points he and Ben Moore needed to investigate. He was right about the size of the problem.

Dave and Karen Awdry were convinced Clive Palmer was a decent bloke who had made one mistake. But Mark had lost count of the number of burglars, car thieves, and shoplifters he'd nicked in Swindon as a uniformed officer in his youth. When he asked his sergeant why most of them had addresses in Oxford, Newbury, Chippenham, and Cirencester, he'd replied:

"You don't dirty your own doorstep, lad, now do you?"

Perhaps Clive Palmer hadn't turned over a new leaf.

Had he attacked another young girl on his travels, and someone traced him to Purton and a field off the High Street? How far did they need to spread the net to catch the potential suspects?

Meanwhile, DI Ben Moore was supervising matters at the crime scene. The uniformed officers had secured the yard's perimeter and the farm buildings. Two Scenes of Crime Officers concentrated on the outside of the caravan and the grounds nearby, collecting evidence.

Ben Moore looked for a familiar face. But, instead, he soon learned that the police surgeon he was used to seeing arrive at a crime scene was in court, and a local GP, Eve Northwood, answered the call for a substitute.

Eve was a no-nonsense woman of few words. She had arrived ten minutes after the uniforms and forensics team in her buttercup yellow Mini Cooper. Eve was suited and booted, ready to enter the caravan. After a brief conversation with Ben to acquaint herself with the known facts of the case, Eve stepped inside.

Ben had heard from his colleague, Gareth Francis, that Eve recorded every step of her initial examination of a crime scene for posterity. She set up her gear on the worktop next to the kitchen sink and approached the body. Ben stood just inside the van door and kept quiet. Eve didn't appreciate idle conversation interrupting her dulcet tones.

Eve's first comment was that she entered the caravan on Tuesday the fifteenth at nine fifty-five. The outside temperature was one-degree centigrade. There was a heater in the corner of the living space, but not switched on.

The deceased lay, fully clothed, in the centre of the van floor. He appeared to be male, between forty and fifty years of age.

The estimated time of death was between eight to twelve hours earlier. She would achieve a more accurate time at autopsy. The preliminary time for that detailed examination would be nine o'clock on Wednesday the sixteenth. That would be subject to rescheduling prior appointments with patients from her GP practice.

The body had been identified one hour earlier by DI Ben Moore after conversations with the victim's landlord and employer.

Clive Palmer had received six stab wounds from the same weapon with a four-inch blade. The first two wounds to the left upper arm were superficial. However, the victim's left carotid artery had ruptured with the third stab wound to the neck. The rapid and massive blood loss which followed proved fatal. The three wounds to the upper torso and lower back were excessive, further evidence this was a brutal attack carried out by a right-handed assailant.

Eve Northwood paused the recording and turned to Ben Moore.

"Can you ask one of the SOCOs to help me turn the body over, please? I want to check for additional wounds. Given the damage to the neck, I'm not surprised at the blood volume, but the van's floor cants towards the front. So I'd expect the blood pool to be greater beyond the victim's body. There appears to be a secondary contributor."

Ben looked outside the van; everyone looked the same in their white suits, boots, and gloves. He called to the nearest person.

Eve Northwood asked the SOCO to identify themselves when they joined her inside for the record.

"Louise Arlett, a junior technician with Gablecross Crime Scene Investigation."

Eve moved to Clive Palmer's shoulders, and Louise tentatively grabbed his ankles.

"Steady," said Eve. "Let's roll him onto his back in three, two, one."

Ben Moore swallowed hard.

Louise Arlett dashed outside, and Eve tutted when she heard the young girl being sick.

"Right, that explains the extra blood situation. The victim's genitals have been removed from his body. The mutilation occurred after the initial attack while the victim was still bleeding out."

Ben left Eve Northwood to complete her initial findings and went outside. Fresh air was in short supply inside the caravan. Ben needed to rid himself of the stench of death and the sight he had witnessed. There didn't appear to be much doubt about the motive for the attack.

Clive Palmer's past had caught up with him in a gruesome way.

Ben spotted Louise Arlett standing on the opposite side of the yard. He walked across to console her.

"I take it today is your first murder scene, Louise? I wouldn't have asked you if I'd known.."

"Yes, I've only been on the job for two months," replied Louise. "I've seen a dead body before and thought I'd be okay, just turning him over. However, nobody warned me who he was. My colleague over there has filled in the details since I came outside. I just hope I haven't obliterated a vital piece of evidence."

"It looked like a vigilante attack as soon as we entered the caravan," said Ben. "We only saw the stab wounds to his back, of course. We can only hope the attacker left evidence behind that allows us to bring him to justice. So far, I have seen no sign of the murder weapon."

"I'd better get back to what I was doing before you called me," said Louise. "We may find it outside."

Ben watched the young girl as she crossed the yard to rejoin her white-suited colleague.

He could only see Louise's piercing blue eyes, but the five-foot-five-inch junior technician had spiked Ben's interest.

"How's it going, boss?"

Mark Harvey was back from The Volunteer.

"Finished at the pub already, Mark?" asked Ben.

"I've got two more calls to make, guv, but although Dave Awdry gave me addresses and rough directions, I thought it safer to use the car's satnav. Is it okay for me to take my car?"

"I suppose so. Here are your keys," said Ben. "Don't kid a kidder. You want to avoid walking around the village in the cold. What did you learn so far?"

Mark referred to his notes and took Ben through his conversation with Dave and Karen Awdry.

"So Palmer was in the bar during the evening, didn't speak to anyone, and there were no altercations," said Ben. "However it played out, things didn't start until he reached the van. Someone jumped Palmer, stabbed him, and chopped off his bits as he died."

"Gross," said Mark with a shudder. "I wonder why they left him lying face down?"

"Good point, Mark," said Ben. "The police surgeon showed Palmer wouldn't have lasted long because of the ruptured artery. However, we do not know whether he was on his back or front after the initial attack. Either way, the killer mutilated the body and went to the trouble of turning him over."

"Perhaps they couldn't stand seeing what they'd done," said Mark.

"When we have time to search Clive Palmer's clothing and the caravan, we need to assess whether anything's missing. His mobile phone's still inside, but perhaps the initial motive was a robbery. So, maybe, the attacker was already inside the van when Clive got home, and matters escalated. The van wasn't locked this morning, was it?"

"No, just stuck. Robbery's a stretch, guv," said Mark. "Although, it explains our earlier query about who Palmer knew well enough to invite inside late at night. But surely, a robber wouldn't mutilate the body?"

"Not unless they hoped to confuse us," said Ben. "Eve Northwood stated there was a gap between the attacks. So his killer could have done the extra cutting to lead us in the wrong direction."

"I'd better get on with the next two names on my list. Emily Chivers, the barmaid, and Tom Angell, local builder and loudmouth."

"What were those other names you mentioned again?" asked Ben. "The drivers somewhere on the road in the county working for Rob Dolman."

"Ken Webb and Peter Wright," said Mark.

"When Eve Northwood has finished here, I'll see Palmer's body off the premises," said Ben. "Then I'll check the uniforms are clued in on what we need from them. Someone needs to hold the fort while the others carry out house-to-house enquiries. Dolman's depot can't be far from here. I'll find it and see whether either of those guys has reported back yet. I'll see you at Gablecross later today."

"Good hunting," said Mark. "Any idea when we'll get the post-mortem?"

"Eve hopes to have it scheduled for nine o'clock tomorrow morning. So we'll go together."

"Terrific," said Mark. "I'll remember not to eat breakfast. You've seen the killer's handiwork. I've got that dubious pleasure ahead of me."

Ben Moore watched Mark Harvey swing his Ford Kuga in an arc and head for the entrance.

"Good," thought Ben as he saw one PCSO heading his way. "Mark remembered we needed to get the uniforms organised."

Happy that the six uniforms would have enough to occupy them until the close of play, Ben then switched his attention to the caravan. Louise Arlett and her colleague had moved from the gravelled area surrounding the van and were ferreting through the undergrowth beyond it on hands and knees.

"Any luck finding the murder weapon?" he shouted.

"Nothing, so far," Louise replied.

Eve Northwood's head appeared around the caravan door.

"I've finished here if your people want to remove the body," she said. "Will I see you in the morning?"

"My sergeant and I will be there," said Ben. "Thanks very much for filling in on short notice."

"No problem. It makes a change from in-growing toenails and varicose veins."

With that, Eve hurried away to her yellow Mini and ripped off her protective clothing before jumping into the driver's seat and roaring off with a cheery wave.

Behind him, Ben heard Louise's colleague call the rest of the forensic team over for a briefing. Ben took a last look around the yard. Everything was under control. The forensic people would be here until it got dark, at least—time to find Rob Dolman's depot.

An elderly lady walking her dog out on the High Street pointed Ben in the opposite direction to The Volunteer, and in ten minutes, he stood in the haulage firm's empty yard. The Portakabin door was locked. Ben called Rob Dolman, but the call went to voicemail.

Ben got the same result when he called Mark Harvey.

"Terrific," thought Ben, "I've got no lift back to Gable-cross, and it's too cold to hang around on the streets. The landlord at The Volunteer might not appreciate having two coppers through the door on the same day. I wonder where Tom Angell drinks?"

The elderly dog-walker was nowhere in sight when Ben reached the main road again. He took a punt that there would be a pub on the road out of the village, and he was in luck. Once he sat in the warm bar with a pint of bitter, he tried Rob Dolman again.

Still no joy. It pleased Ben the haulier didn't use his phone while driving, but it would help the investigation if he could get to as many of Clive Palmer's associates as quickly as possible.

Mark Harvey answered his boss's call at the second time of asking.

"Have you got hold of the barmaid?" Ben asked.

"We're not allowed to mix business with pleasure, guv," said Mark. "Emily's story matched what Dave Awdry told me. Nothing happened in the pub last night, and she didn't see or hear anything when she walked home. Mind you, Emily lives in the opposite direction."

"What about the builder fellow?"

"I can't speak to Tom Angell, guv. His wife says he's

working on an extension in Bishopstone. He won't be back until six this evening."

"Which one?" asked Ben.

"What do you mean, guv?"

"Which Bishopstone? The village on the Oxfordshire border, the other side of Swindon, or the one near Salisbury? You could drive out there this afternoon if it's the nearest one. Fifteen-minute drive tops."

"I'd better check with Tom Angell's wife, guv."

"Do that, and then pick me up from the Royal George."

"Got it, guv."

Chapter Three

Wednesday, 16 December 2015

DI BEN MOORE parked his BMW outside the Gablecross Police Station at eight-fifteen. He crossed the forecourt towards the entrance and scanned the car park for Mark Harvey's Kuga. He hoped Mark wouldn't cut it fine this morning. Eve Northwood didn't suffer late arrivals gladly.

They had returned to the squad room yesterday and debriefed the morning's events. Then, after a coffee and croissant in the café, Mark had driven to Bishopstone to speak with Tom Angell. After he'd left, Ben had finally traced Rob Dolman. The haulier sounded harassed enough, so Ben didn't add to his worries by telling him about the additional injuries inflicted on Palmer's body.

"Do you want me to ask Ken and Peter to stay in the office first thing in the morning until you've spoken to them?" asked Dolman. "Only I've got collections and deliveries scheduled throughout the day. I'm covering what I can, but I can't afford to be without them for too long."

"We're conducting a murder enquiry, Mr Dolman," said Ben. "I won't be available until after the autopsy. You'll have to rework your schedules to free them up to attend Gable-cross at two in the afternoon. Either DS Harvey or I will collect them from Reception. Is that clear?"

Rob Dolman realised his business wasn't Wiltshire Police's priority and reluctantly agreed to spare his two remaining drivers for an hour.

Mark Harvey had arrived at the address he'd been given in Bishopstone village at two o'clock. He noted a flat-bed truck and transit van in the property's driveway carrying signage for Tom Angell & Son–General Builder. When he asked if Tom Angell was around, one bricklayer had pointed to a fair-haired youngster at the foot of a ladder.

It appeared the talkative employer ran a family business.

"Is your father here, Tom?" Mark had asked.

"Who wants to know?"

Mark looked up.

An older version of the lad at the ladder's foot appeared in the open space that would eventually frame a first-floor window.

"Wiltshire Police," said Mark, showing Tom Angell Senior his warrant card. "Can you come down, please, sir? We need a word."

Tom Angell joined him outside the house one minute later. Mark decided it was too cold to stand around chatting. He pointed to the transit van.

"Let's get out of this wind," he said. "The others don't need to hear this."

Once seated inside the van, Tom Angell asked what the visit was about.

"When was the last time you visited The Volunteer in Purton?" asked Mark.

"Six months ago, maybe," replied Tom. "Why?"

"The way this works best, Mr Angell, is for me to ask the questions, and you answer. Can we agree on that?"

"Alright, I stopped drinking there. It's a free country, or at least it used to be."

"Why did you stop using The Volunteer?"

"I didn't like the company," said Tom Angell.

"Did you leave home early this morning to work on this extension?" asked Mark.

"We start work at half-eight every weekday. I suppose Tom and I left the house just after eight. Chris collected the rest of the crew in this transit. We arrived at the same time, twenty-five past."

"Were you here late yesterday afternoon?" asked Mark.

"Chris and the others couldn't do much after it got dark. I sent them home at half-past four. Tom and I finished a few odds and ends, then drove home. Got indoors around six."

"How did you spend the evening?"

"What, all of it?" asked Tom.

"It will help us, sir," said Mark.

"I had a shower and changed, and Tom followed behind. We ate dinner with my wife, Liz, and then Tom went out with his girlfriend. I heard him park his car on the drive at around eleven. I was already in bed."

"When was the last time you saw Clive Palmer?" asked Mark.

"The paedo? The last time I drank in The Volunteer, I reckon. Why? Has someone given the sick devil what for, at last? It wasn't me. Liz will swear I never left the house after I got home. The building trade is hard work. At young Tom's age, I could handle a night out after a day's graft, but not now. I might drop into a pub for a swift pint on the way home, but you lot have eyes and cameras everywhere. I can't afford to lose my licence. Friday and Saturday nights are when I relax and enjoy a good drink."

"Where did you hear about Palmer, anyway?" asked Mark. "Dave Awdry told me you were the one that let everyone in the village know why Palmer had gone to prison."

"I heard Palmer talking in the pub the first week he moved to Purton," said Tom. "Posh bloke, isn't he? He was in there with Ken Webb, one of Dolman's drivers. I heard them discussing the next day's deliveries. I couldn't believe it. Why was an educated bloke working as a delivery driver? It made little sense. Dave, the landlord, told me Palmer lived in a caravan on John Oatley's land. Posh people usually live in houses like the one in front of us. Loads of money coming in, with both the husband and wife working. Two cars, and holidays abroad twice a year. That's like the couple paying for this extension; money's no object. So I asked if anyone knew where Palmer came from."

"Who did you talk with?" asked Mark.

"First, I looked at his caravan one afternoon when I knew he was working. A sign on the back showed he'd bought it from a dealer in Charmouth, Dorset. I gave them a ring and asked if they could remember him. The bloke didn't want to say too much, but he told me he thought Palmer had just left the prison on the Isle of Portland. I looked it up online. Most of the inmates were sex offenders, the dregs of society. I dug more and found Palmer's name in newspaper reports two years earlier. He got sent down for having sex with a child, not just touching her or encouraging her to do things to him. They had full sex several times over six months. Prison's too good for the likes of blokes like Palmer."

"Did you read the full details of the trial?" asked Mark.

"I'd seen enough," said Tom. "He was a paedo. They never change. Every young girl in the village was at risk. It was my duty to warn people. Unfortunately, Dave Awdry and that wife of his had fallen for the smooth-talking devil's story. He was making a fresh start. Was he heck. He'd been caught messing with a schoolgirl somewhere in London, got sent to prison, and thought he could hide away in a village in the country, waiting for another chance to attack a child. I wasn't having that. So I did my best to let people know what he was really like."

"There *were* incidents reported to the police," said Mark. "Did you have anything to do with those?"

"I can't be held responsible for a bunch of teenagers throwing muck at his caravan," said Tom Angell. "My lad wasn't involved before you asked. Although, it wouldn't surprise me if a group of young fathers got together to wreck that caravan of Palmer's one night. The best thing would be to force him out, making it so uncomfortable that he had to move somewhere else. We don't need his sort here."

"Not everything laid at Clive Palmer's door had anything to do with him, though, did it?" said Mark. "Was it you that pointed the finger in his direction when a girl thought she was followed home from the youth centre?"

"It stood to reason, didn't it?" said Tom. "We've only got one paedo in the village, thank goodness."

"Clive Palmer was in The Volunteer, taking part in Quiz Night," said Mark. "You were mistaken with your accusation, and you tried to convince people not to confirm his alibi."

"Who told you that? I bet it was a regular from the pub who doesn't want to get on the wrong side of Karen Awdry."

"What about the rumour you spread when you heard a girl fell off the climbing frame? When that incident occurred, Clive Palmer was setting off from the other side of Salisbury. If the girl had been old enough to describe the man who cleaned the mud and grit from her knees, we'd probably learn he was old enough to be her grandfather."

"Maybe," said Tom Angell, "but no matter what you say, Palmer's done it once; he'll do it again."

"That's not possible," said Mark. "Someone stabbed Palmer in his caravan late last night, around the time young Tom returned home from seeing his girlfriend. Perhaps I should have a word with him before I leave."

"Is Palmer dead?"

"Yes, Mr Angell. It was a brutal attack. We're searching for the murder weapon. Does Tom carry a knife? Would he have one in that toolkit he carries on his waist?"

"Look, I'm not apologising for anything I said about Palmer. I'm glad he's dead. Because that means our young girls are safe now. But my son wasn't in Purton last night; his girlfriend lives in South Marston. So she'll vouch for him, and Liz was still up when Tom got home. If he'd done something like that, she would have known, surely? Tom has sharp blades in his toolkit, but he never carries one when he's not working."

"Our forensic team is still working in the caravan and the surrounding area," said Mark. "If the killer left a scrap of evidence, we'll trace it to them. You were most vociferous in your opposition to Palmer living in the village, Mr Angell, making you our first port-of-call. However, you were genuinely shocked when I told you Palmer had been attacked, and unless that was a performance worthy of an Oscar, I'm certain we need to look elsewhere to find his murderer."

"Can I get back to work now?" asked Tom Angell. "You can go find the real killer. Tell him thanks from me."

With that, Tom got out of the transit, slammed the driver's door, and returned to the house. Tom Junior stood, one hand on his hip, the other holding a nail gun, staring at Mark Harvey as he left the Transit and returned to his Ford Kuga.

Mark had returned to Gablecross, and Ben Moore had agreed with his assessment of the situation. Tom Angell was responsible for hot air but wasn't involved in Palmer's murder. Neither was Tom Junior, who was left-handed.

Ben Moore had reached his desk in the detective squad room. He spotted DS Jake Latimer sitting on the far side of the room.

"Did you hear what we found at Purton yesterday?" asked Ben.

"Only a few rumours in the canteen yesterday lunchtime, but the news was around the station before I went home at six. You were there, so I'd prefer to hear the facts from you. The killer removed Palmer's genitals, did he?"

"That's a fact, Jake."

"Where did he put them? Someone reckoned Eve Northwood fished them out of his throat."

"That's not true," said Ben. "The lower part of his body was a mess, but the bits were there, somewhere. They just weren't attached to him."

"Have you got anyone in the frame yet?" asked Jake.

"Early days," sighed Ben. "Mark thinks we'll have a long list of suspects before we finish. But, so far, we've eliminated two possible names."

The squad room door swung open.

"Blessed traffic," said Mark Harvey. "Morning, Jake.

Okay, boss? Ready for a ten-minute drive to the Great Western? My car's warm and ready to go. The sooner this is over, the better."

"Did you eat a hearty breakfast, Mark?" asked Jake.

"Fat chance of that," said Mark. "Post mortems are bad enough without a spot of mutilation thrown in."

"You can drop by the canteen when you get back," said Jake. "Mushrooms on toast is the special this morning."

Jake quickly ducked the stapler Mark threw in his direction.

"Settle down, children," said Ben. "Come on, Mark, let's get to the hospital morgue. We mustn't keep Eve waiting."

When they arrived, Eve's yellow Mini Cooper was already in the car park near the morgue entrance. Mark had managed the ten-minute journey in seven. They were inside the viewing room at nine when Eve entered the operating theatre.

Eve checked she had the correct corpse on the slab and prepared her equipment. She looked up at the mezzanine where Ben and Mark were standing. Ben saw a slight nod of the head. Not a word passed her lips until she was ready to start. Ben knew they could always listen to the recording if they got called away. The microphone was suspended from the ceiling, a few feet above the body.

Ben listened as Eve took them step-by-step through the procedures as she performed them. Beside him, Mark Harvey sat back, then leaned forward with his head between his knees. Ben would have given odds he wouldn't last the course, but somehow he did.

While Mark fidgeted and Eve worked methodically on Palmer's body, Ben recalled the man's history that he'd researched in detail yesterday evening.

Clive Palmer was born in the Inner London Borough of Wandsworth on April the first, 1967. At eleven years of age, he attended Furzedown Secondary School and was an excellent and popular student. He studied History and Ancient History at Exeter University in 1985. He also secured his Post Graduate Certification for Education. His first teaching post was at a secondary school in Tooting in September 1989.

Clive met Marcia Brophy, a language teacher at the same school, who was to become his wife in 1991. Clive's younger brother, James, was the best man at their registry office wedding. Liam, their first child, arrived in 1992, and their daughter Nicki was born two years later. The family lived in Tooting in a three-bedroomed detached house.

Clive Palmer moved to one of the early Academies set up in London in 2003 to become head of the History Department. Marcia Palmer returned to teaching in 2000 and chose to work as a supply teacher. She worked at dozens of schools across the London area for the next twelve years. It offered the variety she craved. Clive taught the subject he loved at the Academy, and everything was right in their world.

In September 2012, a new school term began, and fifteen-year-old Gemma Long joined the Academy after her parents had moved back to Britain from Germany. Gemma's father had been stationed at Joint Headquarters Rheindahlen. But he had left the Army after twenty-two years before the station closed and the British Armed Forces HQ moved to Bielefeld.

Gemma Long was an attractive and precocious teenager who had caused her parents many sleepless nights in the past two years. The term 'wild child' could have been created with her in mind. Gemma lost her virginity at thirteen and soon confided in her mother she thought she was pregnant. When the pair visited one of the Army camp's female doctors, that proved to be a false alarm.

However, the doctor recommended that if their daughter was likely to remain sexually active despite her age, they should prescribe her the contraceptive pill. Gemma's mother agreed. She kept this information from her husband and consoled herself that her daughter should at least avoid an unwanted pregnancy.

The move back to London seemed the perfect answer, as far as her mother was concerned. Gemma was starting at a new school. Although there were plenty of teenage boys surrounding her, the temptation offered by much older, uniformed soldiers in Germany to whom she was most attracted had been removed.

Within weeks of the start of term, Gemma had become obsessed with her History teacher. She did everything she could to attract his attention in the classroom and the school corridors. Gemma had few close friends in her new school as a new student. She flirted with several boys in her class, antagonising their girlfriends, which was why she did it. Gemma enjoyed causing trouble. She wasn't interested in boys her age, anyway.

The few friends she made warned Gemma she was playing with fire, stalking Mr Palmer in such an obvious way. Someone was bound to notice.

"I'll get to him in time," she told them. "Just wait and see."

Clive Palmer knew well that a pupil was attracted to a teacher from time to time. He accepted every teacher had a duty to make sure they didn't take advantage of that situation. If everything had stayed the same as it had done for the past twenty years, there wouldn't have been an issue.

Clive and Marcia's son, Liam, was now twenty years old, and, disillusioned with his degree course and life in general, he left university to travel the world.

"Liam says he wants to find himself," Clive said to Marcia, shaking his head. "Where did we go wrong?"

Marcia was enduring a particularly tough assignment at a failing school in Wandsworth. She was under pressure and couldn't wait for the teacher she was standing in for to return from maternity leave. So she and Clive argued for the first time in a decade.

The following week, eighteen-year-old Nicki broke up with her childhood sweetheart. Clive returned home to find Marcia and their daughter in tears. He was tired and didn't show the correct amount of sympathy for his daughter's broken heart and his wife's traumatic day with a classroom of feral children. There was another blazing row. Something had to give.

Clive Palmer didn't encourage Gemma Long in any way. Quite the opposite. He continued to do everything to avoid being alone in her company. However, Clive drove pupils on field trips in the school minibus on a couple of occasions each term, and it was during one of these excursions Gemma made her move.

Clive had parked the mini-bus in a multi-storey car park, and with another female teacher, they escorted the boys and girls in their charge to an archaeological site in the neighbourhood. After being there for thirty minutes, Gemma Long complained of feeling dizzy. The female teacher, who didn't drive, asked Clive what they should do.

Gemma said she wanted to go home. So, Clive elected to drive her and return to the site to continue the visit. The teacher agreed to look after the other students in his absence.

When they reached the multi-storey car park, Gemma said she wanted to lie on the back seat of the minibus. Clive told her she needed to sit up and put on her safety belt, or he couldn't start the van. It was too dangerous. Gemma began to cry. He walked to the back of the minibus to find her grinning at him. He sat beside Gemma and asked what she thought she was playing at.

That was when Clive Palmer took his first step on the slippery slope that ended with him being sent to prison. He knew Gemma had tricked him into being alone with her, but the sudden turmoil at home had unsettled him. Clive gave into temptation while he was emotionally vulnerable, but Gemma was in charge from then on.

She made it clear nobody would ever learn of their affair, provided Clive continued to have sex with her. Gemma told her parents she was staying behind to attend an after-school club, which pleased them. In reality, she and Clive Palmer were making out in his car. Gemma entertained Clive in her bedroom when her parents were away for a weekend. Their meetings became more frequent and riskier.

Whispers spread around the school. Gemma couldn't resist bragging that her friends had been wrong. She *had* made Mr Palmer take notice of her, and now she could twist him around her little finger. The whispers reached the staffroom.

Marcia had moved to a safer, better-performing school and spent more time there in the evenings. Clive was too concerned with the risks he'd been taking over the past six months to question whether there was an ulterior motive in her extracurricular activities.

Nicki had moped around the house for weeks after the break-up, but recently she'd secured a job as a chalet host at a ski resort in Austria. They wouldn't see her for four months. Marcia counted the days until the next postcard from Liam. The last one had been from Bangkok a month ago. He sounded more lost than ever.

Palmer's world fell apart in the last week of March 2013 when the school suspended him.

The Metropolitan Police visited the Palmer home on Good Friday. He confessed.

Clive spent four months on remand before the case went to court. A custodial sentence was inevitable. Regardless of Gemma Long's conduct, the law was clear. An underage child cannot consent to a sexual relationship with a teacher because of the power imbalance. Or, to put it another way, a fifteen-year-old child cannot groom an adult.

Palmer served his sentence in HMP The Verne, Portland. On his release, he bought a second-hand car and caravan and drove to Purton via the M5 and M4 to make a fresh start.

Soon after his arrest, Palmer's wife started divorce proceedings. Marcia didn't visit her husband while on remand or attend the court case.

In June, Liam had flown home from New Zealand to stay with his mother until after the trial. Nicki was already home after the skiing season ended but soon left to work in the West Indies. While Clive Palmer languished in Portland, Marcia sold the family house and moved to a smaller property in Putney. She didn't want to encourage the children to pay more than a flying visit. As a result, Liam resumed his travels within a week of his father entering prison.

Ben couldn't find any further updates on the Palmer tribe in the available paperwork. It might be worth trawling through social media for signs of Liam, Nicki, and Marcia tonight when he got home. Although, it was just idle interest rather than relevant to the case.

As Eve Northwood completed the post-mortem and Mark Harvey looked more at ease, Ben recapped what he'd heard while reflecting on Clive Palmer's background.

"So, we learned little more than we knew yesterday," he said. "Palmer died no later than midnight. We know that when he left The Volunteer, he only had a two-hundred-yard walk to his caravan. The fatal attack must have occurred almost as soon as he got inside."

"Cause of death was as Eve thought too," said Mark. "She confirmed nothing was missing from the body. The killer didn't take any bits with him."

"Well, we can't be sure nothing got stolen," said Ben. "We've got his phone, and forensics will have bagged and tagged his clothing and the contents of his pockets. Nobody knew him well enough to know whether he kept money and valuables at the caravan. After the divorce, Palmer needed to open a new bank account, if they had a joint one. Palmer had access to money when he left prison, evidenced by the second-hand car in the outbuilding in Oatley's yard and the caravan. We might need to check his old stamping ground to see if he switched his account once he'd established new roots. There could be debit and credit cards. We need to be stopped. Or we could watch for activity on them for a while."

"You've been busy, guv," said Mark. "I let my mind go blank to avoid thinking about what was happening in the theatre. Is keeping your mind busy a better defence mechanism?"

"I doubt there's much in it, Mark," said Ben. "It's just that I've got much further to go to let my mind go blank."

"Very droll, guv," said Mark. "Any other pearls of wisdom?"

"Why Purton?" asked Ben. "Did Palmer meet someone inside who lives nearby? Or did he have visitors? We need to check with the prison."

"It closed, boss," said Mark. "I doubt anyone kept hold of the visitors' logs."

"Damn," said Ben. "There was no woman in Palmer's life since he left prison, was there?"

"Nobody was mentioned, guv," said Mark. "Dave and Karen Awdry said Palmer was a loner."

"Right," said Ben. "We'll await the forensic results and request the checks on Palmer's bank details and mobile phone logs. Then, let's get back to the office and prepare for this afternoon."

"What about the ex-wife and the other family members, guv?" asked Mark as they left the viewing room.

"All in good time, Mark," said Ben. "London can wait for a day or two. We've still got plenty of suspects closer to Palmer's home to question first."

Mark drove them back to Gablecross, and they spent the rest of the morning filling in reports and requests for information. Then, Mark went to Reception at two o'clock to collect Ken Webb and Peter Wright.

"I'm Detective Sergeant Harvey. Thanks for agreeing to come here today, gents," said Mark. "We won't keep you from your work for too long. Detective Inspector Moore will speak to you, Mr Webb. He's waiting in Interview Room One. You and I will be in Interview Room Two, Mr Wright."

Mark chatted to the two haulage firm employees as they negotiated the corridors inside the building. Whether it put them at ease, Mark couldn't tell. He knew that innocent and guilty visitors lost their sense of direction on the circuitous route adorned with signs and arrows. Several had commented that they never thought they'd find their way out again.

Whoever had designed the system deserved a medal, as far as Mark Harvey was concerned. The battle was half won with some suspects. They were ready to sign a confession as soon as they reached an interview room in exchange for a guide to the exit.

Ben Moore was waiting for Ken Webb when Mark Harvey knocked on the door of Interview Room One. Mark closed the door behind the driver and opened the next door.

"Sit yourself down, Mr Wright," said Mark. "We're having an informal chat on this occasion. I won't be recording this conversation, and you aren't under caution. How long have you worked for Rob Dolman?"

"From the beginning," Peter Wright replied. "Rob started the firm fourteen years ago. We're around the same age. You know the old joke. We went to different schools together. Rob was a local lad, whereas I lived in South Marston. We first bumped into one another as teenagers. He followed the Robins, Swindon Town. I went to several home games each season but wasn't an avid football fan. Ten years later, I was married, living in Blunsdon, and looking for a change of job. Shift work at the Honda factory paid well, but it crippled our social life. My wife had left me, and I heard Rob was looking for drivers. I thought, why not? The job was on weekdays only, and Rob was confident of securing enough clients to mean we would do something different every day. Rob has his head screwed on; he didn't employ too many drivers and get too big, too quickly, as others did. Ken Webb is a decade older than us and was already working in the trade for another firm. Rob drove the firm's third van for the first couple of years until the business got established. Then Mitch Garner joined us after being made redundant from a local engineering firm, and Rob took over the office. Mitch was in his mid-fifties and happy to find something to keep him busy and earn decent money until he could afford to retire. That was how Clive Palmer got the gig with Dolman. Mitch turned sixty-five a couple of months before Palmer landed on Rob's doorstep."

"What did you make of Clive Palmer when you first met him?" asked Mark.

"He seemed okay," replied Wright. "First impressions are usually a good gauge of a person, aren't they? Ken thought he was too posh to be a van driver. I couldn't see what difference it made. We worked for the same firm, but we never worked together. If I got to the depot at the same time as the others, we had a brief chat before Rob handed us the schedule for the day. Then we're in our vans and on our way. Every trip takes a different length of time, so as often as not when I get back to the depot, the only person there will be Rob. I'll be out on my next job before any others arrive back. Nobody hangs around at the end of the day, either. If I've finished my trips by half-past four, I sort out my paperwork, check the board to see what's lined up for the morning and get off home before five. Another evening, I might not get back until half-past five, or even six o'clock, if the traffic's heavy or there was a hiccup at the client's end. I could go a week without seeing Ken, Clive, or Mitch when he was with us."

"In the first few weeks, Dave Awdry told us the three of you drank together in The Volunteer," said Mark.

"Not every night," said Wright. "Ken and I used the pub before Palmer came on the scene. Ken has lived in the village all his life. I moved here after my marriage fell apart.

Nobody was waiting at home for me in the evenings, so I kept Ken company now and then. Mitch had never been a drinker. He cycled home from the depot every evening to his wife. Palmer was on his own in that caravan of his. He said little about where he'd lived before, but it was none of our business. As long as Clive turned up every morning, drove his van, and kept Rob happy, what more did he need to do? If you ask Rob, he'd say the same for Ken and me."

"Those after-work drinks stopped as soon as the rumours started, I take it?"

"Not a bit," said Wright. "Ken and I gave Palmer the benefit of the doubt at first. Rob Dolman did too, and none of his clients ever queried who would drive the van when they arranged a delivery or a collection. So everything carried on as normal for two months at least."

"What happened when Tom Angell could let everyone know where Clive Palmer had spent the past two years?"

"You would have to ask Rob," said Peter Wright. "But I can't recall anyone asking about Palmer while I was driving to businesses around the county. They confined the whispers and hateful comments to this village. You know how it is."

"Nevertheless," said Mark. "You and Ken Webb *did* stop using The Volunteer for a drink after work, didn't you?"

"It was hard not to follow the crowd," said Wright. "Rob Dolman stuck by Palmer, though. He kept saying no matter what people said; Clive had never let him down. Even when there were whispers about another girl getting followed. Nothing happened to her, though, did it? But, of course, if Palmer was a paedophile like Tom Angell said, he wouldn't be capable of stopping at just following the girl home, would he? So Ken suggested we switch pubs to avoid people thinking we were the same as Palmer."

"Rob Dolman was stuck with Palmer, wasn't he?" said

Mark. "Employment law meant sacking him without genuine cause relating to his work performance was out of the question."

"That may be true, but Rob must have known more than he let on. I reckon Palmer filled in the gaps, and Rob believed he'd put his past behind him and wanted to make a fresh start."

"You believe Clive Palmer revealed more to Dolman than he did to the rest of you?"

"It would explain a lot, don't you think?" said Wright.

"Did Palmer say anything to show what he did before he came to Purton?"

"Never, but Clive was a big reader," said Wright. "He left a book in the office one morning when he took the van out. I picked it up, and it was on Ancient History."

"Fact or fiction?" asked Mark.

"Blowed if I know," said Wright. "It was way over my head. Whatever he did before he came here, he used his brain and not his hands."

"Did you ever visit his caravan?" asked Mark.

"I never had an invitation," said Wright. "Ken suggested we take a look one evening when we knew Palmer would get back late to the depot. I peered through the window, but I couldn't see much else apart from a pile of books and magazines on a coffee table."

"What about last week? Did anything unusual happen? Were there any strangers in the village? Did you see Clive Palmer with someone you'd never seen before?"

"No, nothing like that. It was a normal week. Ken and I had a drink in the Royal George on Wednesday night. He was busy at the weekend. His wife wanted him to go Christmas shopping. Clive was at work every day, but we never spoke."

"I suppose Monday was normal too, was it?" asked Mark.

"For me, it was. Three local trips around Swindon and an early finish for a change."

"A quiet night in?"

"I'm single, in my mid-forties, with no family," said Wright. "Of course, I had a quiet night in. Too darned cold to be wandering the streets, anyway. Thank goodness I don't have a dog."

"Why did you mention a dog?" asked Mark.

"Ken and his wife have a dog. The mutt needs walking morning, noon, and night. You wouldn't catch me taking on that level of commitment."

"What time did you get to work the next morning?"

"A couple of minutes early, for a change. Rob was trying to get the office radiator to kick out more heat. I asked what I was scheduled for, and he said I could take my pick off the board as I was early. So I chose the trip to Chilcompton."

"A trip that Ken Webb usually undertook, I believe?" asked Mark.

"Yeah, well, Ken wasn't there, was he? Rob told me to take my pick. That's life."

"What time did you return to the depot?"

"Not before five," said Wright. "I had a few local jobs in Swindon, which I did in the afternoon. Before that, I had stopped at the Leigh Delamere Services on the M4 for lunch."

"So, when did you learn about Clive Palmer's murder?"

"Rob stayed at the depot until Ken, and I returned, as he usually did, and called us into the office to tell us the news. So, we heard Palmer was dead at a quarter past five."

"You must both have been shocked," said Mark.

"Part of me wasn't that surprised," said Wright. "If

Tom Angell was half right about what Palmer had done, then perhaps he had it coming.?"

"Who do you suspect was involved?" asked Mark.

"I haven't had time to give that much thought," said Wright. "It sounds personal, which could mean you're looking for someone from the village who felt strongly a convicted paedophile shouldn't live here. Or someone from his past, perhaps a victim's relative, who discovered where he was living and paid him a call."

"Can anyone vouch for where you were between eleven and midnight on Monday night, Mr Wright?"

"Afraid not," replied Peter Wright. "Just as well. I didn't have a reason to kill him, or I'd be in trouble."

Mark Harvey smiled.

"Don't worry. We'll find evidence to nail the killer, Mr Wright. You've been most helpful. I'll walk you back to reception to save you from getting lost. If Ken Webb isn't already there, you can wait for him if you wish."

"Ken drove us over here," said Wright. "I hope your colleague next door hasn't secured a signed confession. I'll be stranded."

Chapter Four

IN INTERVIEW ROOM ONE, Ben Moore followed a similar line of questioning with a nervous Ken Webb.

"How long have you worked for Rob Dolman?" asked Ben.

"Ever since he set up the firm," replied Ken. "I saw the advert in the newspaper and applied straight away. I'd been driving for a firm in Shrivenham for ages. It felt sensible to have a shorter trip to work each day as I got older, and Rob's work was more varied than the trips I did then. I might as well have been a bus driver."

"Had you known Rob long?" asked Ben.

"All his life," said Ken. "Purton's a big village by some standards, but it's mostly one main road with more roads leading off it as the years go by. I've lived here all my life and watched Rob growing up. His family lived less than one hundred yards from my house. So I had no qualms about switching from my other firm to work for Rob Dolman. He's made of the right stuff."

"How did you get on with Clive Palmer?"

"Clive was a different kettle of fish to Mitch Garner," said Ken. "Oh, you wouldn't know him. Mitch had worked for Rob for around ten years. Rob has never had more than three vans. He handled the local trips in the early days, and Peter and I coped with the rest. Rob's wife dealt with the paperwork from home, but Rob had the Portakabin installed once he'd established a solid business. After that, he became the office manager, and Mitch drove the third van. Mitch retired at the end of February, and Clive arrived at the right time. I couldn't make him out in the beginning. He sounded more like a college professor than a van driver. Once he started working, though, he proved to be a natural. Clive was an excellent driver, and he charmed the customers. Rob always told Peter and me we should be more like Clive."

"You were a regular in The Volunteer in those days, weren't you, Ken?" asked Ben.

"That makes it sound as if I was in there every night," said Ken. "I prefer to say The Volunteer was where I drank the occasional pint. It was closer to my house than the other pubs in the village. I've been going there once, perhaps twice a week, since I was eighteen."

"Why did you move to a pub that was out of your way? That seems strange."

"Peter reckoned people linked us with Clive Palmer too closely if you get my drift," said Ken. "Not at first, but once the rumours surfaced, and Tom Angell painted a lurid picture of Clive's past."

"It was true, though, wasn't it?" said Ben. "Clive Palmer had come to Purton straight from prison for having sex with a young girl."

"I didn't believe it at first. Clive seemed a decent bloke. Rob kept him on at the firm, and John Oatley was happy for him to keep his caravan in the yard. Part of me thought Tom Angell was mistaken, but I felt I should do the same when people I'd lived amongst for decades drifted away from The Volunteer. If they forced Palmer to leave the village, I still had to live there.

"Do you think Clive told Rob Dolman and John Oatley more than he did you and Peter? Would that explain why they gave him a second chance?"

"People who get sent to prison aren't always reliable when it comes to telling the truth," said Ken. "Clive could have spun them a yarn and convinced them it was a terrible miscarriage of justice."

"You didn't think to research the case brought against your colleague?" asked Ben.

"I drive a van for a living, Detective Inspector. I wouldn't have a clue where to start. It was simpler to follow Rob and Dave Awdry's approach to the matter."

"Which was?"

"Clive had never given either cause to turn their back on him. During the ten months he lived in the village, Clive was polite, well-spoken, and a good worker. Something had happened in his past, and he'd moved to Purton to make a fresh start. On Monday night, someone decided that would not happen."

"Did you ever visit the caravan, Mr Webb?" asked Ben.

"Just the once, with Peter. He wanted to look inside, but the curtains and blinds covered most of the window. So Peter could only see books and magazines on a table by peering through a small gap at the bottom. I told him that was no surprise; Clive was an intelligent man. He wouldn't waste his spare time watching rubbish TV in the evenings."

"Did nothing appear strange in the week before Clive's murder? Was there something out of synch with what had gone before?"

"There was another rumour in the village that a mob was gathering to force Palmer to leave," said Ken. "I don't know how much truth there was in that."

"What trips were you responsible for on Monday?"

"Two visits to Swindon in the morning. Rob can supply the details. Then, after lunch, I drove to Downton, on the other side of Salisbury. I got home at six."

"Was your wife with you all evening?" asked Ben.

"Apart from when I took Benji out for a walk. He's our boxer dog, five years old."

"What time would that have been, Mr Webb?"

"Between eight and half-past."

"Why were you late to work on Tuesday?"

"I wasn't late," said Ken. "Peter beat me in by three minutes and nicked the Chilcompton run. He knew how much I enjoyed that trip."

"What's so special about a drive to Chilcompton?" asked Ben.

"It makes a pleasant change from driving in and around Swindon, especially if you've done it most of your working life," said Ken. "Salisbury's a good run too, and one of us had to drive to Winchester every month. We're not stuck in a factory every day or laying bricks in all winds and weather. The West Country has beautiful scenery and picturesque villages dotted around the countryside. Simple pleasures, Detective Inspector, and the variety my job offers is a significant part of its attraction."

"Does Peter Wright see things the same way?"

"I think he'd say that it's a living. Since his wife walked out on him, Peter's been a bitter, lonely soul, not splendid company. He grabbed that Chilcompton trip because he knew I'd be miffed. Also, he took his sweet time getting there and back. Rob had a phone call from a client in Swindon when I was leaving the office after lunch. Peter could have arrived by half-past twelve, but he hadn't arrived at half-past one."

"Interesting," said Ben Moore. "Did Clive Palmer share your views on the driving profession?"

"I often wondered what made him choose this part of the country to settle in," said Ken. "I could understand why he didn't go back to London. Clive said there was nothing for him there anymore. He mentioned a younger brother that kept in touch, but he'd drawn a line under what had gone before he went to prison. Although I imagine working for Rob was light-years from whatever he did before, it suited his purpose. He enjoyed driving around the county to different places most days, and they were new to him. Clive seemed very interested in Purton's history. Well, the history of Wiltshire, in general. He told me things about Stonehenge, Avebury, and Littlecote Roman Villa that I didn't know, and I've lived on their doorstep for over fifty years."

"Clive Palmer had been a schoolteacher before he went to prison," said Ben. "He taught History. The girl he slept with was a student."

"Well, I never," said Ken. "That explains how he knew so much history of the county. He was an idiot to get involved with a girl so young. He should have known better."

"You didn't know he was a teacher?" asked Ben.

"I didn't go digging into the past. Everything I knew came from Tom Angell. The younger ones in the village use the internet every minute of the day. I've never bothered with that. I watch TV for the national news and buy the

Swindon Advertiser for the local stuff. The world keeps spinning without me studying every scrap of news and gossip. There's little I can do to influence which way it's spinning, so I let it pass over my head and get on with life."

"Regardless of the details in the case against Clive Palmer, he deserved to go to prison," said Ben. "You will have heard he died from a savage attack. Who do you know that might be capable of such an attack?"

"It had to be someone from outside the village," said Ken Webb. "Purton has its fair share of tearaways, but it's not the Wild West. Tom Angell did his best to stir the locals into action to get Clive to leave, but he's just a bag of wind. My money would be on someone related to the victim you mentioned. There was only one girl involved, then? Not a lifetime of offences before he got caught."

"I'm sure the entire story will appear in the Swindon Advertiser," said Ben. "We have several lines of enquiry to follow, Mr Webb. However, I feel confident we'll find the person responsible. Many thanks for coming here this afternoon. I'll ask DS Harvey to take you back to Reception."

Ken Webb continued to sit, staring at Ben's desktop as Ben left the room to look for Mark. He found him in the detective squad room with a cup of coffee.

"Ken Webb's ready to leave, Mark," he said. "That coffee will still be warm when you get back. After that, we need to debrief what we both learned."

"OK, guv," said Mark, easing himself gently out of his chair. "Peter Wright's in Reception waiting for Ken. I'll see you in five minutes."

"Great," said Ben. "Bring me a cup of coffee when you're done."

Five minutes later, the two detectives were sitting in Ben's office, comparing notes.

"There are few differences between the two drivers' recollection of the time they worked with Clive Palmer," said Ben. "What did you make of Peter Wright, Mark?"

"He was very laid-back, guv. I told him it was an informal conversation, and he took full advantage. The trouble was, by the end of the meeting; I wondered whether he wasn't being a little glib. Do you know what I mean?"

"I understand the term, Mark," said Ben, "but I didn't speak with him. You did."

"What about Ken Webb?" asked Mark.

"At the start, Webb was nervous, but gradually he relaxed, but I didn't feel he was holding back or trying to avoid certain topics."

"Are we saying we can discount the two of them, guv?" asked Mark.

"There was one thing," said Ben. "On Tuesday morning, Ken Webb arrived at the depot three minutes after Peter Wright. Ken hinted that was unusual. Wright's a single bloke who works for a living rather than lives for work. Rob Dolman allowed him to choose which trip to make, and he opted for one that Ken Webb usually did. Ken thought his colleague did it to annoy him."

"It wouldn't start World War Three, guv,"

"No, but Ken told me Wright was later getting back to Swindon than he should have been. I just wondered if it was significant."

Mark referred to his notes.

"Wright told me he did the Chilcompton run and then used the M4 to return to Swindon. He stopped off at Leigh Delamere Services for lunch. That could explain things."

"Fair enough. Ken wasn't aware of that," said Ben. "He said Wright took advantage of any opportunity to make things easier for himself."

"I suppose if he took longer over the morning trip, he reduced the number Rob could expect him to do in the afternoon."

"I wonder whether Rob Dolman closely checks the breaks his drivers take. Do they have tachographs in small vans like the ones in his fleet?"

"Three vans don't make up a fleet, guv," said Mark, "and as his vans are under three and a half tonnes, they don't need tachos. So Dolman has to rely on his drivers' honesty, I reckon."

"If Ken Webb's right and Rob Dolman asked Peter Wright what he had for lunch that Tuesday, he'd say pizza and chips or something similar."

"Sorry, guv, you've lost me."

"Well, instead of telling the truth, which was an hour and a half or thereabouts."

"Nice one, guv. Another thing we learned was that neither driver checked the story they heard from Tom Angell. Instead, they took it as read and never complained to Rob Dolman that they didn't want to work with Palmer."

"Did you say anything to Wright about the events leading to Palmer getting sent to prison?"

"No, guv," said Mark. "I didn't get the impression he knew much other than what Tom Angell told them. Webb was more interested in whether Palmer had cried on Rob Dolman's shoulder, giving him a sob story he wasn't a threat to the young females in the area. He thought John Oatley must have heard the same story because Tom Angell's revelations swayed neither Dolman nor Oatley. While customers in the pub were leaving in droves rather than be seen in the same bar, Dolman and Oatley backed Clive Palmer throughout."

"Perhaps the forensics people will come up with something," sighed Ben Moore. "Or the murder weapon will surface, covered in fingerprints. We need a break. I can't spot a killer amongst the people we've spoken to so far."

Thursday, 17 December 2015

DI BEN MOORE was back at his desk first thing in the morning. He'd flicked through several hundred social media pages last night, finding nothing that offered a positive line of enquiry in their current case.

A Facebook page revealed that Marcia Brophy had reverted to her maiden name. The supply teacher, aged forty-six, was 'in a relationship with' Adrian Harrold, a thirty-six-year-old Media Studies teacher. The couple lived in Putney. Ben wondered when that relationship had started.

The last post to Liam Palmer's Facebook page was in August, two and a half years ago. Ben couldn't find any other social media sites where Liam was listed. He hoped the young man had found himself and not followed many other young men down a dark hole from which there was only one escape.

The answer turned up on the various accounts where Nicki Palmer was a frequent flyer. Depending on the season, Palmer's daughter was still working in far-flung places as a holiday rep or chalet host. Marcia and Liam were listed among her thousands of friends. The contact with her mother was frequent and friendly enough, but the last contact with Liam had been in January 2014, when he entered a Buddhist monastery in Nepal.

"Morning, guv," said Mark. "Any major break in the case overnight."

"Not a sausage," said Ben. "I expect to receive Palmer's bank details and phone logs in the next thirty minutes."

"What about the clothes he was wearing and the items in his pockets? Where will they be now?"

"Safely locked away in the evidence store, I should hope," said Ben. "We could take a walk there while we're waiting. Come on. The trek will do you good."

They returned to find the reports they were expecting on Ben's desk an hour later.

"Let's hope there's more here than we found in evidence," Mark said. "His bloodstained shirt and body-warmer didn't offer a thing. As for the jeans, they contained little, either. Apart from the key to the caravan, his car keys, a comb, a handkerchief, and eight pounds forty-six pence in cash."

"He dealt in cash for several day-to-day transactions," said Ben. "The barmaid told us he gave her the exact money for his last pint on Monday night."

"I don't use cash much these days, guv," said Mark. "With tap and go on my card, I don't need it."

"I'd feel a prat using my card to buy a newspaper that cost less than a pound," said Ben. "I don't have dozens of coins weighing me down, but half-a-dozen of various denominations can be useful. Maybe Palmer had gathered a pile of shrapnel and was getting rid of them at the pub on Monday night."

"I don't remember a bowl full of coins in the caravan on Tuesday, guv," said Mark.

"Not surprised. You had your eyes closed most of the time. We'll pay a visit later. Forensics will have secured the caravan and its contents for whoever claims Palmer's estate."

"That's not likely to be the ex-wife, guv," said Mark.

"Not everyone makes a will in their forties, Mark. Ken Webb said there was a younger brother. He rang Clive now and then, so we'll have a contact number on that mobile phone."

"What goodies do we have in those reports, guv?" asked Mark.

"Clive Palmer opened an account with the Halifax, in Southside Wandsworth, in August 2012."

"Wasn't he on remand then?"

"There's no law against opening an account while you're in prison," said Ben. "Palmer couldn't open or operate accounts that offer credit facilities. Nor could he open or use store credit cards. We may find his brother played a role in setting that account up for him. The divorce from Marcia was underway, and his solicitor would have warned Palmer he faced a custodial sentence. I see no problem with him planning for life after his divorce."

"Anything stand out on the account itself, guv?" asked Mark.

"His final salary payment from the local authority," said Ben. "Then, while he was on remand, and during his stay in Portland, there was a succession of monthly subscriptions to magazines and book clubs. I presume there were cash withdrawals for odds and ends he could purchase inside. Then, despite his minor share from the divorce proceedings, he got a sizeable cheque. Marcia didn't quite take him to the cleaners. Ah, here we are. Palmer had purchased a second-hand car and the caravan within three days of leaving prison. Since then, Palmer set up a monthly Direct Debit to John Oatley for his rent. The remaining subscriptions appear to have continued as before. Nothing else appears on the account, apart from the money from Rob Dolman and a weekly cash withdrawal for food shopping and beer money."

"No petrol?" asked Mark.

"Palmer drove a van every day," said Ben. "If he enjoyed a drink in the evening. I'd hope he left the car at home."

"Weekends?" asked Mark.

"No sign of him using the card for that," said Ben. "Maybe he paid cash? If he only used the car on rare occasions, he might have watched the gauge like a hawk and put ten quid worth in on the nose."

"Another dead end," said Mark. "Palmer wasn't gambling, wining and dining another bloke's wife, or doing anything to encourage someone from his past to seek him out for revenge. So what did the phone records show?"

"He'd had the phone since 2013," said Ben. "That suggests the Met Police seized his original phone when they arrested him. This pay-as-you-go Samsung has just three contact numbers."

"John Oatley, Rob Dolman, and his brother," said Mark.

"James Palmer," said Ben. "All they show is a bunch of everyday conversations you'd expect between Palmer and the parties involved. If we hoped they would give us a lead on the killer, they're as much use as a chocolate teapot."

"Why don't we use these keys to see what we can find in the car and the caravan, guv?" said Mark.

Ben drove them from Gablecross to Purton. John Oatley had parked an ancient Land Rover in the gateway to deter sightseers. Ben parked close to the Land Rover, and they edged past it to enter the farmyard. The crime scene ticker tape was still much in evidence, but no sign anyone had visited the site.

"The car must be in that shed on the corner," said Mark.

"One key on this keyring will be for that old padlock," said Ben. "Although a swift tug might be enough. I've seen better security on a suitcase at the airport."

Once the padlock was removed, Mark opened the double doors, and both men stepped into the dark interior. Ben opened the driver's door and sat in the driver's seat.

"Are we taking it for a spin, guv?" asked Mark.

"I wanted to check the fuel gauge," said Ben. "Over half a tank. I'll drive it outside. Otherwise, we won't be able to check the boot. This shed is wide but not deep."

Mark stepped outside and waited for his boss to drive out. Then he opened the passenger side door.

"Nothing behind the mirror," said Ben. "An opened packet of mints in the central tray. A biro, two twenty pence pieces, and a ticket for a car park in Swindon, near the theatre. Palmer spent an hour there on Saturday before he died. What is there in the glove box?"

"A folder containing the car's logbook, manual, and service history," said Mark.

"Palmer travelled light, didn't he?" said Ben. "I can't see anything on the back seats or the floor. So let's give the boot the once-over."

The two detectives got out of the car and opened the boot.

"What do you make of that, guv?" asked Mark.

"An old tablecloth, do you reckon?" said Ben. "I wonder what that was used for?"

"I cover the floor of my Kuga's boot with an old sheet

when I'm taking stuff to the recycling centre," said Mark. "Maybe Palmer did the same."

"Your Kuga is your pride and joy, Mark," said Ben. "Palmer's clapped-out second-hand car doesn't deserve to have its floor protected. When was the last time this went through a car wash or had its carpets cleaned? No, this tablecloth covered an item Palmer didn't want the world to see. Something of value, perhaps?"

"If he bought an expensive piece of kit, there's no sign of it on his bank statement," said Mark. "I think you're on the right track, though, guv. Of course, Palmer wouldn't have needed to visit the recycling, would he?"

"Right, I'll get the car back in the shed, Mark. We need to look in the caravan for clues explaining this cloth."

Two minutes later, Ben stood on the step outside the caravan. He remembered the smells and stifling atmosphere the last time he'd been inside the van. Ben moved aside the crime scene tape and opened the door. He let it swing back unhindered.

"Small breaths, guv," said Mark. "It won't be as bad as it was, but let's open a window, anyway."

"You check the right-hand side," said Ben. "I'll handle the left."

"These vans might seem basic," said Mark, "but for Palmer, it had everything he needed. He had his wardrobe, WC, sink and shower in the centre, with his bedroom beyond. The distance separating everything isn't great, but the kitchen area and his living space were adequate for a guy living alone."

Mark and Ben spent the next ten minutes turning the van upside down. Finally, Mark returned to the living space to find Ben thumbing through Palmer's collection of books and magazines.

"Anything, guv?" asked Mark. "Based on what's hanging in his wardrobe, Palmer had two of most things. Two pairs of shoes, trousers, and shorts. He didn't go in for flash gear with designer labels. Just the sort of stuff you would expect a single bloke nearing fifty to have in the closet."

"No secret stash of porn or drugs?" asked Ben.

"Forensics would have bagged and tagged them if he had, guv," said Mark.

"At least one of which should have reached the evidence room," said Ben. "I didn't see things in the fridge or food cupboard to ring alarm bells. Of course, Palmer read a lot, but that shouldn't come as a surprise. Ken Webb told me Palmer was interested in local history and had magazines, books, and brochures for different historic sites across the county."

Mark checked the spines of the books on the only shelf in the van.

"You learned Palmer was a History teacher," he shrugged. "The guy was into the Saxons and the Romans. Well, he had those covered. I'm surprised he didn't apply for Mastermind. Clive Palmer had his specialist subjects covered, didn't he?"

"Do you watch that programme, Mark?" asked Ben.

"Only the last fifteen minutes, when the questions are on general knowledge. At least I've got half a chance to answer a question or two."

"I haven't watched for ages, but I remember a story about a contestant who applied to answer questions on a niche aspect of Anglo-Saxon history. The question setters struggled to compile relevant questions and phoned Aberystwyth University to ask whether they knew the recognised expert on the subject. Dai Jones, they said, he's your man."

"Never heard of him," said Mark.

"The Mastermind people had," said Ben. "Dai Jones was the contestant they were trying to set questions for."

"Nice one. Did you open every one of these books?" asked Mark. "To see if Palmer was hiding something between the pages?"

"Yes, and nothing fell out, apart from a bookmark. So there's nothing here to tell us what might have been hidden in the boot."

"What about any of the official documents people have? Did he have a passport? A large folder containing receipts, invoices, birth certificates, or wedding photos even?"

"If there was something of that nature, I expect forensics is still working on them," said Ben, standing up and preparing to leave. "We might have to wait another day before they make their way into the evidence store. We won't see results until after Christmas."

"Where do we go from here then, guv?" asked Mark.

"I'll drive us back to Gablecross," said Ben. "Then we'll start making calls. James Palmer is first on my list of people to interview. He spoke with his brother as often as anyone outside Purton in the past ten months. So he could give us the answers we need."

Jake Latimer sat nursing a cup of coffee, trying to unthaw his fingers when the two detectives returned to the squad room. Jake thought they cut a disconsolate figure as they shuffled slowly to Ben's office.

"Not making progress then, lads?" he asked.

"It's like trying to knit with fog," said Mark. "Any potential suspects we uncover get eliminated in seconds."

"Are there any likely lads from Purton you should look at?" asked Jake.

"Nobody who's shown themselves capable of a vicious stabbing in the past," said Ben Moore.

"Driving offences, anti-social behaviour, credit card fraud, and a spot of burglary is the pinnacle of their combined achievements," said Mark Harvey.

Jake blew on his coffee while he thought for a while.

"Redman," he said, snapping his fingers. "He doesn't live in Purton, but he's tried his hand at each of the crimes you mentioned, Mark. As a result, Andy Redman has spent nine of the past fifteen years in prison."

Ben Moore was already looking up the details for Andy Redman.

"Why didn't we see this before?" he asked, turning the screen towards Mark.

"Blimey, this Redman character is from a Pinehurst family. He has a younger sister, Patricia, and two older brothers. Andy Redman is Rob Dolman's brother-in-law. Murder is a step up from what he's done in the past, though, guv. If he had an armed robbery, or a spot of GBH, against his name, I'd accept he could be our man, but why would he kill Palmer?"

"Maybe he broke into the caravan hoping to find some-thing worth stealing," said Ben. "He's not the brightest of individuals. Then, Palmer arrived home earlier than expected, and Redman lashed out."

"Not just once, but several times," said Jake. "Why would a thick thief such as Redman go equipped with a knife, let alone carry out the slice and dice that followed?"

"Forensics should have found his prints at the scene," said Ben. "Based on past performance, Redman didn't make much of an attempt to disguise his presence. We'd better pull him in and see what he has to say."

Ben and Mark got ready to leave the office.

"You will mention my contribution when the case is closed, I hope," said Jake Latimer.

"Nobody reads the small print, Jake," said Mark.

They soon found Andy Redman's address and made the ten-minute drive to Pinehurst. A stern-looking older woman answered the door.

"Mrs Redman?" asked Ben.

"What's he done this time?"

"We don't know if your son's done anything," said Ben. "We're hoping he can help us with our enquiries. Is he at home?"

"Try the bookies on Cricklade Road. That's a favourite spot for the afternoon."

"Thank you, Mrs Redman. We're much obliged. Please don't ring him to say we're on our way."

"I'd only be delaying the inevitable," she replied and closed the door.

When Ben parked the car, Andy Redman was standing on the pavement outside the bookies. Redman studied the two detectives as they walked towards him from the vehicle.

"Batman and Robin," he said, taking a long drag on a cigarette. "This will be a first for me. I've heard the names, but our paths have never crossed. So how can I help you, officers?"

"We'd like you to come back to Gablecross," said Ben. "It's quieter for a chat and warmer."

"I've got nothing else to do this afternoon," shrugged Redman, flicking his finished cigarette into a nearby bin. "Will I get a cup of tea at three o'clock?"

Mark glanced at his watch.

"If you give us the right answers, you could be home before three, and your mother can brew you a cuppa."

When they reached Ben Moore's office, Andy Redman slumped into the chair opposite Ben. Mark drew up a chair alongside his boss.

"I've been struggling to think what you think I've done," said Redman.

"Are you not working today?" asked Mark.

"I'm unemployed at present," he replied.

"Yet you can find money to spend in the bookies," said Ben.

"I was standing outside," said Redman. "Perhaps it was convenient to smoke there, where they have a bin."

"Maybe, but you were where your mother said we'd find you," said Mark.

"What do you do to pass the evenings?" asked Ben.

"I walk to my local pub for a pint and watch the football on the big screen. Normal stuff. Why do you need to know?"

"What about Monday evening?" asked Ben. "Was it a late one for you?"

"It was, as it happens. I had a Leo Sayer."

Mark knew what he meant, but Ben Moore was baffled.

"What's a Leo Sayer?" he asked.

"An all-dayer," said Redman. "I had my Giro through and started drinking at home in the morning. I picked up a half-bottle of vodka with the Sun paper from the garage up the road to get things rolling. I couldn't tell you what time I got home. My mother will remember, though. I can make noise when I'm stumbling up the stairs, so she tells me."

"You don't remember where you spent the evening?" asked Ben.

"I remember little after lunchtime," said Redman.

"Did you visit Purton on Monday?" asked Mark.

"Huh, fat lot of good that would do," said Redman. "My sister wouldn't give me the time of day, let alone persuade her husband to give me a job. Instead, he'd rather take on a bloke who's committed crimes far worse than me."

"You knew Clive Palmer?" asked Ben.

"Who hasn't heard about him in Swindon? It was in the papers. Someone sorted him out good and proper. It serves him right. Palmer got what he deserved."

"No, I meant before Monday night," said Ben.

"My mother speaks to Pat every day," said Redman. "She told me Palmer was driving a van for Rob Dolman soon after I left prison. That was three months ago."

"How did you feel about that?" asked Ben.

"Family should come first. So what, anyway, I never met Palmer."

"Did you learn where he lived for the past three months?" asked Mark.

"I heard he had a caravan in Oatley's farmyard," said Redman.

"Would we find a cigarette butt or a fingerprint somewhere in that farmyard, do you think?"

"I wasn't there," said Redman.

"You don't remember where you were," said Mark.

"I think you were up to your old tricks, Redman," said Ben. "You found yourself in Purton on Monday night, spotted Clive Palmer walking home from The Volunteer, and followed him to his caravan. What was it? You hoped to overpower him, steal the money for a taxi back to Pinehurst, and maybe an item or two you could sell for cash in the pub the following night. That's more at your level. But, unfortunately, you were drunk, and things didn't go the way you planned. Palmer resisted, and you grabbed a knife from the kitchen and stabbed him."

"No, that's not what happened," said Andy Redman.

"Oh, so you *were* there," said Ben. "If I've got it wrong, why don't you tell me what happened?"

"No, I meant I wasn't there," said Redman.

"You don't remember where you were, and unless your mother remembers hearing you get home, you don't have an alibi," said Ben.

"Can I have that cup of tea now?" asked Redman.

"Shall I call your solicitor too while we're at it?" asked Mark.

Andy Redman nodded.

Chapter Five

Monday, 17 September 2018

"WAS that when the wheels fell off the investigation?" asked Geoff Mercer.

"They certainly slowed to a walking pace," said Kenneth Truelove. "Redman's solicitor advised his client to adopt the 'no comment' defence in future sessions with DI Moore and DS Harvey."

"Did forensics find any trace of Redman's DNA at the murder scene?" asked Geoff.

"No, and to be honest, if they had identified even a partial fingerprint belonging to a career criminal, then Ben Moore should have received notification by the time they lifted Redman off the street in Pinehurst. They were already forty-eight hours into the case."

"Crime doesn't take ten days off at Christmas," said Geoff. "Why did Moore assume they would need to wait until after the holiday period to get the results from evidence the SOCOs had collected?"

"Budgets weren't any more generous in 2015 than today, Mercer," said the Chief Constable. "I expect those departments had suffered cuts, and one way to keep the service functioning over the last week in December was to operate a skeleton service."

"It makes sense, I suppose. Better to have something than nothing."

"Whatever the nuts and bolts of the departments at Gablecross when Moore and Harvey resumed their investigations, Redman was back home with his mother. She wasn't sure when her son had arrived home on Tuesday night, but it had been while she was still downstairs, and she swore it was earlier than eleven o'clock."

"So, Andy Redman had an alibi of sorts, and Ben Moore had nothing to connect him to the murder scene?"

"Except that, he was a habitual crook related to the victim's employer," said Kenneth.

"A tenuous link, at best," said Geoff. "Where did Moore and Harvey try next?"

"They interviewed James Palmer, the victim's brother, on Monday, the fourth of January. Moore and Harvey travelled to Tooting Bec, London, and visited Palmer at his home address. He confirmed he had never abandoned his brother, unlike Clive's ex-wife and children. James blamed the little minx, as he termed Gemma Long, for his late brother's woes. He insisted she'd waged a lengthy campaign to trap his brother. Ben Moore tried to point out that Clive Palmer should have reported the harassment to his superiors and perhaps have Gemma removed from his classroom, if not from the school. Army kids were always switching schools regularly. They could have removed the potential problem without drawing the attention of her classmates to the matter. James accepted Clive could have handled things better, but Marcia hadn't been entirely honest about why things were less than rosy for Clive at home. James believed the relationship with Adrian Harrold started within weeks of Marcia taking over from another teacher on maternity leave at his school."

"Did Clive Palmer suspect his wife was having an affair with a younger man?" asked Geoff.

"We'll never know," said Kenneth. "Anyway, Clive did what he did and paid the consequences. James continued to visit Clive while he was on remand in Wormwood Scrubs. Moore and Harvey were right. It was James who helped his brother open the personal bank account at a branch in Wandsworth. James liaised with the family solicitor to keep Clive informed about the court case and the divorce. After Clive's trial, James visited Clive in prison in Portland once a month. Clive told James nobody else had applied for permission to visit. He hadn't expected Marcia to do so, but it hurt Clive that his son and daughter never phoned or even wrote to him from the day the police arrested him."

"Did James know why Clive chose to live in Purton?" asked Geoff.

"He knew his brother spent much of his time in prison studying the subject he loved. It was one way to counter the boredom, and many fellow inmates didn't frequent the prison library. Clive lived his life in prison in much the same way he wanted to in Purton. He was polite, never caused the staff a problem, and preferred his own company. James wasn't aware of a particular historic site in Wiltshire that attracted Clive's interest. When he visited his brother a fortnight before his release, Clive mentioned he was thinking of buying a car and caravan."

"Couldn't he have gone to stay with James for a while?" asked Geoff.

"James is married with three children, Mercer," said the Chief Constable. "That was not on the cards. No, James told Ben Moore that Clive wasn't keen on buying a house or a flat in London. He could never teach again, and his family life had gone for good. There was nothing in London for him. Clive was planning to keep on the move, finding temporary work, while he followed his dream of digging deeper into the country's history."

"So, Moore and Harvey were no closer to discovering why Purton was Clive Palmer's first stop?" said Geoff. "I can't see the attraction, can you?"

"One thing Ben Moore added to his final report might be significant," said Kenneth. "He wondered whether Palmer discounted those historic sites in large towns and cities because they were too public. Also, anything worth finding had probably been dug up centuries ago in those large built-up areas. So, for instance, if Palmer was searching for important artefacts, where better to concentrate the search than a village in the countryside?"

"Well, I've lived in Wiltshire for decades and never heard a rumour that the Holy Grail was last seen in Urchfont. I wonder what Gus Freeman will make of this case when you hand it to him?"

"The Clive Palmer folder is going back in my drawer, for now, Mercer," said Kenneth. "Freeman needs to concentrate on the open cases he's still pursuing. He should arrive shortly. Can you ask Vera to get us coffee? I fear we're in for a torrid morning."

Geoff Mercer left the Chief Constable's office and crossed the administration floor to Vera Butler's desk. Vera was just ending a phone call.

"Kenneth would like three coffees when Gus gets here, Vera. Any sign yet?"

"I was just speaking to him," said Vera. "He was visiting an old friend in the hospital."

"That would be Bert Penman," said Geoff. "I know how close those two are. Christine and I were with Gus in the Crime Review Team office yesterday evening when a call came through."

"Christine went with you to the office; that's unusual. What was the occasion?" asked Vera.

"It was meant to be a joint celebration," said Geoff. "Gus and the team had helped close the Danute Zukas case earlier in the day. Just a few loose ends to tie up this week. Then, we were hoping to watch Rick Chalmers arrest the killer of Grant Burnside, but things didn't go as planned. I do not know what the fallout from that will be, but minutes later, Suzie received a phone call to say Bert had tripped and fallen outside the house as he returned from the pub. Irene, his lady friend, heard a loud crack and feared the worst. A broken hip, or leg, could prove fatal for someone in his mid-eighties like Bert."

"Gus found Bert sitting up in bed, complaining he could recover just as well at home," said Vera. "The loud crack Irene North heard was Bert's walking stick snapping. It gave way after months of Bert leaning on it daily, trying to take the weight off his arthritic hip. Bert suffered heavy bruising in his fall but nothing serious. Gus reckons the nurses will be fed up with Bert's moaning by lunchtime. Suzie's on call to fetch Bert from the hospital and return him to Irene. Gus is under instruction to search the hedgerows on the far side of the allotments to find a replacement among the hazel trees."

"Thank goodness Bert's not done something serious," said Geoff. "Heaven knows how Gus would manage without him. He relies on Bert to tell him when to plant everything in his allotment and when to harvest it."

"That's partly true," laughed Vera. "Although, in Gus's defence, he has written most of Bert's advice in a notebook he keeps in his garden shed. Gus is driving back from the hospital and expects to arrive at London Road in twenty minutes. I'll get Kassie organised to bring the coffee into Kenneth's office. She's got a surprise for you boys today after her weekend's baking."

"My day gets better by the minute," said Geoff.

Geoff Mercer returned to the Chief Constable's office to pass on the news.

"We can't allow ourselves to get distracted by Kassie's baked goods, Mercer," said Kenneth. "It's imperative we find and arrest Stan Jones. However, I spotted something else as I glanced at the Palmer file before putting it away. At the end of January 2016, Ben Moore made a second high-profile campaign for information. Moore was convinced that people were unwilling to provide information because of Palmer's past. James Palmer wrote to the editor of several daily newspapers in the New Year, complaining about how the media covered the case. As there was no public support for information to catch his brother's killer, James accused the press of sensationalising the story to sell newspapers. Many social media posts had appeared online, which even approved of the murder. Ben Moore appealed for anyone who had information about the murder to come forward. He said murder was murder regardless of who we are and what we've done in our lives. The guilty party shouldn't escape justice."

"How did that appeal go?" asked Geoff.

"No better than what had gone before," said Kenneth. "The writing was on the wall. Moore and Harvey never found the murder weapon, and the mystery of the tablecloth in the car's boot remained unsolved. By the end of February, they had been reassigned to other cases."

A knock at the door heralded the arrival of Gus Freeman.

"Did Vera pass on the message?" he asked. "I drove to Swindon first thing to visit Bert Penman."

"We got the message," said Geoff. "Glad to hear he's okay."

"I can't say I'm happy with getting relegated on the list of your priorities, Freeman," said Kenneth. "If you had delayed this meeting for a lead in a murder case, fine, but a broken walking stick belonging to an eighty-five-year-old villager is galling."

"I apologise, sir," said Gus. "My decision-making must have been affected by the overtime I worked at the weekend."

"Oh well, I suppose I should congratulate you on clearing up that nest of vipers at The Haven. DS Mercer dropped Natasha Zukas at my place mid-afternoon yesterday. My wife and I drove her to the airport, and she's back in Kaunas with her mother. What a delightful young lady she was, too. One can only imagine how much her sister could have achieved if she hadn't fallen under the spell of that evil Simeon Lane."

"I phoned DS Hardy before I left Urchfont for Swindon this morning," said Gus. "My team is tying up loose ends. DS Davis will visit Nyx today to update David Hodges, the manager, and Phoebe Sawyer, his barmaid. I've offered Neil the chance to pop back on Friday evening to speak to Gloria and Jane, two of the regulars who were very fond of Danute Zukas."

"What about Terry West's death?" asked Geoff.

"I've asked DS Hardy to look into that with Lydia

Logan Barre," said Gus. "My bet is Brother Ralph was involved, but time will tell."

"Do you have an explanation for the Larcombe Manor mystery, Freeman?" asked the Chief Constable. "I had to suffer a tirade from my opposite number in Avon & Somerset Police late last night. I'd only just got back from Bristol International. She'd heard a rumour that a rogue camera feed of the raid was in the public domain. She must have been mistaken because I assured her we weren't responsible.

"I'm as much in the dark as you, sir," said Gus, crossing his fingers. "I can assure you any live feed of the raid was *not* in the public domain. Only police personnel could have seen the footage. Avon & Somerset's intelligence must have been misinformed. I'll ask DS Sherman to get to the bottom of it, sir. The sooner that case gets resolved, the better."

"Right, now where's this blessed coffee? I thought Vera was handling it, Mercer?"

"Kassie Trotter's doing the rounds, sir," said Geoff. "She has a surprise for us."

"Not another lovebird?" asked Gus.

Geoff heard Kassie's dulcet tones outside the door. He got up and opened it before she could knock.

"Good morning, everyone," said Kassie. "What a great start to the week. Three coffees coming up. Would you like to see what I made for you yesterday afternoon?"

Kassie placed a tray with three coffees on Kenneth's desk and then whipped away the tea cloth covering her secret stash of cakes. She couldn't be too careful with DI Packenham on the prowl.

"Voila," said Kassie.

"What are they?" asked Geoff Mercer.

"Black bun," said Kassie. "It looks like a loaf, doesn't it?

But it's a rich treat using raisins, currants, spices, and black treacle. The subtle spice flavours I've added will tickle your taste buds."

Gus could see Geoff wasn't convinced. Kassie was already wheeling her trolley towards the door. Kenneth had got out of his chair and was poised to open the bottom drawer of his filing cabinet. When the door closed behind Kassie, the Chief Constable brought a bottle and glasses back to the desk.

"They traditionally served black bun at Hogmanay," he said. "People often took it with them when first-footing. In Scottish, Northern English, and Manx folklore, the first-footer entered the household on New Year's Day. It was seen as a bringer of good fortune for the year ahead. Coffee won't cut it on this occasion; only single malt."

"Should I lock the door, sir?" asked Gus. "In case Amazing Grace wants to cross the threshold."

"Life's boring without risk, Freeman," said Kenneth. "If she doesn't knock first, there'll be trouble."

"Make mine a double, sir," said Geoff. "Does black bun taste better than it looks?"

"Och aye," said Kenneth, pouring generous measures of whisky for each.

"I thought you were born in Taunton, sir," said Geoff.

"True, but I married a Scottish lass. My wife came from Dunfermline."

"You learn something new every day," said Gus.

"I warned Mercer this morning could be torrid," said the Chief Constable picking a wedge of cake from the tray Kassie left behind. "Let me update you on the latest murders attributed to Stan Jones. On November the eighth, 2014, Agnetha Larsen's body was discovered in a toilet at a service station beside the E20 motorway in Denmark. The service station lay on the Zealand side of the Great Belt, the strait that separates Zealand and Funen. Someone had strangled Ms Larsen with her tights. Agnetha was twenty-eight, and her sister Hanna identified her body as their parents died in a car accident in 2009. Hanna told the police the gold Lutheran cross Agnetha always wore was not among her belongings."

"Another trophy," said Geoff. "What did Agnetha do for a living?"

"She was an artisan baker with a shop in the Odense Walking Street Quarter," said Kenneth.

"How on earth did she run into Stan Jones?" asked Gus.

"Odense is the third-largest city in Denmark," said Kenneth. "It's not a surprise for Jones to have made a truck delivery to a business in the city. The Danish police say they found Agnetha's car in the service station car park. They believe Jones spotted her in a restaurant or a shop, followed her to the restrooms and seized an opportunity to strike. The post-mortem showed Agnetha died between ten and midnight. So, there was a good chance that footfall in the building was light then. The young woman was in the wrong place at the wrong time."

"That fills one of our gaps," said Gus. "You told me on Friday there were two murders. I'm guessing the next one is more recent?"

"Last year," said Kenneth. "November the twenty-fourth. Julia Truman was a nineteen-year-old student from Bodmin. Julia was studying Business Management at Penryn Campus, Falmouth. Police believe she hitched a lift on the A30 on her way home for the weekend. Jones would have used the M5 to Exeter and the A30 to reach Falmouth, although we have not identified which business he was visiting. Devon & Cornwall Police spoke to an eyewitness who saw a young woman climbing into the cab of a truck at around six in the evening."

"Did they get the registration?" asked Geoff.

Kenneth shook his head.

"Julia didn't reach home, and her parents didn't raise the alarm because they didn't know their daughter was planning on paying a brief visit. It was Monday lunchtime before anyone asked why she wasn't on campus. Then, outside Bodmin, the landlord of the Lanivet Inn on Truro Road found Julia's body in a commercial waste bin at the rear of his car park. A shocking discovery, I imagine, when discarding rubbish from the weekend trade. The young girl died from strangulation less than four miles from home. Her father noticed a nine-carat gold pendant missing when he identified his daughter's body."

"The same method as several of the others," said Gus. "Another trophy and the last piece of the November jigsaw."

"It has to be the last, Freeman," said the Chief Constable.

"I'll drink to that," said Gus.

"Me too," said Geoff. "Do you know this cake is tastier than I thought, and it goes well with the whisky."

"How can we hope to progress the Stan Jones case, sir?" asked Gus. "We have a long list of murdered women whose deaths occurred during November, plus details of trophies he removed from the bodies. You've asked the Major Crimes people to pursue the case, and apart from adding possible names to the list, they don't appear to be any closer to locating Jones and his truck."

"Gus has a point, sir," said Geoff Mercer. "We don't have anyone from London Road seconded to the MCIT investigation. If we did, we would understand what methods they're using to narrow the search."

"We can't spare anyone at present," said the Chief Constable. "Unless you have a Detective Inspector with time on their hands, Mercer?"

"DI Packenham might act as our liaison officer with the investigation, sir," said Geoff. "Although, I'd prefer a Detective Sergeant on the inside. Someone with a closer affiliation to Gus and his team."

"I don't believe the MCIT would welcome DS Chalmers with open arms, Mercer," said Kenneth. "You know the type of person running the show."

"More a Brendan Curran type of police officer than a Gus Freeman sort, sir," said Geoff. "Maybe that's why progress has been so slow?"

"Careful, Mercer," said Kenneth. "my Glen Scotia is a tad stronger than your usual tipple. We can't ruffle the feathers of our nation's finest. DI Packenham ticks most of the boxes MCIT will look for. She needs to contact Leo Gibbs, the National SIO Adviser who assembled the Jones case team. I'm sure Grace will know the right things to say and which subjects to avoid, but I can rely on you to mark her card, Mercer. It would help the career of everyone involved if Grace could help get this case resolved quickly."

"I'll get started as soon as we finish here, sir," said Geoff.

"How much surveillance has Gablecross provided, sir?" asked Gus. "Are Eddie Dolman and Jeff Hughes safe? What about the lorry park Jones frequents? Do they have unmarked cars patrolling that part of Swindon on the lookout for Jones? He has to visit Station Road at some point, even if he's not there to spend quality time with his father."

"I don't know the details, Freeman," said Kenneth. "But

as it's a matter we can control without referring to the MCIT investigators, I suggest DS Mercer liaises with Rebecca Gregory, the ACC at Gablecross. It shouldn't take long for them to find a suitable match in the command structure."

"That translates as someone I can speak to without asking for an interpreter, I imagine," said Gus.

"Just tread carefully, Freeman," sighed Kenneth. "I'm still hoping to retire with a shred of respect attached to my time in the force. Right, let's finish our drinks and clear the desk."

"My coffee's still drinkable," said Gus. "We can avoid Kassie Trotter's acid tongue if we empty these cups."

"Good thinking, Gus," said Geoff. "I'll grab that last wedge of cake and take it to my office for later. I've got a pack of extra-strong mints in my desk drawer; I'll bring them back."

"Thank you, Mercer," said Kenneth, and Geoff Mercer left the room.

"I know you're keen to learn what's next for you, Freeman, but I insist you concentrate on tying a neat bow on the Zukas case first. Then, it would be best if you worked with whichever name ACC Gregory puts forward. Under no circumstance can Stan Jones visit his father, stalk Chaloner's friends' home address and log their movements before carrying out another revenge attack this November. Is that clear?"

"Crystal clear, sir," said Gus.

"One more thing before you leave, Freeman," said the Chief Constable. "DS Chalmers has taken three days' holiday owed him. We're unsure whether he'll return to the Lymington area to rejoin the teams watching for refugees crossing the Channel. I presume he'll be at home today.

Can you speak to him about last night's fiasco? Who was responsible? How do we extricate ourselves from this interminable Burnside saga? Please remember what happened when you visited those same premises in July. The last thing we want to do is rattle Brendan Curran's cage again."

"I continue to tread with care on every task you hand me, sir," said Gus. "Like Rick Chalmers, I don't understand how the manor house came to be empty. According to Rick, the Avon & Somerset team conducted several weeks of extensive surveillance and observed families and married couples living in the main house, plus many staff and patients in buildings on the grounds. Yet, if the charity was moving, there was no sign spotted during that period of surveillance."

"I'll leave it with you, Freeman," said Kenneth Truelove. "Let me know immediately if the situation changes in the coming days. Either way, you can update me on your progress next Monday morning at the usual time. Then, if you've finally ticked off two of your three open cases, I'll let you loose on another unsolved murder."

Geoff Mercer had returned from his office. He offered an extra-strong mint to Gus and the Chief Constable.

"DI Packenham is waiting in my office, sir," he said. "I'll pave the way for her to provide a link between us and the MCIT."

"If it means she'll be out of Vera and Kassie's hair, you'll have their undying gratitude, Geoff," said Gus. "Can you ask Grace to start by getting those investigators to take shorter lunch breaks? Oh, and let us know where Stan Jones and his truck are by tomorrow morning?"

"The impossible we can do at once," said Geoff. "Miracles can take a little longer."

"Playtime's over, gentlemen," said Kenneth. "Get on with it."

Gus and Geoff left the Chief Constable stowing his bottle of Glen Scotia in the bottom drawer of his filing cabinet. Gus wondered how he'd explain away the empty glasses they'd left on the tray with the coffee cups.

"I'll talk to you later, Gus," said Geoff. "Are you driving straight to the office?"

"Not after that glass of whisky. My first port-of-call will be Rick Chalmer's flat," said Gus. "While I'm in Devizes, I might as well get the first of Kenneth's tasks underway. Let's hope Rick hasn't flown to sunnier climes."

Gus ignored his Ford Focus and headed towards the town centre. He spotted Suzie's Golf still in the car park. Bert Penman hadn't escaped from the Great Western Hospital in Swindon yet.

Gus was standing on the pavement outside Rick's flat within minutes, and he rang the Detective Sergeant first, hoping he was out of bed and ready to leave for a brisk walk to the nearest café. The rescheduling of his regular weekly session with Kenneth Truelove meant Gus had only had a wedge of black bun since breakfast.

He was in luck. Rick emerged from the front door with one arm in his battered leather jacket sleeve. Gus watched him chase the other sleeve for several seconds before completing the task.

"Did you have a late night?" asked Gus.

"We had nothing to celebrate," said Rick. "The Avon & Somerset crowd weren't keen to drown their sorrows, so I was home by eleven."

"The Chief Constable told me you had three days holiday due. Were you thinking of going somewhere?"

"The pubs haven't closed overnight, have they?" asked Rick.

"In that case, I can save you from yourself," said Gus. "The boss also asked me to get you to explain what went wrong with last night's raid. He's eager to draw a line under the whole affair. I thought we'd find a café, grab a bite to eat, and you can talk me through what we need to do to put paid to it once and for all."

"There's a place just around the next corner that serves a decent all-day breakfast, guv," said Rick, "and it won't cost an arm and a leg."

"Is that the one next to the pub where you bumped into Neil Davis recently?"

"Possibly," said Rick with a grin. "Where's your car, anyway, guv?"

"At London Road, I thought the walk would do me good. It depends on how long we took to talk through last night, but either I'll drive to the office for an hour or go straight home."

They passed the pub on their left, and soon Rick was holding the café door open for Gus.

"After you, guv. When you return to fetch the car, I'll pop next door for a swift pint."

"I doubt you'll ever change," said Gus.

"I thought that about you, guv," said Rick, "but rumour has it you're going to be a father. So congratulations. I may surprise you and settle down one day, too."

"They serve an unhealthy all-day breakfast here, you said?"

"I did, guv," said Rick. "I didn't say I'd settle down today, though, did I?"

Chapter Six

IN THE CRIME Review Team office, Alex Hardy had briefed the team with the message he'd received from Gus as soon as everyone arrived.

"I don't mind driving into Bath today to tell Hodges and his second-in-command the latest," said Neil. "Are you sure Gus said I had to go back on Friday night, Alex?"

"It wasn't a direct order, Neil," said Alex. "Gus thought you might want to let Graham and Jerry know Danute's killer had been brought to book."

"I'll call ahead to check when Phoebe Sawyer will be at Nyx," said Neil. "I don't want to make two journeys. So, I'll have a quiet word with Phoebe afterwards and ask her to update anyone who knew Danute while she worked there. That should cover it."

"What have you heard from The Haven since Saturday afternoon, Alex?" asked Luke.

"Very little," Alex replied. "Lydia and I will check with the officer in charge of Saturday's raid for the latest. Then we must interview the three main protagonists. Gus believes one of them was responsible for Terry West's death."

"I couldn't stop worrying about Gus's friend, Mr Penman, last night," said Blessing Umeh. "After Jamie dropped me off at the farm, I mentioned what had happened to John and Jackie Ferris. Just the way they looked at one another gave me goosebumps. It was clear they feared the worst."

"If what Gus says about Bert Penman is true, then he's a durable old soul," said Lydia. "Perhaps he'll survive the lot of us."

The office phone interrupted the conversation, and Alex answered.

"Yes, she's here," he said. "Just one moment. Blessing, it's PC George Collins for you."

"What on earth can that man want?" tutted Blessing. "Unless he will apologise for his crass behaviour last week."

Blessing picked up the phone.

"Detective Constable Blessing Umeh, speaking. What is it?"

"Hello, Blessing," said George. "You showed me up last week, and I know I cut corners and miss the obvious. But I will try to do better, I promise. At the weekend, I searched through the CCTV footage we had in storage. Danute was talking to her friends. They were near the church on Stallard Street. A bloke that's been in trouble for issuing dodgy MOT certificates was standing by a people carrier. He appeared to be shouting at Danute to get in the van. Laura and Natalia wanted her to stay with them. Danute went with him, of course."

"When was this, George?" asked Blessing.

"The Saturday night when Danute was seen standing

near the park entrance," said George. "There's more. I found Gibbons again on Sunday afternoon."

"Gibbons?" asked Blessing. "What, Ralph Gibbons?"

"That's him," said George. "He's a mechanic, although I'd never travel in a motor he repaired. He had a lock-up garage on Shails Lane at one time. Anyway, a speed camera caught him on Bradford Road at one-thirty-eight. Gibbons was driving, and another guy was in the passenger seat. When I asked forensics to tinker with the photo, I could see someone in the back seat. It was Danute Zukas, and she was crying."

"George Collins, you're a star," said Blessing. "Hang on to everything you've got. Can you see whether Gibbons still has that lock-up if you get a chance? I'll be in touch."

"That sounded good news," said Alex.

"I wouldn't have believed it possible," said Blessing. "Last week, I couldn't get him to raise a finger, and now George spent the weekend on the case without being asked. Gibbons and Gee don't have a hope now. We can place them in a car with Danute Zukas, heading towards The Haven, less than ten minutes after Laura Boyd said they took Danute away from her house in Gloucester Road. The sighting George has for later on Saturday night consolidates their movements. We have irrefutable evidence Brother Ralph collected the girls and returned them to The Haven."

"What was that about a lock-up?" asked Alex.

"George Collins said Ralph Gibbons was a disreputable mechanic," said Blessing. "The police at Polebarn Road and Gibbons had crossed paths over MOT certificates issued for cars that should never have been on the road. If Gibbons hung onto that lock-up after he joined Simeon Lane and the others at The Haven, I thought that might have been where he stored a printing press."

"If Collins comes back with further information, we'll pay the place a visit," said Alex. "I love it when a plan comes together."

Neil Davis left the office at a quarter to eleven. David Hodges had confirmed that he and Phoebe Sawyer would be ready and waiting. Naturally, they were keen to hear from Neil.

Alex and Lydia weren't far behind Neil as they went downstairs in the lift and took Lydia's Mini for the trip to London Road.

"Who are we going to see?" asked Lydia as she overtook a milk float on the outskirts of town. Alex closed his eyes when he saw the Ocado delivery van heading towards them, flashing its lights.

"If we get there in one piece, we're meeting Jared Hawkins," said Alex.

"Jared *was* a hunk, wasn't he?" said Lydia. "The name suits him."

"I can't say I noticed," said Alex. "ARU personnel are like PE teachers."

"I know what you mean," laughed Lydia. "PE teachers can't resist wearing shorts throughout the year, showing off their toned calves and thighs. And that's just the girls. The ARU guys wore short-sleeved t-shirts and the ever-present Kevlar stab vests on the raid."

"Any excuse to show off their guns," said Alex. "If you challenged Jared Hawkins, he'd say he was exercising his right to 'bare' arms."

"That was poor, Alex. Although, they work out far more than Luke or Neil ever do," said Lydia.

"I'm spending less time in the gym these days, too," said Alex.

"The effort you put in to get back to full fitness paid off, darling," said Lydia. "It was a long, hard road, but we got through it together."

"I couldn't have made it without you," said Alex.

Lydia swung the Mini through the London Road entrance and searched for parking near the Hub building.

"No sign of Gus's Focus here yet," she said. "He must still be at the hospital in Swindon."

Alex's phone buzzed in his pocket.

"That might be him," he said.

Lydia found a parking space, and they were soon heading to the main building where Jared Hawkins and Annie Matthews, his second-in-command, had agreed to meet them.

"Gus is on his way back from Swindon," said Alex. "He just texted me with one update I need to pass on to Blessing. Bert Penman broke nothing more serious than his walking stick."

"That's a relief," said Lydia. "All we have to do now is negotiate Reception."

A phone call from the front desk brought Annie Matthews from the Armed Response Unit to collect them.

"We normally blindfold visitors," she joked, "but Jared said I could trust you not to reveal our secrets."

When the four police personnel were seated in Jared Hawkins's light, airy office, Alex told the ARU team leader what Blessing Umeh had learned this morning.

"Another piece of solid evidence is always useful," said Jared. "Gibbons isn't going anywhere, so we can wait for further news from Polebarn Road and then look inside this unit of his at our leisure. I'm happy to leave that to your team, Alex. If it impedes Gus Freeman's next case, he can always pass it onto DS Mercer. You said on the phone that you wanted to speak with Lane, Gibbons and Gee. Was that concerning where they got their leaflets printed or the money trail?"

"No," said Alex. "Gus had a hunch Terry West's death wasn't an accident. So they have tasked us to pursue that line of enquiry, and the three principal men at The Haven were the most likely suspects."

"Given what you've learned about Gibbons, he's the one I'd concentrate on," said Annie Matthews. "West died in a car crash where brake failure was a major contributor, together with the volume of alcohol he had consumed."

"The three men you want to speak to are in the custody suite on your doorstep," said Jared. "They will transfer to HMP Erlestoke later in the week. So if you want to get to Gibbons quickly, I should head back to your office and make the call."

"I'll call before we leave here," said Alex. "In the meantime, can you tell us what happened after we left you at The Haven on Saturday?"

"We removed the ringleaders, as you know," said Jared, "but a high percentage of the others were happy to continue living there. Because they had given themselves to the cause, they weren't ready to return to the world they had rejected."

"Every man, woman and child we spoke to had been drugged," said Annie. "LSD was the chief weapon in Brother Simeon's arsenal. If there's one thing cults are known for, they can dictate their followers' thoughts, attitudes, and behaviours. Cult leaders dedicate themselves to mastering the art of mind control. There were many ways to control the group of individuals at The Haven. First, Lane looked to separate members from their loved ones at those Sunday meetings. They soon isolated new members at the remote manor house, then they were confused and disorientated by the narcotics Lane supplied."

"Narcotics cause significant psychological alterations in human behaviour," said Jared. "These changes are rarely positive. When the members were hooked, the drug became their God. Brother Simeon established himself as a God-like figure in their lives. He controlled the supply of drugs, and they became reliant on him. Keeping him happy was paramount. The drugs made Danute Zukas and the others vulnerable. They would never have done what they did before he'd established that dependency. He was as much a monster as Manson or any other cult leader over the years."

"Do you think the brothers and sisters who stayed behind will eventually leave The Haven and return to their families?" asked Lydia.

"We've contacted the right people to handle what lies ahead for them," said Annie. "We removed every scrap of narcotics from The Haven on Saturday."

Alex Hardy knew what Annie Matthews meant. It took weeks to release himself from the grip prescription meds had on him after the pain from his injuries became too much to bear.

There were tough times ahead for the men and women Lane had brainwashed.

"Did you find any link to the computer equipment and documentation to help trace the funds available to The Haven?" asked Alex.

"We planned to visit the office premises in Bradford-on-Avon this morning," said Jared. "DS Mercer asked DI John Cook from Polebarn Road to handle it. We're waiting to hear from him."

"Variety is the spice of life," said Lydia. "It will be the first time Cook has escaped the office in ages."

"Was there anything else we can help you with?" asked Jared.

"I'll call the custody suite," said Alex. "Perhaps we can pay Gibbons a visit before we return to the office."

A klaxon sounded outside the building. Lydia sensed movement around her as she listened to Alex on the phone.

"What's happening?" she asked their hosts.

Jared and Annie had already donned their Kevlar vests and were preparing to leave.

"A bloke has barricaded himself in his flat with his two-year-old son," said Jared, reading the message on his phone. "When the boy's mother arrived to collect the lad after the weekend, her ex-partner attacked her and left her bleeding in the stairwell outside the first-floor flat. We'll see you off the premises, but you might need to run to keep up."

Alex and Lydia hurried outside. An ARU van screeched to a halt, and Jared and Annie jumped inside to join the rest of their team. They were heading for the car park exit before Lydia could catch her breath.

"Exciting stuff," she said.

"We can't see Gibbons for another hour at least," said Alex. "He wants to wait for his solicitor."

"I'll drive carefully on the way back," said Lydia. "We could visit the office if you wish to fill in time?"

"There's a Greggs on the outskirts of town, isn't there? Let's grab a bite to eat."

When they arrived at the custody suite, Alex spotted a Lexus parked outside.

"I bet that doesn't belong to anyone working here," he said.

"The Haven's finances must be healthy," said Lydia, "if they can afford a solicitor with such expensive tastes."

Alex and Lydia entered the building and identified themselves to the officer at the front desk.

"We were expecting you. Please wait."

"You've been here before, haven't you?" asked Alex as they sat in Reception.

"Yes," said Lydia. "When Gus interviewed James Bosworth and Krystal Warner. That's an afternoon I'll never forget. Gus was awesome."

The young officer soon returned. He pointed to the door at the far end of the corridor, where another officer stood waiting. Lydia and Alex began the long march.

"This was the point at which James and Krystal passed one another," said Lydia. "Gus timed it to perfection. He'd sown the seeds of doubt in her mind, and it wasn't long before he'd gained a confession."

"I have read the Freeman Files report, you know," said Alex.

"It's not the same as being there," said Lydia.

Ralph Gibbons and his solicitor waited in the interview room. Neither man looked happy to be there.

Lydia checked the recording equipment was set up correctly. Alex thought Brother Ralph looked less foreboding in a grey sweatshirt and sweatpants.

"Thank you for agreeing to speak with us this afternoon, Mr Gibbons," said Alex. "For the record, I'm DS Alex Hardy. My colleague is Lydia Logan Barre."

Alex nodded towards the solicitor.

"Digby Ballard-Hayes, Ralph's solicitor. I'm aware of my client's charges, and he's already pleaded guilty. I cannot see why this interview is necessary. Who do you work for? I've never seen either of you before."

"We report to Gus Freeman with Wiltshire Police's Crime Review Team," said Alex. "Chief Constable

Kenneth Truelove created the team to take a fresh look at unsolved murder cases."

"Unsolved murder cases? I repeat. I fail to see why this interview is necessary. My client has not been charged with murder. It was Simeon Lane who killed that young girl. My client was under Lane's spell and helped dispose of the body. He regrets his actions and is seeking help with his drug addiction."

"When you got arrested on Saturday, Mr Gibbons, we removed several sets of keys from your jacket pocket."

"So what?" replied Ralph Gibbons.

"We checked the vehicles parked outside The Haven to confirm which ones you drove."

Lydia watched Alex hold his notebook at an angle to shield the page from Gibbons and his solicitor. Alex continued to read from the blank piece of paper.

"So, we could check the contents of your BMW and the minivan you drove when you ferried the young women in your charge into town."

"You won't find anything worthwhile," scoffed Gibbons.

Digby Ballard-Hayes placed a hand on Ralph's arm.

"They're trying to goad you, Ralph. Don't bite."

"We aren't concerned with the keys that belonged to various rooms within The Haven, but we know one set of keys was for the office space you rented in Bradford-on-Avon. What can you tell us about that?"

"We needed somewhere with access to a computer and printer to check our general accounts," said Gibbons. "Simeon told me we only needed to check basic house-keeping items and the production of our leaflets and flyers. We couldn't grow all the food we required, so someone had to get the best deals on the food and drink we bought. James and I shared that task between us, plus the sourcing of the materials for our flowers. It was hard work. Everyone at The Haven had agreed to adopt a spartan lifestyle."

"We saw how the brothers and sisters lived at The Haven," said Lydia. "Conditions were far more comfortable in the apartments you, James, and Simeon occupied, though, weren't they?"

"No comment."

"We haven't completed scrutinising every document at the office yet," said Alex. "No doubt we'll discover the trail to the money for the cars, minivans, and much more. So let's put that aside for now and concentrate on the keys to the lock-up in Trowbridge. Do you remember that place, Ralph? You got into trouble when you issued MOT certificates for cars heading for the scrapyard."

" No comment."

"We intend to have a forensic team in that lock-up tomorrow. My boss has a hunch we might find the tools you used on a Toyota back in 2015."

"I never had a Toyota in that garage back then," said Gibbons. "I finished with the motor trade racket long ago. That was way before I met Simeon and saw the light."

"Perhaps," said Alex. "But you hung onto the lock-up, and the keys, didn't you? You never know when the tools you accumulate over the years will come in handy. Do you know what I think we'll find? A well-stocked toolkit with your fingerprints on it and everything inside."

"My client has already said he used to work at that lock-up, DS Hardy," said Ballard-Hayes. "Of course, you would find his prints on tools he owned when he worked as a mechanic."

"What if we found flecks of paint on the tools, Ralph?" asked Alex. "The tests would take time, but if Gus Freeman's right, we'd be able to identify a particular car you worked on from those flecks of paint."

"No comment," said Gibbons.

"Is this fishing expedition over, DS Hardy?" asked Ballard-Hayes.

"You may not have met DI West, sir, but he was a detective at Manvers Street, Bath. Terry West drove a clapped-out Toyota," said Alex. "He left Bear Flat and drove out of Bath searching for The Haven. Terry knew it had to be somewhere remote. What happened, Ralph? Did Terry stumble across the manor house, and you and James realised he could cause problems if you let him get away?"

"No comment," said Gibbons.

"You can relax, Ralph," said Alex. "We haven't checked inside the lock-up yet, and when we do, we don't expect to find those tools. After all, someone had to maintain the vehicles at The Haven, didn't they? I'm surprised Simeon trusted you to keep the vans on the road, given your history."

"That's not fair," said Gibbons. "I was an excellent mechanic. Times were hard, and when someone offered me several hundred quid to overlook the faults I'd found during his annual inspection, it was too much to turn down. Word got around, and I made more money from dodgy MOT certificates than from tinkering with engines twelve hours a day - until I got caught."

"Where did you store your tools at The Haven?" asked Lydia.

"In the shed at the back of the house, next to the car park," said Gibbons.

"We will find that evidence, Ralph," said Alex. "You know that, don't you? If one speck of paint remains on either of the tools used on that Toyota…."

"Okay, Okay," shouted Gibbons. "James spotted the car parked up the hill in the lane leading to the house. We used to take turns patrolling the grounds in the evenings. In case a brother or sister tried to leave. James found me working on a van in the car park and asked what he should do. I walked outside the main gates with him, but the driver wasn't in the car. He suddenly emerged from the bushes. I think he'd been relieving himself. It was plain he'd been drinking. He muttered something about the flowers and that he couldn't sleep nights without nightmares over the murder he'd never solved. James knew immediately he meant Danni. He persuaded Terry West to spend time inside The Haven; to prove to him that we lived a simple life and thrived in a world without modern technology. James nodded towards the Toyota. I realised what he wanted me to do."

"I'd like to talk to my client, DS Hardy," said the solicitor.

"No," sighed Gibbons. "I need to get it off my chest. I waited until James had walked through the gates, and then I ran around to the rear of the main building to fetch my tool kit. It took me minutes to finish the job that wear-and-tear and lack of maintenance had almost completed. I was confident the Toyota wouldn't reach Bath without breaking down. It wasn't my aim to cause a fatal crash, although I believe that was what James had in mind."

"A jury will decide whether that was the case or not, Ralph," said Alex.

"What happened next?" asked Lydia.

"James brought West outside the estate's walls again and walked him to his car. James invited West to return at any time if he wished to learn more. The man was in no state to drive, but he turned that Toyota around and headed for the main road. We heard the news about the crash late the following day."

"I insist I be allowed to speak with my client now, DS Hardy," said Ballard-Hayes.

"Carry on," said Alex. "We're finished for now. Ralph will transfer to HMP Erlestoke later in the week. We'll continue searching for evidence to confirm your client's version of events. Our boss, or another detective from London Road, will advise you when we're ready to visit him to add further charges to the list. I'll tell the custody officer you'll need a few minutes with your client before he's returned to the cells."

Alex and Lydia left the interview room. After Alex had spoken to the custody officer, they walked along the long corridor towards the exit.

"We did it, Alex," said Lydia.

"Only because I played a hunch that Ralph's previous trade had to have been useful at The Haven."

"Jared and Annie never mentioned the tools or the shed," said Lydia. "They *will* still be there, won't they?"

"I hope so," said Alex. "Whether we'll find anything incriminating on the tools I mentioned, I do not know. We've got a confession on record from Ralph Gibbons that he tampered with the brakes on Terry West's Toyota. A jury might believe he only meant to disable the car. Ralph Gibbons sounded as if he'd decided he wanted a clean slate. I reckon Ralph will co-operate. I'll suggest to DS Mercer they need to squeeze Gibbons for information on The Haven's finances. He tried to make out that the office in Bradford-on-Avon was a minor cog in the organisation. I can't believe he doesn't know where Simeon Lane was hiding the rest of the money."

Lydia drove them to the car park at the rear of the Old

Police Station. When they exited the lift, Luke and Blessing were the only ones in the office.

"Have you heard from Gus?" asked Alex.

"Nothing yet, Alex," said Luke. "Neil rang to say he's returning from Bath."

"I expect Mr and Mrs Ferris will have heard by the time you get home, Blessing," said Alex, "but Bert Penman wasn't badly hurt last night. The loud crack his friend heard was Bert's walking stick snapping."

"Oh, thank goodness," said Blessing. "Did you two make any progress?"

"We spent time with the ARU personnel at London Road," said Lydia. "Then Alex got a confession from Brother Ralph when we interviewed him at the custody suite. Ralph Gibbons was responsible for Terry West's death."

"Well done," said Luke. "You've had a better time than we have stuck in the office."

"We'll get our contributions into the Freeman Files," said Alex. "There are a couple of loose ends to deal with before we close the file completely. First, we must find the keys to the lock-up among items taken from Gibbons on Saturday."

"That's right," said Lydia. "He didn't bat an eyelid when you mentioned those. Brother Ralph would have said straight away if they hadn't been in his jacket pocket."

"Then, I must ask Jared Hawkins where they removed the evidence from The Haven. Ralph's tool kit will be among that, and we can get forensics to search for finger-prints and anything to link Ralph's tools to Terry West's Toyota. They will need to liaise with Manvers Street and whoever did the test on the vehicle at the crash site in 2015."

"I can see you're going to be busy," said Luke. "Until Gus returns with a fresh case, Blessing and I are at a loose end."

"I wonder when Gus will be back?" asked Blessing. "When he meets with the Chief Constable, they usually have a working lunch, and he's not in the office before three o'clock."

"That schedule went out of the window when Gus raced to Swindon to check on his old friend," said Lydia. "Maybe they won't finish until late, and Gus will drive straight home to Urchfont."

"I think we need to concentrate on getting the Zukas case out of our hair," said Alex. "I'll call Jared and locate the items we need before keying in my report. Luke, I want you and Blessing to pick up the keys for the lock-up in Trowbridge and the tool kit from the shed at The Haven. Blessing, perhaps you could persuade George Collins to accompany you to Shails Lane? I doubt you'll find anything relating to the case, but an inventory of whatever you find inside should be on record at Polebarn Road for future reference."

"Got it, Alex," said Blessing.

"Do you want me to organise forensic tests on any relevant tools I find in this tool kit, Alex?" asked Luke.

"Yes, please, Luke," said Alex. "Sorry, we have got nothing more exciting at present."

They heard the lift descend to the ground floor.

Neil Davis emerged a minute later.

"Mission accomplished," he said. "David Hodges and Phoebe know everything we know."

"Not quite," said Alex. "Ralph Gibbons has admitted he tampered with the brakes on Terry West's car. So, Phoebe Sawyer can get closure on how her friend died."

"I should call her," said Neil. "What was the name of the DS that worked with West? Can anyone remember?"

"Erica Barge," said Lydia. "You visited her place, Alex. Wasn't she considering quitting the police to open a restaurant with her husband?"

"That's right," said Alex. "Look, someone needs to go to Manvers Street to join the dots between the original crash investigation and the evidence we gather from Ralph Gibbons' tools. I suggest Neil tags along with you, Luke."

"That's fine with me," said Neil. "I could drink a river dry. Anyone else for a coffee?"

While Neil beavered away in the restroom, the lift descended to the ground floor.

"You'd better tell Neil that Gus is on his way," said Alex.

Sure enough, Gus exited the lift minutes later, and Lydia noticed their leader wasn't carrying the usual large folder.

"A change of plan, folks," said Gus.

"Neil's in negotiations with the Gaggia, guv," said Lydia. "With luck, we'll each have a coffee soon, and you can tell us the news."

Gus sat at his desk and waited. Finally, Neil emerged from the restroom with six coffees.

"Welcome back, guv," he said. "What's the latest?"

Gus explained that Kenneth Truelove wouldn't give them a fresh case until they'd finished at least two of the cases they had outstanding. He told them DI Packenham was now the liaison between London Road and the Major Crimes Team assigned to the Stan Jones case.

"I'm not sure what that will achieve, guv," said Neil. "I reckon Stan Jones is controlling the agenda. We'll have to wait until he visits his father to renew his Swindon Advertiser subscription. The police didn't get Al Capone for the murders he committed, did they? They got him for tax evasion."

"The Chief Constable thinks we should watch any potential targets in Swindon, as well as his father's house, Neil," said Gus. "He wants us to be pro-active. Grace will try to warn us that Jones is visiting the area. If he does, we have to capture him without incident. To make sure he doesn't sneak into Swindon unnoticed to check out the whereabouts of Richard Chaloner's close friends, for instance, we'll need ACC Gregory to give us a contact at Gablecross to keep us in the loop at all times."

"Lydia and I can offer a crumb of comfort, guv," said Alex.

He explained what had happened at the custody suite earlier in the afternoon.

"Terrific," said Gus. "I knew Terry West's death wasn't accidental. Good work, you two."

Alex outlined the tasks he'd assigned to Neil, Luke, and Blessing.

"That should bring the affair to a successful conclusion," said Gus. "One down, two left to tackle."

Gus looked across the room to Luke Sherman.

"Luke, you're the right man for the next job, according to Geoff Mercer," said Gus. "I spent time with your ex-colleague, Rick Chalmers, earlier, and we spoke at length about the fiasco at Larcombe Manor last night."

"Is Rick not going back to Lymington, guv?" asked Luke.

"The Chief Constable was unsure, Luke. Geoff Mercer thought a fresh pair of eyes was required, no matter what Rick was doing next. Why did the raid fail in such a spectacular fashion? How did a hundred people disappear like that? Rick was adamant the information from Avon &

Somerset was sound. The man responsible for Grant Burnside's death should have been there last night. I want you to find him, Luke, and arrest him."

"Will I need to liaise with Portishead, guv?" asked Luke.

"I'm sure DS Mercer will sanction that, Luke, and if you need to work undercover, that will receive a green light, as well. Are you happy to go ahead?"

"Of course, guv," said Luke.

"It's been an odd day," said Gus. "Let's tidy up any reports we need to get into the files and head home at four. Everyone has plenty of work ahead of them tomorrow."

Chapter Seven

GUS WASN'T FAR behind the others when the office emptied one minute after four. He called Suzie to tell her he was finishing early. She texted him to say she would collect Bert Penman from the Great Western Hospital after work.

"That's me told," thought Gus as he eased the Focus into the late afternoon traffic.

If Suzie left London Road at five o'clock, she wouldn't be back at Bert's house before half-past six. Gus wondered whether Irene North was at home, waiting for Bertie's return, or sat at his bedside. There was only one way to find out.

Gus drove through Devizes, passed the London Road HQ without slowing, and pulled up outside Bert's house at twenty to five. The curtain twitched in the front room. Irene appeared at the front door before Gus got halfway up the path.

"Mr Freeman," she said. "Bert won't be home just yet. Your Miss Ferris has offered to collect him."

"So I hear, Irene," said Gus. "What a relief to learn it

was that wretched walking stick Bert kept waving around that you heard. It could have been far worse. He wants me to search for a replacement, but it might be better if you persuade him to stop avoiding the doctor. That hip of his won't get any better."

"I told Bertie I would look after him while he recovered from the operation," said Irene. "He's a stubborn so-and-so. Bertie reckons there are people in far worse pain than him. So he'll keep badgering you until he has another stick to lean on."

Gus knew Irene was right. These past couple of years, it had been amusing watching Bert dovetail his visits to The Lamb to avoid the occasions when the local GP was in the bar. Stubborn was the right word. Like many of his contemporaries, Bert was hospital averse and relied on his parents' traditional remedies - plenty of red meat, fruit, vegetables straight from the land, and cider.

"Suzie won't be here for two hours," said Gus. "I'll look along the hedgerows next to the church. If I find something suitable, I'll bring it for his master to decide. Do you need any help to get the place ready?"

"Bertie might struggle with the stairs, Mr Freeman," said Irene. "Perhaps you could persuade him to sleep downstairs?"

"Have you spoken to Brett since you heard Bert was coming home?" asked Gus.

"I kept him in touch," said Irene, "but he will be in Wootton Bassett at the surgery until half-past five. Then he's coming straight here once he gets away."

"Good," said Gus. "Between us, we should be able to get Bert's bed moved downstairs. Then, if it's ready for him when he gets home, he'll be stuck with it until Brett and I move it upstairs again. It will be his only choice, won't it?"

"Bertie won't be happy," said Irene, "but we have an understanding, Mr Freeman. Our bedroom doors stay closed once we've said goodnight on the landing."

"If Brett's getting here at six, I'll start hunting for hazel trees," said Gus. "I'll be back in time to help him with the move."

"Right you are, Mr Freeman," said Irene. "I'll make a start and bring his bedding down. After that, you boys can do the heavy work."

Gus left Irene standing at the door and returned to the Focus. As he drove along the lane to the allotments, he wondered whether Irene still hankered after persuading Bert to make an honest woman of her.

The evenings were drawing in, but the allotments were bathed in sunshine when Gus arrived. He opened his shed and found a pair of secateurs, gloves, and a saw. Then, as he set off towards the hedges on the far side, he heard a familiar voice.

"Good evening, Gus. You're home early."

"Ah, Reverend," said Gus. "Just the woman I was hoping to see."

"Now, which is it?" said Clemency. "You want to arrange for the reading of the banns for the wedding? Or find a suitable date next year for the christening?"

"Not so fast, Reverend," said Gus. "No, it concerns Bert Penman. Suzie will deliver Bert to his door at around six-thirty. Brett should be there by six, and Irene wants to get Bert's bed downstairs before he arrives. It will make things easier for him until the heavy bruising subsides. Also, unless I'm in luck, he won't have a stick to lean on while he's recuperating."

"I suppose you want me to help Irene persuade Bert to do as he's told," said Clemency.

"Would you? Oh, it's grand of you to offer," said Gus.

Clemency Bentham shook her head and laughed.

"Suzie often says you're incorrigible. I intended to drop in on Bert to welcome him home, and then Brett and I were off to the cinema. Mamma Mia's showing in Devizes."

"I remember the last film I sat through at the cinema," Gus said. "Tess was desperate to watch it. It sounded interesting. I enjoy a good courtroom drama, like Twelve Angry Men, but this one proved to be a major disappointment."

"What was it called, Gus?" asked Clemency.

"Kramer versus Kramer," said Gus.

Gus left Clemency shaking her head, gathered his tools, and walked to the far side of the field. He'd seen Bert's walking stick on dozens of occasions. The dimensions weren't an issue, but how to tell whether what he was looking at in the hedgerow was willow, hazel, or ash? That was a different matter.

Gus returned to Bert's house with half a dozen possible sticks on the back seat of the Focus. Brett's car was already parked outside, and the Reverend's bicycle was leaning against the side of the house. He rang the doorbell.

"Brett's in his grandfather's bedroom with Clemency," said Irene.

"Don't worry," said Gus. "I'll knock."

"Get on with you," said Irene, cuffing Gus on the shoulder.

Fifteen minutes later, Bert's bed was in situ; pillows plumped, ready for the wounded soldier's return.

"We were cutting things fine," said Clemency. "That's Suzie's Golf in the lane if I'm not mistaken."

Irene went outside to welcome Bert home. Gus watched from the front room window as Bert levered himself out of the Golf's passenger seat and stood beside the open door.

Suzie retrieved an aluminium walking frame from the back seat, and Bert gingerly made his way up the path to the door.

Brett and Clemency helped Bert sit in his familiar chair by the fireplace in the front room.

"I made you a cup of tea, Bert," said Clemency, placing a mug on the small table beside him.

"Very neighbourly of you, Reverend," said Bert. "You needn't have gone to all *that* trouble."

He was nodding towards the bed.

"You won't be able to manage the stairs, Bert," said Suzie. "And the doctor suggested you use the walking frame for a week."

"I'll be up and about in no time," said Bert. "My right buttock resembles a large posy of purple and yellow pansies, but I'll be right as rain once I have my new walking stick."

"We think you should listen to the doctor, Bertie," said Irene. "You'll be comfortable down here, and if you stop snoring, I can always check you're still alright."

"Hmph," said Bert. "Two bedroom doors don't mellow the sound of your snoring, Irene North, and you know it."

"If you check on Bert, remember to put on your dressing gown, Irene," said Suzie. "The doctor said Bert should avoid too much excitement for a while."

"As everything seems back to normal, we'll get off," said Brett.

"We are going to the cinema, Bert," said Clemency.

Suzie watched Irene move her chair closer to Bert.

"That's a signal for us to leave, Gus," she said.

"I've got samples in the car, sir, if you have time?" Gus said to Bert.

"They won't walk in here by themselves, Mr Freeman. Let the dog see the rabbit."

Gus fetched the pieces of tree branch that most closely matched Bert's broken stick.

"Will one of these be any good, Bert?" asked Gus.

"That piece of hazel looks just the ticket, Mr Freeman," said Bert. "Irene can use the rest as kindling when we need to light a winter fire."

Gus was happy to have got one right out of six.

"Put this in a safe place, Irene," said Gus, handing her the chosen item. "Don't let Bert have it back until his bruises have faded."

"I know Bertie too well," said Irene, "I'll keep hold of it for three days longer than that. I can't take his word that they've faded."

"You have an understanding," said Gus.

"Correct," said Bert and Irene in unison.

Gus and Suzie left the old couple alone and walked outside to their cars.

"What do you fancy?" he asked. "Park the cars at the bungalow and walk to the Lamb for a meal?"

"Yes, please," said Suzie. "I'm famished. Then you can tell me about your day."

Tuesday, 18 September 2018

"A QUIET NIGHT IN TONIGHT?" asked Gus as he and Suzie stood beside their cars at twenty-past eight.

"That sounds good," she replied. "Will you cook this evening, or shall I?"

"Leave it to me," said Gus.

They drove into Devizes in convoy, and Gus flashed his headlights as Suzie turned into the Wiltshire Police HQ. He continued through the town centre to arrive at the Old Police Station car park at two minutes to nine.

Blessing Umeh's Nissan was parked in the extreme left-hand space reserved for CRT personnel, and Lydia's red Mini sat at the opposite end. Gus opted to grab the centre spot. Neil and Luke were cutting it fine, but he was confident they would arrive before he reached the first floor.

"Morning, guv," said Alex. "Did Bert Penman get home safely?"

"Bruised but unbowed," said Gus. "Where's Blessing? Her car's downstairs."

"PC Collins was waiting for her when she arrived, guv," said Lydia. "He's driven them to Devizes to collect the keys and then to Trowbridge to examine Gibbons' lock-up."

"Blessing has had a remarkable effect on that young man," said Gus.

The lift descended to the ground floor, and Neil Davis emerged two minutes later.

"Any sign of Luke when you drove in, Neil?" asked Gus.

"I thought he'd be first in this morning, guv," said Alex. "Luke perked up after you gave him that new assignment yesterday afternoon."

"He was fed-up with having nothing to do, guv," said Lydia.

"Luke has had itchy feet for a while," said Gus. "DS Mercer thought a spot of undercover work would keep him attached to this team a little longer. I've been meaning to sit with Luke for a heart-to-heart for a week or two to remind him he's a valuable team member. But sometimes the case we're working on changes gear swiftly, and my spare time disappears in a flash."

The doorbell on the ground floor rang.

"We're not expecting visitors, are we, guv?" asked Lydia. "That looks like a woman on the camera."

Gus walked closer to the screen in the corner of the office.

"Amazing Grace," he groaned. "What have we done to deserve this?"

"Do you want me to collect her, guv?" asked Lydia.

"Alex should go, Lydia, as your longer skirt appears to be at the cleaners."

Minutes later, Alex exited the lift with DI Packenham as she entered the Crime Review Team office for the first time.

"Ah, Mr Freeman," she said. "So this is where you hide."

"I hope you're here to give us good news," said Gus. "You've contacted Leo Gibbs, and he's located Stan Jones; am I right?"

"Not quite," said Grace. "I thought there were more of you. Or do you work flexi-time? That's frowned upon at London Road, you know. If we allowed standards to slip, police support services personnel would start asking to work from home. That would never do."

"We have one staff member on her way to Trowbridge to search a place of interest related to our latest case," said Gus. "We *were* wondering what had happened to DS Sherman. He's not usually late."

"It sounds as if Luke's on his way up, guv," said Neil.

The lift doors opened, and Luke Sherman walked into the office.

"What on earth has happened, Luke?" asked Lydia, jumping from her chair and running to her colleague.

Luke looked like he'd gone twelve rounds with someone taller and heavier.

"Nicky and I have split up," he said. "I told him about

the prospect of me going undercover, guv. I knew he wouldn't be happy, but he went ballistic and started throwing things—plates, punches, and expletives. We'd already argued at the weekend because I worked Saturday and Sunday. He said the job always came first, and it was over if we couldn't have the social life we did when we first got together. So I packed a bag and left. Sorry, I was late, guv, but it took longer to drive here from Swindon than I thought."

Lydia squeezed Luke's arm. She'd guessed there was something more than a friendship starting between Luke and someone he'd met at Gablecross. Maybe that was where he went last night. At least they were both police officers and understood the problems. What would that mean for Luke and the Crime Review Team from now on?

"Are you okay to work today, Luke?" asked Gus.

"I'll arrange for Neil to collect the items we need from the evidence room, guv, and stay in the office if I may. I'm a quick healer and should be back in action later in the week."

"We'll share the workload between us, guv," said Neil. "There's nothing this team can't handle."

DI Packenham sat next to Gus Freeman, watching and listening.

She hadn't seen eye-to-eye with Gus Freeman from the first day they'd met. He didn't march to the same beat as modern high-ranking officers, yet the men and women surrounding him seemed to go above and beyond. So what was it he had that inspired such unswerving loyalty?

"Can we get to business now, Mr Freeman?" she asked.

The office phone rang. Gus gave her a look that suggested she needed to wait until he'd answered.

"Freeman speaking," said Gus. "Good morning, ma'am.

Of course, DI Francis is an officer I've met in the past. I'd be happy to work with him on the Jones case. Thank you for the call. Goodbye."

"Was that ACC Gregory from Gablecross?" asked Grace.

"Rebecca?" said Gus. "Yes, I was expecting her call. Now, what was it you wanted to discuss, Ms Packenham?"

Alex Hardy turned to Lydia and hoped DI Packenham didn't see him grinning.

"Gareth is to be our liaison officer, then," he said. "Gus said he'd improved somewhat since he worked at London Road. We bumped into Gareth on the Stacey Read case and left on speaking terms. Gus still doesn't think Gareth will ever make an outstanding detective, but he's an excellent researcher. That talent could be useful this time around."

Lydia wondered whether it would be wise to interrupt Gus and Grace with an offer to provide coffee. She didn't want the efficiency expert to think that was all they did here.

Luke was sitting at his desk, and Lydia sensed he had more he wanted to say, but not in front of a stranger. So she tapped on his desk as she headed for the restroom. Luke joined her one minute later.

"What does the other guy look like?" asked Lydia.

"I didn't hit Nicky. I just waited until the storm abated, then got out. Heaven knows what would have happened if I had lost it, too."

"How could you just stand there and take it?"

"Deep down, I knew Nicky was right," said Luke. "The job came first in our relationship. I can't see that ever changing."

"Where did you stay last night, Luke?" asked Lydia.

"At Tom Spencer's place," replied Luke. "We met on the

Chaloner case. Tom was working on thefts of large agricultural vehicles from farms in North Wiltshire, and we bumped into one another while I was visiting Jake Latimer. Tom asked me for a drink, and I told him I was in a relationship and getting married. Nicky and I hadn't spoken about setting a date for weeks because things were going downhill. So, last week, I drove to Swindon to meet with Tom. Nothing happened; we met in a pub, talked, and got to know one another. Then, last night, I knew I had to get out of the house, and without calling one of the team, I was out of options. I called Tom. He was happy for me to sleep on the sofa last night after we'd talked. We talked again this morning over breakfast."

"What are your plans?" asked Lydia.

"I'm going to retrieve my things from Warminster and look for a place in Swindon. I've got to ask DS Mercer to transfer me to Shrivenham to work out of Gablecross. That shouldn't prevent me from working on his proposed undercover assignment. While I work on putting the Burnside case to bed, I'll retain contact with Gus and the rest of you. I'll miss this place, but Alex is the senior team member, and Gus will only stay in charge for a short period. A parting of the ways was inevitable, and the split with Nicky brought things to a head sooner than I expected."

"And Tom Spencer?"

"It's too early to say, Lydia," said Luke.

Lydia hugged her colleague.

"Ouch," said Luke. "Not too hard. My ribs are killing me."

"Do you think we should take coffees back for the gang, plus Amazing Grace?"

"While you crank up the Gaggia, I'll see what the Detective Inspector wants," said Luke.

He left Lydia in the restroom and approached Gus's desk.

"How do you take your coffee, DI Packenham?"

"I don't, DS Sherman. I only drink green tea."

"A green tea it shall be," said Luke.

Neil was ready to leave for Devizes.

"I'll grab a coffee later, Luke. I should be back before lunch, and we'll sift through the evidence together."

Luke gave Neil the thumbs up and returned to the restroom.

Gus wondered if Geoff Mercer had provided stocks of other hot drinks when the office opened. If so, it was six months since anyone had wanted to try whichever varieties were available. Perhaps he could blame Geoff if Grace disapproved.

"Take me through the sequence of murders your team and MCIT have attributed to Stan Jones," said Grace.

"Emma Fox died in 2007. We believe she was the first victim. Her family said her gold necklace of a fox with its brush covered in red stones was missing. Molly Phelps died in 2010, and someone had removed her choker chain and cross from her body."

"Both these attacks took place in November," said Grace, "near a UK motorway?"

"Correct," said Gus. "Both victims were similar in build and appearance to Tara Laing, the girl who jilted Jones on their wedding day. Jones works in Europe and the UK; his next victim was Petra Fischer in 2012. Petra always wore a gold chain that wasn't found with her body or belongings."

"How do you explain the gaps?"

"Jones carried the trauma of the firework injuries with him throughout his teens and early twenties. Then his only girlfriend left him, and his mother died. With little to occupy his mind as he drove thousands of miles home and abroad, the pain he felt centred on Tara Laing. She had robbed him of the future he thought lay ahead. He blamed her for his mother's untimely demise. It was two years before he snapped and attacked Emma Fox. So why did he wait three years before attacking Molly Phelps? Maybe it was as simple as not finding a girl who reminded him of Tara?"

"Or we haven't found all the bodies yet," said Grace.

"Time will tell. The brutal nature of the murder of Sammy Yendell in South Wales in 2013 pointed to an escalation in Jones's actions. Jones took a charm bracelet on that occasion, and since then, he's murdered someone in November every year. Agnetha Larsen, in 2014, wore a gold Lutheran cross; Zoe Dubois, in 2015, another gold necklace. The first suggestion that Jones had switched his attention from Tara Laing to the boys who scarred him for life with that firework was in 2016 when he shot Richard Chaloner. That's the only time Jones has used a weapon, although after he'd strangled Sammy Yendall, he smashed her face with an iron bar. Last November, it was Julia Truman, a university student. Once again, her father noticed something missing. Jones has taken trophies from each victim. Eve Chaloner had bought her husband a gold chain months before Jones gunned him down."

Luke was back from the restroom. He placed a black coffee next to Gus and something unpleasant in a cup near DI Packenham.

"I can see why these two men in Swindon are in danger," said Grace. "I'm sure you will get full cooperation from DI Francis in keeping them safe, especially with ACC Gregory in your corner. However, I'm at a loss to see how to protect any girl who bears a resemblance to Tara Laing.

After all, they could live in one of almost thirty countries where Jones drives his truck. The motorway systems are so widespread and the traffic volume so high, it's like looking for a needle in a haystack."

"I appreciate the difficulties MCIT faces," said Gus, "but the Chief Constable wants Jones in a cell before November. So what have you learned about how Leo Gibbs handles matters?"

"A National SIO Adviser moves in circles where plain English is avoided at all costs," said Grace. "Gibbs reminded me of the Schengen Information System that we've operated under since 2001. Unfortunately, he lost me when he mentioned SIRENE, but Gibbs explained how it applied to Jones's case when he saw my bemused expression."

"I'm bemused too, so please enlighten me," said Gus.

"It stands for Supplementary Information Request at the National Entries, and whether it will still be in place when we extricate ourselves from the ongoing negotiations with the European Union, I don't know. The process is as complicated as it sounds. It could take years for law enforcement to find Jones and his truck in the affected countries. His name is on the list, but that list is very long."

"That's not what Kenneth Truelove wants to hear," said Gus.

"What's the alternative?" asked Grace.

"What would bring Jones to Swindon?" asked Gus. "He's only got one home, apart from the cab of his truck, and that's in Station Road. What if his father was taken ill? Or the council demolished that row of terraced houses to make way for a multi-storey car park or a new school? Another option might be to involve Eddie Dolman and Jeff Hughes. Arrange for their faces to get plastered over the front page of the Swindon Advertiser. Richard Chaloner made generous contributions to local charities to assuage his guilt over his part in the firework incident. That's what we believe enraged Jones in the first place. Why else would he switch from killing Tara Laing over and over to targeting Chaloner?"

"We'd need the local newspaper to cooperate for either piece of subterfuge," said Grace. "I don't like using his father to trap Jones. Stan Jones senior does not know his son's a serial killer. As for a rumour about knocking the street down, we'd never get the paper to publish it. Anyway, there are a dozen other places Jones could check online to confirm something of that nature. We couldn't hope to close every loophole. So no, your last idea is best."

"I know," said Gus. "I was only kidding about the others. Dolman and Hughes will have every reason to cooperate. If we need to stump up some cash to bolster their charity donation, it will be a small price to pay to remove the risk of them going the same way as Richard Chaloner. It's a win-win for those two. Can I make one suggestion when you arrange this with Gareth Francis?"

"With Gareth? What about Leo Gibbs?"

"Leave Gibbs filling out paperwork and dreaming up more pointless six-letter acronyms. I reckon a nice touch would be to get the Swindon Advertiser photographer on board and make sure the lads are wearing a heavy gold chain or cross. Jones will have to remove a piece of jewellery. Gazing at those trophies and reliving when the light leaves his victim's eyes gets him through the next twelve months."

"It doesn't bear thinking about, does it?" said Grace.

"It's best if you don't," said Gus. "Concentrate on finding the criminal's weakness. We know Stan monitors

Swindon news. A human interest story on the inside page with Dolman and Hughes will do the job just as well as a front-page headline. It will be less suspicious. Jones hasn't been home for a while and is due any day. DS Davis spoke with his father a few weeks back, and old Stan had mail put aside for his boy. So, it's a given that he'll pay a flying visit before driving off who knows where. Once he's paid that visit, our chance will have gone. Stan will be on the open road, November just around the corner, and a Tara Laing look-alike will die a painful death."

"Not if I can help it," said Grace.

"That's the spirit," said Gus. "You're getting the hang of it now."

Gus detected a hint of a smile on Grace's lips but dismissed it as a verdict on the green tea.

"The walls of this office are very busy, Mr Freeman. I recognise the street map of Swindon. Are the other maps, images, and lists attributed to the case DS Davis is handling?"

"The far wall relates to Danute Zukas and The Haven," said Gus.

"And the wall between the restroom door and the fire door?"

"Not my finest hour," sighed Gus. "The Chief Constable is eager to get closure on the Grant Burnside killing, but that manor house refused to give up its secrets on Sunday evening. We'll get the blighter one day."

"So the CRT doesn't have a one hundred percent success rate?"

"Show me a detective who does," said Gus.

"Touché. I'd better drive to Shrivenham," she said. "I'll speak to Gareth Francis and meet with the gentlemen concerned as soon as possible."

"The Advertiser is still a daily paper, Ms Packenham," said Gus. "If Gareth is busy making lists, and you miss the deadline for tomorrow, you only have to wait twenty-four hours."

"Stan Jones could be driving to Swindon as we speak, Mr Freeman. So we might not have a moment to lose."

"Agreed. One of my colleagues will see you out, Ms Packenham," said Gus.

Alex saw Grace gathering her things together and approached Gus's desk.

"All finished? I'll accompany you in the lift and see you get your car safely back to the main road."

"Is that necessary?" asked Grace.

"The locals aren't keen on the CRT taking up valuable parking spaces, and their driving can be careless in the confined space left. I'll bring my camera if we need to record any bumps or scratches you've suffered."

Grace's face paled, and she hurried to the lift with Alex.

Lydia couldn't contain the laughter after the lift doors closed behind them.

"I don't know what's got into him, guv," she said. "He's usually so serious."

Two minutes later, Alex reappeared with Blessing Umeh.

"Amazing Grace escaped unharmed," he said. "By the way, guv, she suggested that Luke ask London Road for housing support if his relationship has broken beyond repair. He can't sofa-surf with his mates."

"I understand, Alex. It's a pity she had to be here when Luke arrived. But, unfortunately, we can't keep it in-house now. I need to report the matter to DS Mercer."

"OMG," cried Blessing when she spotted Luke.

"It's a long story, Blessing," said Luke. "Best kept for later."

"What news from the shed, Blessing?" asked Gus.

"Nothing but spiders, guv," shuddered Blessing, "and a few newspapers from seven years ago. Gibbons hasn't been using that shed since he joined The Haven."

"Well, we tried," said Gus.

"I asked George Collins to get DI Cook to let us know what he finds at that office in Bradford-on-Avon, guv," said Blessing. "You should get a phone call after lunch."

"Thank you, Blessing. You can put your finishing touches to the files. We're almost there."

"Got it, guv," said Blessing.

She was itching to hear what had happened to Luke, but he was staring at the screen in front of him.

"Anything you can give me to do, guv?" asked Lydia.

"Ms Packenham commented on the volume of wall art," said Gus. "I think we can dispense with the contents of the far wall now. We can cope with whatever DI Cook uncovers and the results of our search through the evidence removed from The Haven without the visual stimuli."

"I'll clear the decks ready for the next case, guv," said Lydia.

"Did your conversation with Grace bring us closer to resolving the Stan Jones saga, guv?" asked Alex.

"Perhaps, Alex," said Gus. "We're going to tempt Jones to return to Swindon by using Dolman and Hughes as bait. Don't worry. It's not as dangerous as it sounds. Gareth Francis has enough resources at his disposal to see they come to no harm. If we can get Jones on our patch targeting one of Richard Chaloner's associates, we save a young woman who could live in one of thirty different countries. The guy in charge of our MCIT crew has already admitted to Amazing Grace their chances of locating Jones are slim. I expect to see an advert in the Swindon Advertiser by tomorrow with a photograph and article featuring Dolman and Hughes, which will infuriate Jones and bring him home on the double."

"The net's closing then, guv," said Alex.

"I'll be able to clear the wall beside me too, guv," said Lydia.

"One wall at a time, Lydia," said Gus, casting a wistful glance at the photographs of Larcombe Manor on the left-hand wall.

He wondered what progress Luke Sherman might make with the assignment he'd handed him yesterday. Could that even go ahead after last night's events? He decided to call Geoff Mercer from the restroom later. He didn't want Luke to overhear the conversation.

Neil Davis returned to the office at noon. He carried two folders balanced on top of a clear polythene evidence box.

"Is that all of it?" asked Luke.

"Don't be daft," said Neil. "I need you to come with me. We've got half-a-dozen boxes to carry up yet."

Luke and Neil disappeared downstairs to the car park. Gus grabbed the opportunity to call Geoff Mercer.

"What a mess," said Geoff after Gus had told him the news. "Luke needs to take advantage of the police accommodation we have available in the Swindon area. Did he mention anything about what he plans to do long-term?"

"I suspect Luke had an in-depth conversation with one team member, but DI Packenham was here when he arrived, so Luke didn't elaborate."

"I think it best Luke come to my office this afternoon, Gus. Make it four o'clock, and then he can go to Swindon and start sorting his life out. I'll keep you informed of what he intends to do next."

Gus ended the call as Neil and Luke exited the lift with the six evidence boxes. Lydia ran to help carry them to the side tables by the back wall.

"That should keep you busy for the rest of the afternoon, Neil," said Gus. "Luke, you can help him until half-past three, and then you need to leave for London Road. DS Mercer should have arranged appropriate accommodation for you by then. He wishes to speak with you about last night and, among other things, the undercover role."

"That's fair enough, guv," said Luke. "I was going to call, anyway."

Blessing looked at Lydia, but her colleague was giving nothing away. Luke and Neil started opening evidence boxes while Alex updated his digital files.

The young detective sensed her boss was standing by her desk.

"Don't worry, Blessing," Gus said quietly, "the storm will pass."

Chapter Eight

DI JOHN COOK was true to his word. Gus received a phone call from Polebarn Road at two o'clock.

"We spent a valuable morning in Bradford-on-Avon this morning, Mr Freeman," said John. "I took a forensic accountant with me. Although the computers owned by Lane and The Haven were password-protected, she soon got into the system. As a result, we have everything you might need on the day-to-day running of affairs in Avoncliff, plus a complete record of how many flowers they produced and the different leaflets and brochures they printed. The most telling files she accessed belonged to Simeon Lane himself. As you would imagine, the charity received twenty percent of the donations they collected, and Lane siphoned the rest into an offshore account in the Channel Islands. Last Saturday's balance at close of business was over three and a half million pounds."

"Good work, John," said Gus. "The brethren who elected to stay on at The Haven might have difficulty accessing even a small amount of that money. They would need to petition the courts. Have you finished at the offices now?"

"Yes," said Cook. "We removed the evidence we could carry. I've arranged for the rest to be collected. We can hold them in storage until the courts decide what to do with them. I wouldn't mind having the printer in my office. It was a cracker. No, I couldn't afford to stay out of the office any longer. I've got a meeting at two-thirty and another at four."

"It's all go, isn't John?" said Gus. "Thanks again."

Gus ended the call and wondered when John Cook would be on his next course.

"Another line can be drawn underneath The Haven case then, guv?" asked Alex.

"The financial jigsaw is virtually complete," said Gus. "When I take the final reports to the Chief Constable next Monday, we're sure to receive one green light."

Luke left the office at three-thirty to drive to Devizes for his appointment with Geoff Mercer.

Neil Davis walked across to Gus's desk.

"Can you spare me five minutes, guv?" he asked.

"You're going to ask about Luke, I suppose?" asked Gus.

"Lydia reckons he's going to ask for a transfer to Gable-cross," said Neil.

"Restroom gossip, Neil?"

"None of us wants to see him go, guv," said Neil. "I know Luke wasn't with us at the start, but he's been terrific to work with."

"Luke saved my life, Neil," said Gus. "I wanted to let him show he was more than a bodyguard with a gun. He's done that and more besides. We were a man short when Alex was side-lined and when you took time off after your father was murdered. We couldn't have coped without the fourth detective. I wasn't sure about Blessing joining us at first because she was so young, but Lydia vouched for her, and that was enough for me to give her a go. Look at Blessing now. She'll be a Detective Sergeant within twelve months, which was another reason Luke wondered where he fitted into the picture. The Chief Constable has always had Lydia in his sights too. She will move up the ladder before Kenneth Truelove retires. That's a given. We can't hope to keep the same team forever. All I can do is offer unbreakable justification for a replacement officer for every person who leaves. If we ever lost the support of the Chief Constable and DS Mercer, instead of maintaining the status quo, the whole initiative could get disbanded."

"If you left us, we 'd be finished anyway, guv," said Neil.

"Very nice of you to say so, Neil," said Gus, "but I'm keeping tabs on officers I've met who I think could take the CRT forward after my return to life as a retiree. I'm confident Maxine Devereux would do an excellent job. If she returns from maternity leave, she will become a Detective Inspector. Maxine wouldn't need to carry a library card or call on a senior officer to make an arrest."

"Maxine had a glowing reputation, guv," said Neil.

"Her appointment might cause as many problems as it solves," said Gus. "Alex is the next cab off the rank. If Geoff Mercer brought in a DI from outside, Alex would need to move to take his next step."

"Thank goodness I don't have to worry about things like that, guv. I'm a plodder, like my father, and destined to be a sergeant until I draw my pension."

"If I believed that, you wouldn't be here, Neil. When I first set foot in this office, Geoff Mercer handed me three names and made it sound like a fait accompli. But, if I had found a square peg in a round hole among you, their feet wouldn't have touched. So don't sell yourself short, Neil. You have a bright future ahead."

"I'd better get on with sifting through this evidence then, guv. Luke and I found Ralph Gibbons' toolkit, but we're not sure what we're looking for."

"Call Manvers Street, Neil," said Gus. "Ask whether DS Barge is still there. If she is, ask her for the name of the mechanic who dealt with Terry Walsh's car after the crash. They'll tell you which tools you need to check. If not, badger another DS in Bath until you find the right person."

"OK, guv," said Neil.

The afternoon drifted on, and the next time Gus looked at the clock, it was five to five. What was it he was supposed to remember today?

He travelled in the lift with Blessing Umeh, and when they got outside, it came to him.

"I've done it again," he said. "I made a mental note on my way to work this morning to decide what I was cooking for Suzie this evening. We'll reach the bungalow within minutes of one another at half-past five, and I haven't given it a thought."

"You need to write mental notes at your age, guv," said Blessing as she opened her car door.

"That would be a great idea, Blessing," said Gus. "But how would I remember where I put the pieces of paper?"

"Do you still have that list of phone numbers in the kitchen? The one you mentioned when we were in the Waggon & Horses. Tell Suzie you decided on a takeaway."

"You could have saved my bacon, Blessing. Let's hope Suzie can find something among the menus to match her cravings."

Wednesday, 19 September 2018

"A CHINESE MEAL and a chat about DI Packenham wasn't what I imagined when I drove home from work yesterday," said Suzie.

"Her mere presence in the CRT office was enough to make me forget to plan the culinary delights I promised, sweetheart," said Gus as he waited for Suzie to finish putting on her uniform.

"Do you think your scheme to lure Stan Jones home will work?"

"Stranger things have happened," said Gus. "I meant to remind Grace that she'd look stupid if Jones reached home, collected his mail, and disappeared again while she had dozens of officers protecting Dolman and Hughes."

"Surely, it would help if Gareth Francis had officers posted near the house and at the lorry park? That's on the outskirts of Swindon somewhere, isn't it? They could arrest him as soon as he parks his truck."

"Jones has avoided the police for over a decade," said Gus. "He'd spot a uniform a mile off. A runaway truck could pose a threat to the public. Gareth will have carried out a risk assessment. His best chance of taking Jones without incident is when he reaches his father's door. Any suspicious person or vehicle within a hundred yards of either place would cause Jones to abort his visit."

"I remember you telling me Jones never rang his father, and old Stan had no means of contacting him. Could we…."

"Stan Senior doesn't know his son is a killer, Suzie," said Gus. "I toyed with telling him so that I could suggest Gareth put someone inside the house. It might work, but we can't tell what Stan's reaction might be. He could suffer a heart attack. I don't want his death on my conscience, regardless of what his son's done."

"What do I have to look forward to tonight?" asked Suzie as they walked outside.

"A visit to The Lamb is in order, I reckon," said Gus.

"Good," said Suzie. "That means no conversation about Amazing Grace, but a catch-up on how Bert's getting on and whether Mamma Mia was a hit with Brett and Clemency."

"Riveting," said Gus. "I'm sorry we don't have a new case to mull over. However, the ways things are progressing, we could be on target for next Monday."

"Fingers crossed," said Suzie.

Gus followed Suzie's Golf through the gateway and along the lane. He would be in the office by nine. Another day of chasing shadows, preventing them from tying a neat bow on their outstanding cases. Perhaps another day closer to Luke Sherman leaving the Crime Review Team.

Alex and Lydia were already upstairs when Gus exited the lift.

"Have you seen the Advertiser this morning, guv?" asked Alex.

"I never read a newspaper first thing in the morning, Alex," said Gus. "I find it kills my hopes for a good day."

"Amazing Grace came up trumps, guv," said Lydia. "They've printed a story about Jeff Hughes. Hughes and his partner, Lamai, are photographed at the Folk Club at Highworth. Although the place has been running successfully for years, finances were struggling. Hughes has stepped in with a five-thousand-pound donation to save it. It showed Jeff Hughes passing a cheque to the Folk Club chairperson. I don't know how he felt wearing an open-necked shirt and a gold medallion, guv, but you can't miss it."

"Excellent," said Gus. "Now we've set the trap. We wait. I'll call Gareth Francis to see what he's got planned."

"What about DI Packenham, guv?" asked Alex.

"I expect she's cosying up to the National SIO Adviser," said Gus. "If this ploy is successful, Grace won't miss the opportunity of letting Leo Gibbs know how much of a part she played in the show. It could be a foot on the next rung of the ladder for an ambitious officer like Grace."

"That was your idea, guv," said Lydia.

"It hasn't worked yet, Lydia," said Gus, "and I have no wish to be anywhere near a ladder, thank you."

Neil and Blessing arrived together one minute later.

"Luke's car has just pulled into the car park, guv," said Neil.

"Good," said Gus, "everyone's on time. I suppose you've seen the Advertiser, Neil?"

"Is it in the newsagents in Devizes this early?" asked Neil.

"The online version is available, Neil," said Lydia.

"That's another reason I wouldn't have seen it," said Gus.

Luke came through the lift doors before Lydia could comment. She knew Gus wasn't a complete technophobe. He liked to be portrayed as a dinosaur, but they had often used the internet and social media to help solve their cases.

"A slight improvement this morning, DS Sherman," said Gus.

"You mean I'm on time, and the bruises are fading, guv," said Luke. "Do you want me to tell you about my meeting with DS Mercer, or has he called you already?"

"Let's get everyone settled first, Luke."

"No problem, guv."

"Alex, can you get things organised, please? I want to catch DI Francis before he gets too engrossed in the hunt for the elusive trucker."

"Leave it with me, guv," said Alex.

Gus called Gablecross, and Gareth Francis answered on the second ring.

"You're wide awake, Gareth," said Gus, "that's good to hear."

"Gus Freeman, as I live and breathe," said Gareth. "I should have guessed DI Packenham didn't come up with the newspaper idea herself. When did you two speak?"

"Yesterday morning, Gareth, done and dusted by mid-morning."

"DI Packenham called me before lunch, and we pulled out the stops. At first, Hughes wasn't sold on the idea, but his girlfriend twisted his arm. Lamai appreciated that Eddie and Jeff could be in danger if Jones were crazy enough to murder Richard. By the time we reached Highworth, Hughes had called Eddie Dolman and brought him up to speed. He agreed to donate half of the five grand."

"The gold medallion was a nice touch," said Gus. "That should spark Jones's interest."

"The medallion belonged to my late father," said Gareth. "I'd never wear it. They look naff, but when I showed it to DI Packenham, she thought it was perfect for Hughes. He offered me twenty quid for it after the photo was taken. It had no sentimental value, so how could I refuse?"

"That could work to our advantage, Gareth," said Gus. "If Jones escapes your first line of defence and reaches Jeff Hughes, and he's still wearing it, Jones won't suspect we have conned him."

"I hadn't thought of that," said Gareth.

"Do you have people watching the lorry park?" asked Gus.

"Parks, plural, Gus," said Gareth. "We can't rely on Jones being a creature of habit. If he's escaped justice for this long, it's because he never sticks to the same routes, service stations, and overnight lorry parks."

"That's a fair point, Gareth," said Gus.

"We're monitoring the CCTV coverage of every potential site where Jones might park his truck. I'll call you as soon as we spot him. Let's hope he was driving in this country when he accessed the Advertiser online this morning. The hours are counting down, Gus."

"We live in hope, Gareth," said Gus. "How are you handling the surveillance of the three target properties?"

"PCSO Travers is coordinating that, Gus. He reports to me. You identified a genuine talent there. We have high hopes for the young man."

"You seem to have covered the angles, Gareth," said Gus. "I look forward to hearing from you soon."

"I'll call you, don't worry. Meanwhile, I have research to carry out. Have a nice day."

Gus ended the call before he said something rude.

"I've spoken to DS Barge, guv," said Neil. "She sent her love. The switch to restauranteur is three months away. They hope to open before the holiday season. Erica has given me the number for the mechanic who worked on Terry West's Toyota. I'm calling him now."

"Thanks, Neil," said Gus. "Good hunting."

Gus caught Luke's attention, and Luke came to sit beside him.

"Where did you sleep last night?" asked Gus.

"DS Spencer helped me collect a few more essentials

from Warminster, guv. Nicky wasn't home. I called to say I would drop in, and he made himself scarce. Tom dropped me outside my new digs in Shrivenham, and I'm adapting to my enforced bachelor lifestyle."

"I'm glad DS Mercer could get you somewhere suitable at short notice. Unfortunately, you're not the first copper to suffer a broken relationship, Luke. There are undoubtedly others in the same boat, as well as the stubbornly single male and female officers. What else did you and Geoff discuss?"

"I've officially applied to transfer to Gablecross, guv. I hope you won't object. A complete change of scene is in order. I've loved working with the team, but the break-up with Nicky seems the right time to make a move."

"I understand, Luke. We'll miss you, but I've been in this game long enough to know nothing is ever forever. Football teams win trophy after trophy with a particular set of lads, but the time comes when one of them feels he needs to move on. Provided the manager finds the right replacement, there's no reason why that winning habit can't continue. At least, I think that's what Neil reckoned. He's our sporting metaphor expert. So, if we find the right person to fill your shoes, we'll continue to solve cases the Chief Constable hands me."

"I'm sure you will, guv. DS Mercer discussed the Larcombe Manor affair with me too, and I'm meeting an ACC at Portishead on Monday. Just a preliminary meeting. Nothing concrete will be agreed upon until I've moved to Gablecross."

"Good luck, Luke. I want the Burnside business put to bed before I hang up my boots."

"Got it, guv," said Luke. "I don't know when my

transfer will get confirmed. I'll keep giving you one hundred percent until then."

Luke returned to his desk. Gus looked up to find Neil hovering by his chair.

"I think I might have found something, guv," said Neil.

"What do we have here?" asked Gus, inspecting the evidence bag Neil handed him.

"That's one tool Howard Ellis suggested we inspect, guv. Ellis was the mechanic who examined the Toyota after the crash."

"What colour would you call that?" asked Gus.

"I'm hoping it's a blue slate metallic paint from a 1993 Toyota Corolla," said Neil.

"Wouldn't there have been a lot of Corollas on the road in the UK in 2015, Neil," said Gus.

"Maybe, guv, but not at The Haven. We know DI West didn't look after his car. The Toyota was due an MOT eight weeks after Terry died and was decrepit. The tools in Ralph Gibbons' toolkit only got used on vehicles owned by the charity. For this tool to carry that specific colour code has to mean Ralph used it on a Toyota Corolla that visited The Haven. Gibbons told us he kept the toolkit in the shed behind the manor house for running repairs. We can place the Corolla at The Haven the night Terry West died. Howard Ellis is convinced this is the tool Gibbons used to cause the brake failure, leading to West's death."

"If you can get confirmation that that's the right colour code, you might have him, Neil. Well done. I told you, you're a good detective."

Gus felt things had gathered pace today.

Thanks to DI Packenham's swift response to Gus's suggestion, Gareth Francis was on the ball in Swindon.

Neil might have brought the Terry West matter to a satisfactory conclusion.

Luke had his accommodation sorted, and although he was soon on his way to a new police station, Luke would still chase the sniper Rusty Scott.

All things being considered, things were moving in the right direction in their three cases.

The phone rang, and as Gus listened to Gareth Francis with an update, he remembered why people said you should never speak too soon.

"We've got a problem, Gus," said Gareth. "We haven't caught Jones and his truck on CCTV at lorry parks within the Swindon area. However, Travers extended the search by twenty miles, and we're awaiting confirmation, but it appears Jones parked his truck late last night in a lorry park in Faringdon, on Southampton Street."

"Does that mean he's on foot in Swindon as we speak?"

"Travers says as Jones knows the area so well, he'd be aware he could get a bus from the Market Place in Faringdon to Swindon that would arrive here after midnight. The bus journey takes just under forty minutes. I sent an officer to check which bus covered that route last night. We can check the onboard cameras to identify Jones and learn where he got off."

"Have you strengthened the protection for Dolman and Hughes?"

"Of course, but there's been no sign of Jones anywhere in Swindon. It makes me wonder."

"What have you done about the truck?" asked Gus.

"The area is secured, Gus. I'm waiting to hear from DI Packenham whether I'm authorised to impound the vehicle and search it. Wiltshire handed the case to MCIT, and my boss is concerned we're exceeding our brief."

"So, Rebecca Gregory wants the glory to go to MCIT, who failed to find Jones and were unaware he was less than fifteen miles from two of his likely targets. Make a name for yourself, Gareth. Slap a Denver Boot on the truck, and search it from top to bottom. Strip it apart as if you had received intelligence it contained twenty-five kilos of cocaine in a hidden compartment. We must find those trophies."

"I'll check with ACC Gregory," said Gareth. "As I say, I'm wondering why we haven't caught Jones on camera today. You know how extensive Swindon's CCTV coverage is. Swindon is the third most-watched place in the UK outside London, with over six hundred cameras around the town. A camera for every three hundred people. I can't explain why we haven't spotted him. With his scarring, even partially covered by facial hair, he should be easier to locate than most of our citizens."

"Where's Travers now?" asked Gus.

"He's still trawling through CCTV footage. I've got as many people as we can spare helping out. But, with so many cameras, it will take time. Time we might not have."

"What did your research tell you, Gareth?"

"I know you're mocking me. But as we hadn't found a sighting of Jones, I listed places he might go outside Swindon. I didn't get far with it, I'm afraid."

Gus thought for a moment.

"I could have missed the obvious, Gareth. I assumed Jones would continue to murder his victims in November. We're now assuming that our ploy to encourage his return to Station Road with Jeff Hughes and his medallion led to him parking his truck in Faringdon last night. What if Jones has tired of killing young women who remind him of Tara Laing?"

"You think he could search for Tara herself?" said Gareth.

"Tara Laing lives in splendid isolation on the remote island of Barra, in the Outer Hebrides," said Gus. "The nearest place to her property with a name on the map is Buaile nam Bodach. That's Gaelic for something like the ghost's milking parlour. Tara wanted to get as far from her old life as possible. Whether she feared retribution from Stan Jones, who can say?"

"An island off the west coast of Scotland that can only be reached by ferry," said Gareth. "Give me half an hour, Gus. Then, I'll get back to you."

Gus ended the call and scratched his head.

"Problem, guv?" asked Alex.

"Stan Jones arrived in Swindon at midnight. He hasn't been seen anywhere near Station Road or lurking near the home of Jeff Hughes."

"How did he get there, guv," asked Alex.

"On a bus from Faringdon."

"Jones could have been on a platform at the railway station within two minutes, guv," said Alex. "I've taken advantage of the bus station being so close myself when I worked at Shrivenham. It's on the same S6 bus route."

"Local knowledge always helps, Alex," said Gus.

He called Gareth Francis, but his phone was engaged.

"How do I get hold of that young lad, Travers? When we were on the Stacey Read case, did we get a number for him?"

"Can't remember asking for it, guv," said Lydia. "Jake would know where to reach him."

Gus called the detective squad room. Jake Latimer answered.

"Another day in the office, Jake?" asked Gus.

"Paperwork is the bane of my life, guv," said Jake. "How can I help?"

"I need a number for Travers. It's urgent."

"He's in the office, Gus. Hold on."

Ten seconds later, PCSO Travers was on the line.

"Good morning, Mr Freeman. What do you need?"

"Check the cameras at the railway station. You have a narrow time-frame between twelve-fifteen this morning and one o'clock, at the most. Jones knew what he was doing. He arrived out of town by bus, then dashed from the bus station to catch a train heading north."

"We're ahead of you, sir," said Travers. "I accessed the onboard camera on the last S6 bus running last night, and we've got Stan Jones seated in the fourth row downstairs. He kept his head down throughout the journey and wore a peaked baseball cap. When Jones stood to get off the bus, I could see he wore black gloves, jeans, and a camouflage jacket zipped up to the neck. As Jones reached the driver, he turned slightly to drop his ticket in the waste bin and exposed the right side of his face for a second. I'd swear it was Jones, sir."

"Have you got him on CCTV on the platform?" asked Gus.

"We do. Jones boarded the twelve-thirty-eight train to Glasgow. The station manager told DI Francis that was a one-stop service which arrived in Glasgow at seven forty-eight this morning."

"What's Gareth doing now?" asked Gus. "I tried to call him, but he was engaged."

"You know DI Francis, Mr Freeman. He loves to work on puzzles such as this one. He's followed your thoughts on where Jones was heading. There are several ferries to Barra each day, so he's working out when each of them leaves the mainland and arrives on the island. He's phoning the local police to make sure they arrest Jones the second he reaches the ferry port."

"I'll let you get on, Travers," said Gus. "The net is closing. Good work."

"Thank you, Mr Freeman," said Travers.

Gus ended the call but didn't have time to tell the others about the progress. His phone rang again.

"Gus? It's Gareth. I don't know whether you've heard, but Jones arrived in Glasgow just before eight this morning. I've calculated the quickest route for our man to follow if he's heading for Barra. Jones will board the ferry at Oban, and to reach there by train will take three and a quarter hours. We knew he was a cunning devil. Jones left Glasgow Central for Oban at five minutes past eight. He didn't hang around on the station platforms for long. Oban police have plain-clothes detectives on the scene. I've sent them the images PCSO Travers captured from the bus journey. Jones was carrying a bag over his shoulder. He might have changed clothing on the train. One thing he can't disguise is his face. I'm waiting for a phone call from DI Angus McLeod soon after eleven-thirty. Sit tight, and I'll convey the good news in a while."

"Good work, Gareth," said Gus. "What progress on the truck search?"

"ACC Gregory was wary of acting without first advising the Major Crimes people. So I'm waiting for the go-ahead. Although, I'm not sure the ACC will hear back today. MCIT has many boxes to tick before they can decide."

"Hold on, Gareth," said Gus. "Can I hear a dog barking?"

"I can't hear anything, Gus. It must be outside your office."

"No, it's definitely in a lorry park in Faringdon. Do you think the driver has left his dog in his cab? Of course, the sun's not as hot as in high summer, but we wouldn't want the animal to suffer, would we?"

"That's sneaky, Gus. I'm not sure what Major Crimes would say."

"If Rebecca Gregory gets a green light, it will be irrelevant," said Gus. "Trophies, Gareth. That's what we need."

"I'll send Jake Latimer and two uniformed officers to investigate," said Gareth, "with orders to make as little mess as possible. There has to be valuable evidence inside that vehicle. Jones picked up the latest victim as she hitchhiked her way home from Falmouth."

"I can trust you to think of everything, Gareth," said Gus.

"I haven't called Barra yet, to get the local police to send someone to Tara Laing's place."

"We don't need to alarm the lady unduly," said Gus. "If Jones somehow evades the people in Oban, you still have six to eight hours to alert Barra. They can arrest Jones when he steps off the ferry. Let's hope McLeod gets our man as soon as he reaches the ferry terminal. I'll be poised with my hand, ready to answer your call in around forty minutes."

"What happens if MCIT refuses permission to search the truck? They'll never swallow the barking dog story."

"If you and Rebecca Gregory can produce Stan Jones and the trophies, I don't think you'll hear a complaint, Gareth," said Gus. "They made zero progress in a week despite their available resources. You two have wrapped it up inside twelve hours."

"PCSO Travers deserves credit, Gus."

"He does."

"What about DI Packenham?"

"What about her?" said Gus. "If Stan Jones parked his truck in Faringdon before midnight last night, there's no way he'd seen Jeff Hughes and his partner in that Swindon Advertiser article. I'll never know whether my bright idea would have worked, but as long as we get the right result, I can live with that."

"I've just thought of something," said Gareth.

"You were lucky to get twenty quid for that medallion?"

"No," said Gareth, "I was wondering whether the Folk Club has banked that five grand cheque yet."

"The answer, my friend, is blowing in the wind," said Gus. "Roll on eleven-thirty."

Chapter Nine

GUS SAT BACK in his chair and sighed a deep sigh.

"Your phone is red-hot this morning, guv," said Blessing. "Do you have time for a coffee?"

"Always, Blessing," said Gus. "Does anyone else want to take a break until we hear from Gablecross? Stan Jones is trying to reach Barra and Tara Laing. Oban police are lying in wait at the ferry terminal. The nightmare will soon be over for Tara, Chaloner's accomplices, and young European women."

"His arrest will bring closure for the families of his victims," said Lydia.

"It's not just the ability to return jewellery he took from the body," said Luke. "They've suffered the loss of their loved one once. Now the trauma those girls went through will get aired in court. The families have to endure further suffering."

"The suffering never ends, Luke," said Alex.

Blessing returned from the restroom with the coffee.

"Could there be another twist yet, guv?" asked Neil.

"It feels like the endgame, Neil. We're still in September. If Jones planned to attack Tara in November in line with his other killings, he'd seek a contract that took his truck as close to Oban, or one of the other ferry ports, as possible. It doesn't fit the pattern."

"Do you think Jones wants to get caught?" asked Blessing.

"I wouldn't go that far, Blessing," said Luke. "The planning that went into getting to Swindon, then to Glasgow, suggests his focus was on reaching Tara Laing. I believe Jones hoped he could rid himself of the urge to lash out every November by killing her."

"We'll learn more when Jones is in custody," said Gus. "How long will it take Jake Latimer to get to that lorry park in Faringdon, Alex?"

"Twenty-five minutes, guv," said Alex.

Lydia watched the clock on the far wall tick past half-past eleven.

Blessing collected the empty coffee cups and paused by Neil's desk before disappearing behind the restroom door.

When Gus's phone rang, Neil heard a cup smash as it hit the floor.

When he turned around, Blessing stood in the doorway with a tea towel in her hand.

"Hang on, Gareth," said Gus, "I'll put you on speakerphone."

"Angus McLeod rang just now to confirm Stan Jones was in custody. The platform at the train station wasn't crowded, even by Swindon standards, but his officers had been warned Jones should be considered dangerous. They elected to follow him on the short walk to the ferry terminal. DI McLeod signalled to move in when Jones didn't have a civilian within five yards of him. Other officers joined their colleagues, pinned Jones to the floor in seconds, handcuffed him, and returned him to the police station in Albany Street."

"Has DI McLeod spoken to Jones yet?" asked Gus.

"No, Gus. Rebecca Gregory is arranging for Jones to be collected from Oban and returned to Gablecross."

"Did Jones say anything?" asked Alex.

"No. Angus McLeod told me Jones looked relieved it was over. He made no attempt to resist arrest and has only spoken to confirm his name and that he understands why he's being held."

"Was there anything in the shoulder bag except a change of clothing?" asked Gus.

"I'm afraid so," said Gareth. "Jones had a cloth bag at the bottom which contained several jewellery items."

"He had the trophies with him?"

"Yes, Gus, but when I gave Angus the list DI Packenham provided me yesterday, Angus said there were more pieces left after he'd moved those to one side."

"We've got more victims to identify," said Alex.

"Three more," said Lydia.

"The jewellery items will travel south with Jones," said Gareth. "We'll ask where the bodies are buried, but I doubt Jones will cooperate. So I fear we will have to search through missing persons from November in the years concerned and show the parents the items to identify the victims."

"Have you remembered to call Jake Latimer?" asked Gus.

"I asked Travers to call as soon as I got off the phone with DI McLeod. Jake said they had located Jones's truck, and an officer used his baton to smash the driver's window. I told Jake to tell him to stop."

"Good," said Gus.

"Not really," said Gareth. "The officer took two swings before he heard Jake. The window didn't break, but it looked a mess. ACC Gregory still hasn't heard from MCIT. There could be an almighty row over this."

"Never mind," said Gus. "Get Rebecca Gregory to tell Leo Gibbs it was kids. Anti-social behaviour is one of the biggest headaches you've got in Swindon, isn't it?"

"I'd have to make sure nobody saw the CCTV images, Gus," said Gareth.

"Your secret's safe with me, Gareth."

"Hmph. Until you want a favour."

"It's the result that matters," said Gus. "Can I make a suggestion? When Jones and his cloth bag return to Gable-cross, put DS Latimer on the three jewellery items. He could do with something to motivate him. We don't need to hand the final pieces of the jigsaw over to MCIT. We'll handle it in-house. I'm sure Rebecca will approve."

"Jake has never found a new partner since he split with Theo Hickerton," said Gareth.

"Why not pair him with a Detective Constable?" said Gus.

"We don't have one spare at present," said Gareth.

"If only you had a bright PCSO studying at night school who could do the job standing on his head."

"Travers?" said Gareth. "I'll suggest it to the ACC. He's talented but inexperienced. Latimer knows all the tricks in the book. It could be a disaster."

"Or it could be the dream team. Go on. You know it makes sense."

"Are we still on speakerphone?" asked Gareth.

"Of course," said Gus.

"I'll just say goodbye for now, then."

Gus ended the call.

"We've got our man, guv," said Alex. "Even if our worst fears were realised. The first murder was in 2007, as we thought, and Jones has struck every year since."

"Julia Truman was the last to suffer," said Gus. "Now we can leave things to Gablecross. They can interview Jones, try to discover where the three remaining bodies can be found, and prepare a watertight case the Crown Prosecution Service can't lose."

"Time for us to move on, guv," said Lydia.

"I'll call London Road," said Gus, "to get a message to the Chief Constable. He needs to inform Leo Gibbs at the National Crime Agency that we no longer require the assistance of MCIT. So Jake Latimer can cope with tracing the owners of the trophies Jones has kept."

"With Travers's help," said Lydia. "The only police officer in the UK known by a single name."

Gus called Vera Butler. She told him Kenneth was with the Police and Crime Commissioner. She would pass on the message and tell Gus when her boss was next available. All he could do now was wait.

"We will soon reunite Eve Chaloner with the gold chain she bought her husband, guv," said Blessing.

"That's not a job I'd want, guv," said Lydia.

"I've informed dozens of people a family member has died, Lydia," said Gus. "Whether they were involved in a car or motorcycle crash or murdered. It's always gut-wrenching, and it never gets easier. Those trophies won't bring back Richard Chaloner or the murdered girls, but I've never met a family yet that didn't want to receive an item with their loved one when they died. I've often wondered whether they stored them away, never to see the light of day, had them buried with the departed, or treasured those items for as long as they lived. To my shame, I've never returned to any of those people to ask."

"If we got that involved in every case we dealt with, we'd never last the course," said Alex.

"Can I clear the wall now, guv?" asked Lydia.

"You may, Lydia," said Gus, knowing Alex was right.

The mood in the office was subdued for the next hour.

The team updated their digital files. Each was glad to draw a line under their part in what started as a review of the Richard Chaloner murder.

None of them had realised how protracted and complicated that review would be.

Neil Davis had contributed nothing to the Stan Jones case for several days; he'd spent time adding details to his files relating to Terry West's death. Then, as the afternoon wound to a close, Neil received a call from a forensic officer at London Road.

As soon as Neil looked towards him and smiled, Gus could tell it was good news.

"Game, set, and match," said Neil. "The blue slate metallic paint came from a 1993 Toyota Corolla, and Gibbon's prints are all over the tool handle. My contact at London Road also confirmed the mechanic, Howard Ellis, had partial prints he'd recovered from the bodywork and underside of West's Toyota, for which they didn't seek a match. They deemed the crash an accident, so it wasn't relevant. London Road has attributed these partials to Gibbons. I'll add the finishing touches to my report, and you can deliver the completed folder to the Chief Constable when you see him."

"Excellent, Neil," said Gus. "Your news is like the sun reappearing after days of heavy cloud. It lifts the spirits."

Gus left the office at five o'clock. He wanted to get home to tell Suzie about the excellent news.

Lydia and Alex were still removing the maps and photographs from the right-hand wall. Luke and Blessing were chatting and didn't seem in a rush to go home.

Gus remembered Luke giving Blessing a lift to work when her Nissan was in the garage. That wouldn't happen again now that Luke was living in Shrivenham.

Neil Davis was happy in his work, updating his files with the evidence that would see Ralph Gibbons tried for the murder of DI West.

Gus made a mental note to get Neil to call Erica Barge. But, as he travelled down in the lift, he searched his jacket pockets for a pen and paper without luck. Suzie breezed through the door at twenty to six, ten minutes after Gus had reached the bungalow.

"I know you have something to tell me," she said, giving him a big hug. "The news flew around the offices at London Road this afternoon. DI Packenham was livid. She blamed you, of course."

"Gareth Francis called to say they had arrested Jones in Oban at a quarter to twelve," said Gus. "Gablecross did the hard graft. They found the truck in Faringdon, followed Jones from Swindon station to Glasgow, and reasoned he was on his way to Barra in the Outer Hebrides. Major Crimes and DI Packenham didn't raise a finger. Jones had arrived in town before the Jeff Hughes article appeared."

"Grace thinks you should have told her what was happening, and Leo Gibbs wasn't happy being kept in the dark. After all, Kenneth had handed the case to MCIT, as it was too big for Wiltshire Police to handle."

"Neither of the people you've mentioned can point the

finger at the Crime Review Team," said Gus. "We weren't party to any operations that went on today."

Suzie looked at Gus's hands.

"Are you crossing your fingers, Gus Freeman? Who are you trying to kid? Everyone at London Road knows a puppet master was pulling the strings, having a quiet word in Gareth Francis's ear. He could never have done it by himself. You directed operations from the Old Police Station office, didn't you?"

"I couldn't possibly comment," said Gus. "We were bringing a killer to justice. Our focus was on Ralph Gibbons, who we can now prove tampered with Terry West's brakes, causing the fatal accident he had after he drove away from The Haven."

"We hadn't heard that news in the office," said Suzie. "Two successes in one day. Kenneth *will* be pleased. I wonder when he'll hand you another murder to solve?"

"I called Vera, but Kenneth was otherwise engaged. Maybe tomorrow. Who knows? Forget about work now. Let's shower, get changed, and walk to The Lamb. I need sustenance and conversation."

Gus and Suzie always enjoyed Wednesday nights at the pub. Brett and Clemency never missed the opportunity to join them to discuss every subject under the sun–except work. Bert Penman and Irene North were already there when Gus and Suzie walked into the bar at seven-thirty.

"He's getting better every day, Mr Freeman," said Irene.

"My new walking stick's a real help, Mr.... Gus," said Bert. "You found a good one there."

"If you need help with your allotment, Bert, don't be afraid to ask," said Gus.

"I'll cope, Gus," said Bert. "Irene came with me this

afternoon while I pottered around. She worries that I'll do too much but a little and often won't tax me.

"How was the film the other evening?" asked Suzie.

"Brett fell asleep halfway through," said Clemency.

"I enjoyed what I saw," said Brett, "but it had been a long day, and it was so warm in the cinema."

"I like Pierce Brosnan," said Clemency. "so it was no hardship to stay awake."

"Has he been in anything else?" asked Gus.

Brett laughed.

"I never know whether to believe you, Gus. Don't you ever watch films on TV?"

"I'd rather listen to music," said Gus. "Then I can close my eyes to ponder a case without flashing images disturbing my concentration."

"I thought we weren't mentioning work?" said Suzie.

"Gus is a deep-thinking man, Miss Suzie," said Bert. "He needs steak and a glass of Malbec tonight, I reckon. What might you fancy? We're paying since you put your-selves out to get me home from the hospital and sorted my sleeping quarters."

"That's very kind of you, Bert," said Suzie. "I'd like the fish special and a slimline tonic."

Thursday, 20 September 2018

"WHAT TIME TONIGHT, GUS?"

"I can't see why I should be later than five-thirty," said Gus.

"My turn to cook," said Suzie. She opened the front door and dashed to her Golf as the heavens opened.

Gus stood in the doorway and watched Suzie drive through the gateway. There was something he had to do. He popped back to the kitchen, found a scrap of paper and a pencil, and wrote Erica's name. Gus slipped the piece into his trouser pocket and checked the state of the weather through the window. It was still raining, but not enough to warrant taking a raincoat. He stepped outside and made his way around the corner to the Focus.

Thirty minutes later, Gus parked behind the Old Police Station. The delay meant he was the last to arrive. The others were discussing something that happened last night when Gus reached the office. Conversation ceased as soon as he sat at his desk.

"Don't stop on my account," he said.

"Luke saw something last night, guv," said Lydia. "While he was picking up a takeaway in Shrivenham."

"I wasn't hungry when I got home after work," said Luke. "I still had things to do at my digs to get everything how I like it. That took longer than I thought, and I was starving. It was almost ten o'clock when I drove to the nearest Indian. Guess who I saw leaving a pub on the other side of the road?"

"The student formerly known as Travers?" asked Gus.

"No, guv. Gareth Francis and Rebecca Gregory," said Luke.

"Nothing odd about a boss having a drink with their team to celebrate a win," said Gus. "Perhaps the others had left already or were still inside the pub drinking it dry."

"That's not how it looked, guv," said Luke.

"They're both single," said Gus. "Best not to jump to conclusions."

Gus's phone rang.

"Freeman?" said the Chief Constable. "I want you in my office in thirty minutes."

"On my way, sir," said Gus.

Gus replaced the phone.

"Do we have everything ready for me to take to London Road?" he asked.

A chorus of affirmative answers helped put his day back on track. Gus donned his jacket, collected the case folders, and headed for the lift. As the doors opened, he remembered the scrap of paper.

"Neil," he called. "Remember to tell DS Barge the good news about the Terry West case, won't you?"

"Got it, guv," said Neil.

Gus returned to the car park he'd left five minutes earlier and drove towards Devizes.

This morning, a senior sergeant that Gus knew well was on the Reception desk at London Road. The Gods were with him. He was bounding up the stairs to the mezzanine in one minute. He saw Kenneth Truelove standing outside his office door as he passed Vera's desk.

Did that mean rain? Gus could never remember.

"Mercer will join us in a moment," said Kenneth as he walked inside and stood by the window. Gus placed the folders on Kenneth's desk before taking a seat.

"What do you have there?" asked Kenneth.

"The blue folder contains the complete works of the Richard Chaloner case and the supplementary enquiry that led to the capture of his killer, Stan Jones, yesterday lunchtime," said Gus. "The red folder covers the investigation into the murder of Danute Zukas, plus the forensic accounting analysis of The Haven's activities. You will also find Neil Davis's supplementary report regarding DI West's death. Finally, charges can now be brought against Ralph

Gibbons for Terry's murder. Sorry it took so long, sir, but they were tougher nuts to crack than the others you've handed me."

A knock on the door heralded the arrival of Geoff Mercer.

"Did you know about this, Mercer?" asked Kenneth.

"I heard the rumours, sir," said Geoff.

"You're supposed to be in charge of Freeman. We can't afford to have a loose cannon on the team."

"Have I missed something, sir?" asked Gus.

"Vera Butler passed on your message yesterday afternoon, Freeman. I called Leo Gibbs and told him what progress ACC Gregory and her team had made. He wasn't best pleased. Gibbs had people working undercover in Swindon. They were unaware of what was happening at the Faringdon lorry park."

Good job, too, Gus thought.

"As for DI Packenham, she went above and beyond to get Hughes and Dolman on board with your scheme. While Grace awaited news from the MCIT crew, hoping Jones had taken the bait and was returning to his father's house, Jones was on a train to Glasgow and onward to Oban, where DI McLeod arrested him."

"May I butt in, sir?" said Gus. "I'm sorry if DI Packenham's nose is out of joint, but that's tough. Jones was already on his way to Barra from wherever he was before he reached Faringdon. They did not copy him into the memos flying between London Road, Gablecross and the National Crime Agency hallowed halls. The newspaper article might have worked if he wasn't already planning to murder Tara Laing. But, in the event, it was irrelevant. Jones is safely under lock and key. He can't harm Tara Laing or the two men in Swindon. Ten young women are dead, and we've only identified seven of them so far. Jones won't add to that number. ACC Gregory and the detectives she had working on the operation will continue to do a good job. I'm confident they can use the trophies recovered to locate the three missing victims. After that, Leo Gibbs and his people can concentrate on organised crime and agree with their European counterparts how to continue cooperating, so evil men like Jones don't have free rein to kill on both sides of the Channel after Brexit."

"Quite," said Geoff Mercer.

"My meeting with the PCC yesterday afternoon was unscheduled, Freeman. The story was breaking, and he was getting edgy. So I'll try to tame the storm," said Kenneth. "I suppose you've done what I asked despite not following standard procedure. You've brought two of the three outstanding cases to a successful conclusion. What progress has been made on the one that remains?"

"Luke Sherman will continue to carry that enquiry forward, sir," said Geoff Mercer. "He's applied to transfer to Gablecross, and I'm working out the details. Luke's liaising with Portishead and will meet next week with the ACC responsible for the Larcombe Manor operation."

"Luke had itchy feet earlier in the year, sir," said Gus. "A personal matter brought things to a head. I didn't want to lose him, but he's ambitious, and who am I to stand in his way?"

"I couldn't have put it better myself, Freeman," said Kenneth. "How do you intend to replace him? Another DS, perhaps?"

"DC Umeh could put in for her sergeant's exam, sir," said Gus. "That would take time. However, I need someone with more experience to replace DS Sherman. But, of course, you know better than I do how long I can remain in position. So it might be sensible to recruit a Detective Inspector who could run the CRT after you've retired. You keep telling me my hopes of staying in the job will rapidly diminish once I lose your protection."

"He's a crafty devil, isn't he, Mercer?" said the Chief Constable. "He's got someone in mind already."

"They would need to be someone Gus respected, sir," said Geoff. "I can only think of one that didn't get criticised when we debriefed any completed file folders from CRT."

"And the winner is?" asked Kenneth.

"Someone unsure whether she wants to return to work after maternity leave, sir," said Gus. "Maxine Devereux."

Kenneth Truelove looked at Geoff Mercer.

"I don't believe it," he said. "Freeman is proposing we replace him with a young woman who ticks every box his detractors claimed he didn't."

"Maxine is an excellent detective," said Gus. "Her approach might differ from mine in some respects. However, I hope to have time to show that our methods have merit. Between now and when you retire, Alex, Lydia, Neil and Blessing can help me make Maxine an even better detective."

"I would have to fend off requests to poach the services of Ms Logan Barre," said Kenneth. "Two ACCs at London Road are keen to add her name to their departments, and South Wales Police have their eye on her following the Kendall case."

"I'm sure you'll do what's best, sir," said Gus.

Kenneth moved the folders Gus had delivered and placed them on his in-tray. Then he opened the top drawer of his desk.

"I sometimes wonder whether you're more trouble than

you're worth, Freeman," he said. "If you keep delivering the goods, I suppose I'm stuck with you."

"What do we have this time, sir?" asked Gus, accepting the folder from the Chief Constable and flicking through the pages.

"A case from December, three years ago," said Kenneth. "The victim was Clive Palmer, an ex-teacher from London. He was forty-eight when he died in the village of Purton. Palmer was stabbed several times, and his body was mutilated post-mortem."

"What was Palmer doing in Purton?" asked Gus.

"He had moved there ten months earlier," said Kenneth. "Palmer left prison in Portland after serving eighteen months. He had a six-month affair with one of his students; Gemma Long was fifteen years old. Palmer's name went on the Sex Offenders Register. His marriage ended, and he started afresh in a quiet village where nobody knew him."

"The murder you described sounds personal," said Gus. "Was he re-offending? Were detectives searching for a relative of a victim or a vigilante? Who caught the case?"

"DI Moore from Gablecross headed the initial investigation, assisted by DS Mark Harvey. Palmer arrived in Purton with a car and a caravan. He approached John Oatley, a local farmer, who was happy to rent a barn to Palmer to garage his car, and a space in the corner of the farmyard to house his caravan. Palmer secured a driving job with a haulier based in the village. Rob Dolman told Moore and Harvey that Palmer was an excellent driver, never any trouble, and clients confirmed he was always polite and helpful."

"He upset somebody," said Gus, "if they did what I can see in this crime scene photograph. You could have warned me."

"Palmer settled into village life," said Kenneth, "and for the first few months, he socialised with Ken Webb and Peter Wright. They were the other two drivers employed by Dolman."

"Any relation to Eddie Dolman?"

"Dolman's not an uncommon surname in the county, Gus," said Geoff Mercer. "They might be distant cousins, but we don't believe they knew one another."

"What changed?" asked Gus.

"A local builder called Tom Angell learned why Palmer had gone to jail and told everyone Palmer was a paedophile. Customers left The Volunteer pub rather than mix with him, or they stayed and gave Palmer a hard time. Webb and Wright drank elsewhere and stopped speaking to him, but Dolman and Oatley never wavered in their support. Palmer continued to live in his van in the farmyard and drive for Dolman. The landlord at The Volunteer, Dave Awdry, and his wife, Karen, shared the same opinion. The Clive Palmer they saw in the bar was a good worker, paid his rent on time, and was a polite, intelligent man. He continued to be welcome in the pub until the night he died."

"Did they know the full story?" asked Gus.

"Perhaps they were naïve," said Kenneth. "Tom Angell didn't know the entire story, but that didn't stop him from whipping up a storm when a young girl thought someone followed her home from the youth club. First, the kids vandalised Palmer's van. Then a youngster hurt herself in a playground, and a stranger helped her to her feet. They blamed Palmer for both attacks, yet he wasn't in Purton on either occasion."

"How did Moore and Harvey handle the investigation?" asked Gus.

"They interviewed everyone in the village who had

come into contact with Palmer during the ten months he lived there," said Kenneth. "Palmer has a brother, James, who lives in Tooting Bec. Moore and Harvey visited him for more background on Gemma Long. They looked at the ex-wife and her new partner and soon discounted their involvement and that of Palmer's two children."

"Was Tom Angell ever a suspect?" asked Gus.

"Not really. Tom Angell was a loudmouth who didn't have the facts. Moore and Harvey did eventually make an arrest. Rob Dolman's brother-in-law, Andy Redman, has been in trouble with the law since he was a teenager. At first, he appeared to have means, motive, and opportunity."

"What went wrong?"

"When he's not behind bars, Redman spends most of his time getting drunk. He knew Palmer worked for his sister's husband and often went in for a spot of breaking and entering. Redman was drinking throughout the day and couldn't be sure he didn't visit Purton on the night in question. His mother gave him an alibi. She said Andy arrived home drunk before she went to bed at eleven. No way could Redman have committed the murder. Dave Awdry at The Volunteer said Palmer was the last to leave. Palmer reached his caravan at eleven. Eve Northwood adjudged the time of death to be around midnight."

"That was it? They didn't put anyone else in the frame?"

"The case followed the familiar pattern, Gus," said Geoff. "Time ran out. Other cases with a greater chance of success took priority. I want to think the victim's past wasn't the reason behind the enquiry getting shelved as quickly as it did."

"We'll need to study this file closely," said Gus. "I sense there was more to the Gemma Long case than it would appear. Someone from London, connected to Long and her family, could have travelled to Purton to attack Palmer and mutilate his body. I think that was unlikely. So that leaves us with the villagers. Who did he cross swords with that wanted to kill him? You said there was no truth in the rumours Palmer had picked up from where he left off. He wasn't targeting young females in Purton?"

"There was no evidence of that whatsoever, Gus," said Geoff.

"Why did he move to Purton?" asked Gus.

"That was the question DI Moore and DS Harvey asked," said Kenneth. "Palmer had been a history teacher before he went to prison. Dave Awdry told the police Palmer was a regular at the Quiz Night in the pub. He answered every question but crossed out enough answers to avoid winning. He didn't want the hassle. So nobody spoke to him, and Karen Awdry marked Palmer's quiz sheet because everyone else refused."

"What did he do in his spare time?" asked Gus.

"Palmer read a lot," said Kenneth. "One driver said he was interested in ancient history. At weekends, he believed Palmer visited historic sites around the county. When Moore and Harvey searched the caravan, they found books, magazines, and brochures on the same subject. James Palmer told them his brother had spent most of his sentence in the prison library. He was an avid reader."

"I wonder what he was looking for?" said Gus.

"There was one item that puzzled Moore and Harvey," said Kenneth. "When they searched the boot of his car, they found an old tablecloth. There was nothing under it nor in it. Ben Moore couldn't find a receipt or a record in Palmer's bank account to explain what he may have hidden there."

"Why did it have to be something he'd hidden?" asked

Gus. "I lay an old cloth in the boot of my Focus when I'm taking items to the recycling centre."

"Ben Moore knew that the farmer, John Oatley, had waste bins and compost heaps on his land," said Geoff Mercer. "Palmer didn't have a lawn to mow or small trees to prune. So he never needed to make a special trip to recycle anything. Ben just thought it was odd."

"We'll need to pick this file apart and identify the people we need to re-interview. The murder was only three years ago. I imagine the vast majority you mentioned are still in the same place?"

"Rob Dolman has three drivers working for him," said Kenneth, scanning the report in front of him. "He replaced Clive Palmer one month after the murder with a girl called Emily Chivers. She used to serve behind the bar at The Volunteer. Ken Webb is still with Dolman, but Peter Wright left the firm early in 2017. Wright was single and fed up with driving for a living. His whereabouts are unknown. Dave and Karen Awdry got most of their regulars back at The Volunteer after Palmer's death, and the pub is hanging on by its fingernails like most places these days. John Oatley retires this year, and his sons will take over the day-to-day running of the farm. He plans to see the world, so you must catch him before he packs his bags."

"I presume the car and caravan belonging to Palmer are long gone?" asked Gus.

"Afraid so," said Kenneth.

"Wonderful," said Gus. "This should be a cinch."

Chapter Ten

GUS RETURNED to the Old Police Station office with the Clive Palmer folder.

He'd stopped to chat with Vera before leaving London Road. Kassie was at the dentist, explaining why the mezzanine was so quiet.

"Another visit to Kenneth without getting a cup of coffee and a buffet lunch," said Vera.

"We've both had a busy couple of days," said Gus. "The PCC and the NCA have hassled Kenneth. He's asked me to check for low-flying three-letter initials heading his way."

"You're not in Amazing Grace's good books either."

"I'll live," said Gus. "Give Kassie my best wishes when she returns. With luck, our routine will return to normal by my next visit. A fresh case means a fresh start."

With that, Gus waved the case folder and trotted down the stairs.

DI Packenham stood at the end of the passageway to Geoff Mercer's old office and scowled.

Vera hoped Gus was right.

When Gus arrived in the office, the conversation ceased again.

"I'll start thinking you're talking about me," he said.

"No, guv," said Neil Davis. "We can see you've brought a fresh case for us to tackle."

"Who's the victim, guv?" asked Lydia Logan Barre.

"Clive Palmer," said Gus. "Does the name ring a bell?"

"I remember that one, guv," said Neil. "Didn't the killer separate Palmer from his crown jewels?"

"The crime scene photos aren't for the squeamish, Neil," said Gus. "Do you know Ben Moore, or Mark Harvey, who worked on that case?"

"I've known Mark Harvey for several years, guv. We're the same age, give or take a month. Ben Moore was his DI, wasn't he? He came from Marlborough, I believe."

"Perhaps you could contact Gablecross and go through the case with the pair of them."

"Leave that to me, guv," said Neil.

"Do I sit this one out, guv?" asked Luke.

"We'll lose you for a day next week when you visit Portishead, Luke," said Gus. "It's possible ACC Gregory will call you to Gablecross for a meeting to discuss your transfer date. So we'll keep you in the loop, but Alex can take over the task of setting up the interview schedule for this case."

"Where did this murder take place, guv?" asked Lydia.

"Purton," said Gus. "We should have a map that covers the relevant area. The victim came from Wandsworth via HMP The Verne in Portland. Clive Palmer was born in 1967 and was a history teacher. Once we've extracted the items we need to post on the boards and the wall, we'll better understand why Palmer's life had such a dramatic change of direction. The original investigation never determined whether the motive for the murder originated in Wandsworth or Purton. I suggest we eliminate one of those options as quickly as possible. Alex, we'll need interviews with his brother and ex-wife. You and Lydia can travel to London to cover those. I'll take Blessing with me to Purton and talk to the people who knew Palmer during his last ten months. Perhaps we can shake loose facts that didn't emerge in the first few weeks of 2016. We can't see the wood for the trees at present."

The office became a hive of activity as the team followed a well-practised system.

Neil Davis had called DS Mark Harvey and copied the investigation report summary.

"I'm meeting Ben Moore and Mark this afternoon, guv," he said. "They're with different teams now, so it might not be possible to grab a moment with them together."

"Would Melody object if you needed a quick drink after work, Neil? A soft drink or half a pint?"

"She wouldn't encourage it, guv, but I might get away with it, just the once."

"See what you can do, Neil," said Gus.

"Will do, guv."

"They found the body lying face-down on the floor of the caravan, guv. Is that right?"

"Yes, Lydia. They didn't discover the mutilation until the body was turned."

"Which came first, guv?" asked Blessing.

"Palmer died seconds after the knife slash to the neck. The on-call police surgeon, Eve Northwood, determined a gap between the two attacks. The knife wounds occurred in one frenzied assault. Then the mutilation followed later."

"Did the same person do it?" asked Blessing.

"The same blade caused the wounds, Blessing," said

Gus. "Forensics couldn't find evidence there were more than two people in the caravan."

"Why did they turn the body over?" asked Lydia.

"Why indeed," said Gus. "However, we need to find out why Palmer was killed and the motive for the mutilation."

"Did police rule out a robbery, guv?" asked Lydia. "Was there anything taken?"

"There was little to take," said Gus. "Palmer had few possessions after his wife divorced him. He bought a second-hand car and the caravan soon after leaving prison and drove to Purton. Why he chose that particular village is a mystery. His wages as a van driver for Rob Dolman helped pay a monthly rent to the farmer who agreed to garage the car and park the caravan. For good reason, Palmer lived a quiet life and didn't socialise other than walking to The Volunteer for a couple of pints several nights a week. The caravan contained books, magazines, and brochures on ancient history, his clothes and toiletries. A mobile phone, wallet, cash, and keys were found inside the caravan. Robbery didn't appear to be the motive."

"What about DNA, guv?" asked Blessing. "Apart from Palmer, was there no trace of the killer or others who had been in the caravan?"

"Forensics believed the killer wore gloves," said Gus. "When you read the reports in more detail, you'll learn that Monday, the fourteenth of December, was one of the coldest nights of the winter. The only identifiable traces they collected belonged to Palmer. His prints were on record, and the caravan had had several owners, none of whom had been in trouble with the law."

"I don't imagine Palmer had many visitors anyway, guv," said Neil. "Not after the locals learned about his past."

"When you're happy that everything we need is in plain

sight on the boards or the rear wall, I think we should familiarise ourselves with the details of the case. A complete read-through of the witness statements and the observations of the police surgeon and the Gablecross detectives. Neil's going to disappear to Swindon in a few minutes. I noticed that he's copied the report summary, which will give him enough to start the ball rolling with Moore and Harvey."

"I'll call James Palmer and Marcia Brophy, guv," said Alex, referring to the murder file. "Lydia and I will drive to London first thing. We'll try to get back to the office before you leave for the weekend."

"You know the drill, Alex," said Gus. "Ask nicely, and if they aren't keen to cooperate...."

"Tell them they can attend the nearest police station and be interviewed under caution," said Lydia. "It's up to them."

Neil Davis left the office and drove Gablecross.

Alex fixed a meeting in Tooting Bec for eleven in the morning and one in Putney at half-past one in the afternoon.

Meanwhile, the others ploughed through the murder file reports for the rest of the afternoon.

"Neil must have stayed in Shrivenham, guv," said Luke. "He didn't make it back."

"You've had three hours digesting the Palmer case," said Gus, looking around the room. "Any observations?"

"I wondered whether we should add Gemma Long to the list of people to interview, guv," said Alex. "It doesn't appear Moore and Harvey considered she might have been involved."

"You're not suggesting she murdered Palmer, are you?" asked Blessing.

"Palmer's younger brother painted a different picture of

Gemma," said Lydia. "She wasn't innocent, based on her life in Germany."

"What if Gemma's father decided the punishment Palmer received wasn't enough?" asked Alex. "How old was Gemma when Palmer died? Nineteen or twenty? Maybe she persuaded a boyfriend that an eighteen-month sentence was a joke. The investigation ignored her altogether."

"The murder file shows that nobody the detectives interviewed saw a stranger in the village on Monday the fourteenth," said Gus. "It appears Moore and Harvey accepted James Palmer's assessment of Gemma Long's character and continued to look elsewhere for the killer. Follow your gut, Alex."

"Got it, guv. It could be a long day tomorrow."

"Time to go home," said Gus. "I'll see some of you in the morning."

Friday, 21 September 2018

GUS GAVE Suzie a wave as she turned into the car park at London Road. They had spent a quiet night at the bungalow, discussing the Palmer case over pitta bread with mashed tuna and salad.

As he drove towards the office, Gus had to admit they couldn't decide the best place to start the search. Suzie thought it unlikely anyone from Clive Palmer's past would have been responsible.

"Palmer was a teacher; he should have spotted the dangers," she argued, "but he ignored them and carried on with the girl for six months. Palmer deserved to go to prison. Reading between the lines, I reckon the wife was having an affair, but that's irrelevant. She's made a new life. Therefore, I would discount her. She'd already done okay out of the divorce. Why bother? As for Gemma Long, she had nothing to gain, either. Her father might have had a motive, but it wouldn't take a minute to check his alibi. My guess is someone in Purton wanted him dead. Why Palmer went there after he left prison beats me."

That was one thing they agreed on. Gus hoped they would learn the answer when he and Blessing visited the village.

Neil was upstairs in the office when Gus exited the lift.

"Debrief, guv?"

"Hold your horses for one minute. Luke and Blessing were just entering the car park."

When the others joined them, Gus gave Neil a nod.

"I spoke with DS Mark Harvey first, guv," said Neil. "They received a call from Rob Dolman first thing on Tuesday morning. He'd walked to the farmyard to see why Palmer hadn't turned up for work. Dolman didn't follow the herd; he was concerned about Palmer. The locals hadn't accepted the ex-teacher as one of their own. There were a few minor incidents where uniforms needed to get involved, but they were unfounded, and Palmer held down a job with Dolman's haulage firm for ten months. Mark entered the caravan and discovered Clive Palmer's body lying face-down on the floor in a large pool of blood. Someone had stabbed him at least six times in the neck, upper arms and back. There were no signs of a break-in, nothing had been disturbed, and there were no signs of a struggle. He and Ben Moore first thought Palmer got home, and his attacker jumped him, giving him no chance to defend himself. But Palmer had few friends in the village, so it made just as much sense that Palmer knew his assailant and invited him inside. Right from the outset, nothing looked straight-forward."

"Who did they speak to next?" asked Gus.

"Mark said he and Ben went outside, called Gablecross for the cavalry, and spoke to Rob Dolman and John Oatley. Oatley had been there when they arrived. He'd spotted Dolman by the caravan as he drove past in his Land Rover. John Oatley knew Palmer used The Volunteer pub and said he would have arrived soon after eleven if he was drinking there last night. When Mark asked where Oatley had been last night, he said he finished work at around six, made a meal, and watched television for two hours before bed at ten. He didn't see a soul until he spoke to Rob Dolman."

"What did Rob Dolman tell them?" asked Gus.

"Mark asked him where he was, and Dolman said he was at home with his wife and children. He left the office at six and didn't step outside the door until a quarter to eight when he walked to the depot."

"Where did Mark go next?" asked Gus.

"The vehicles from Gablecross were on the outskirts of the village. Mark heard the sirens. He went to The Volunteer to talk to Dave Awdry, the landlord, and his wife, Karen. Awdry confirmed Palmer was in the bar from half-past eight until closing time. Mark asked Awdry why he and his wife didn't treat Palmer the same as the landlords of the other pubs in the village. Dave and Karen Awdry reckoned Clive broke the law and served his sentence. So he'd paid his debt to society and was making a fresh start. Mark asked whether they had regretted their decision when the truth came out. The couple pointed out that Rob Dolman hadn't changed his mind, nor had John Oatley. Palmer had never given either of them cause to think he was anything other than a decent bloke. There was no trouble in The Volunteer that night. Mark told them Palmer had been murdered within an hour of leaving the pub. They were shocked. He spoke to Emily Chivers next; she was the barmaid on duty that night. Her story matched Dave Awdry's."

"Nothing significant so far, guv," said Blessing.

"Mark had to chase Tom Angell, the builder who discovered where Palmer had spent the eighteen months before moving to the village. He told Mark he hadn't visited The Volunteer for six months when he caught up with him. Tom Angell said he and his son arrived home at six, and he spent the evening with his wife. Their son went out with his girlfriend, and arrived home at eleven, just after Tom and his wife went to bed."

"Another dead end," said Blessing.

"Mark asked Angell how he learned about Palmer's past," said Neil. "He told Mark that Palmer was too well-spoken. He heard him in the bar with Ken Webb, one of Dolman's drivers. Angell couldn't understand why an educated bloke worked as a delivery driver. He thought Palmer should live in a detached house, not in an old caravan in John Oatley's farmyard. Angell went to the trouble of inspecting the van one day while Palmer was at work. He traced the van to a firm in Charmouth, Dorset, spoke to the dealer, and learned that Palmer had gone straight from the prison in Portland. Angell soon discovered that most of the inmates were sex offenders. He dug deeper and found Palmer's name in newspaper reports from 2013. Angell started a campaign to force Palmer to leave the village. He thought if Palmer had done it once, he'd do it again. When Mark told Angell that Palmer was dead, he wasn't sorry to hear the news."

"Did the alibis check out?" asked Gus.

"They did, guv," said Neil. "On Wednesday morning,

Eve Northwood did the post-mortem. Palmer died no later than midnight, and the cause of death was as stated at the scene. They still had to check the phone's contents, Palmer's clothing, and the inside of the caravan. Ben wanted to confirm nothing was missing. He also asked about Purton. Why did Palmer move there? Had he met someone while in prison, or did he have visitors? Ben parked that while they interviewed Rob Dolman's two drivers. Mark spoke to Peter Wright."

"He's the one who quit driving, isn't he?" asked Blessing.

"Yes," said Neil. "Wright had worked for Dolman for fourteen years. When he was married, Wright worked at the Honda factory, but he fancied a change of scene after the marriage ended. Rob Dolman still drove a van with Ken Webb and Wright in those days. Dolman eventually took over the office duties from his wife. Another driver took his place in the third van and retired shortly before Palmer arrived in the village. Wright's first impressions of Palmer were neutral. The drivers didn't ride together. They carried out whichever trips Rob Dolman allotted them and only bumped into one another at the start and end of the day. Sometimes, not even then. He confirmed he and Ken Webb had visited The Volunteer for a drink with Clive Palmer once or twice a week in the first couple of months. Mark said Wright's view was as long as Palmer turned up every morning, drove his van, and kept Rob happy, what more did he need to do? The same went for him and Ken Webb. When Mark asked if he'd moved to another pub, Wright said he went because Ken Webb thought it best. Palmer might move on, but they still had to live in the village. Mark asked Wright if he'd ever visited Palmer's caravan. He admitted going with Ken Webb and peeking through the window one evening, but all he could see was a coffee table covered in books."

"I wonder if we could see those books, guv?" asked Blessing.

"They could be in evidence, Blessing," said Gus.

"Mark asked Wright where he was on Monday night, guv," said Neil. "He didn't have an alibi. Wright was single, in his mid-forties, with no family. He stayed home that evening because it was too cold to go out. Wright was earlier than usual getting to work the next morning. He spoke to Rob Dolman in the office, picked a trip to Chilcompton off the board, and left. He had a few jobs in Swindon in the afternoon and returned to the yard at around five. Rob stayed at the depot until Webb and Wright returned and told them Clive Palmer was dead."

"That Chilcompton trip was one Ken Webb usually took, wasn't it?" said Gus. "I'm sure I read that yesterday afternoon."

"Rob told Wright to take his pick since Ken Webb wasn't there, guv," said Neil. "That was it for Wright's interview, apart from Mark asking him who might have killed Palmer. Wright thought it was personal. Someone from the village who felt a convicted paedophile shouldn't live there. Or someone from his past, perhaps a victim's relative, who discovered where he was living."

"Someone like Gemma Long's father, guv," said Blessing.

"I'll message Alex," said Gus. "He can check him out. What did you do next, Neil?"

"Had a coffee with Jake Latimer until DI Moore was free, guv. Only fifteen minutes. Honest."

"I'll believe you; thousands wouldn't," said Gus.

"Mark couldn't spare me any more time, guv, but he

agreed to meet for a drink after work to run through what he and Ben worked on together after the initial rush of interviews."

"Fair enough," said Gus. "What did you learn from DI Moore?"

"Ben confirmed everything Mark told me about the time they spent together at the murder scene and the autopsy," said Neil. "After Mark left to walk to The Volunteer, Ben organised the uniformed officers, secured the perimeter, and watched the Scenes of Crime Officers working outside the caravan, collecting evidence. Eve Northwood estimated the time of death to be eight to twelve hours earlier. Eve said Clive Palmer had received six stab wounds from the same weapon. The first two wounds to the left upper arm were superficial. Palmer had his left carotid artery severed by the third stab wound. The rapid and massive blood loss proved fatal. The wounds to the back were unnecessary. Eve described it as a brutal attack by a right-handed assailant using a four-inch blade. A female SOCO entered the caravan to help Eve turn the body. Eve thought the way Palmer's blood had pooled indicated a wound she hadn't yet identified."

"That's when they found the mutilation," said Blessing.

"Not a pretty sight," said Neil. "The female SOCO threw up outside the caravan. Ben Moore returned to Gablecross and attended the post-mortem with Mark Harvey the following morning. As for the interviews in the afternoon, Ben Moore followed a similar line of questioning with Ken Webb. He'd been with Rob Dolman from the start. Webb worked for a firm in Shrivenham before that. Webb had known Rob since he was a youngster. He was older than Wright and Dolman by ten years. Webb told Ben

Palmer spoke like a college professor but handled a van as if he'd been doing it forever."

"The murder file shows Palmer drove the school minibus," said Blessing. "Perhaps it wasn't such a surprise he adapted so well."

"True," said Gus, "and neither of his colleagues knew what driving experience he had. Palmer had a clean licence, and Dolman didn't need the registration and make of every vehicle Palmer had driven since passing his test. What did Moore ask next, Neil?"

"He asked Webb about The Volunteer," said Neil. "I've just realised something, guv. Wright said they switched to another pub in the village because of Webb's concerns."

"He pointed out that the villagers might take against them if they continued to support Palmer," said Gus. "What have you spotted?"

"Webb told Ben Moore that Wright reckoned people linked them with Palmer because of his past. He didn't want to be labelled a paedophile, and Webb went along with switching pubs although The Volunteer had been his local for over thirty years."

"There's a slight discrepancy there," said Gus. "I wonder why Moore and Harvey didn't spot it?"

"I can ask them later, guv," said Neil. "Webb's story about the visit to the caravan matched what Wright had told Mark. Ben Moore questioned Webb about where he was during the day on Monday. He said he visited Swindon twice in the morning, then, after lunch, drove to Downton. Webb got home at six and stayed indoors with his wife, except for a short walk with their dog. Ben's attention turned to Tuesday morning. He asked Webb why the Chilcompton trip was so popular. Webb told Ben that the longer trips came as a blessed relief after driving around Swindon throughout his working life."

"Webb was disappointed Wright had grabbed that job from the board, though, wasn't he?"

"Ben Moore didn't get the impression it rankled with Webb for more than a few minutes, guv," said Neil. "Although Webb and Wright weren't bosom pals. Since Wright's marriage ended, he said he was bitter and lonely and wasn't great company. Ben noted that Webb said Wright took longer over the Chilcompton trip than necessary. However, that was explained later when he compared notes with Mark Harvey. Wright had stopped at one of the services on the M4 for lunch on his way back. As far as Ben could tell, Rob Dolman wasn't aware of that, but Webb said it was typical of Wright. Driving was a job, nothing more, and if he could squeeze in an extended break during the day without the boss knowing, it was fair game."

"A year later, and he'd had enough," said Blessing. "Wright couldn't have known the police would look at how he spent every hour of that day. For all we know, Wright did something similar every day of the week."

"Did Moore ask anything directly related to Palmer?" asked Gus.

"Palmer told Webb there was nothing for him in London anymore. He mentioned his younger brother and that they spoke occasionally, but nobody else from his previous life. Palmer told Webb he enjoyed driving around Wiltshire, visiting different places, because he was interested in the region's history."

"Did Moore ask who Ken Webb thought murdered Clive Palmer?" asked Gus.

"Webb insisted it had to be someone from outside the village," said Neil. "Despite Tom Angell trying to stir the villagers into forcing Palmer to leave, there wasn't enough venom in opposition to Palmer's presence to result in such a brutal attack. Webb thought someone related to the young girl Palmer was involved with was responsible."

"How much did Webb know of Palmer's case?" asked Blessing.

"Only what Tom Angell told anyone prepared to listen," said Neil. "Neither Webb nor Wright bothered to check the details. Ben told Ken Webb bits of the Gemma Long story, and that's why Webb suggested something connected the killer to Gemma Long. Palmer had only been involved with one girl. He wasn't a repeat offender, so Webb thought it obvious that was where the police should be looking."

"That sounds as if Moore and Harvey ended their interviews at the same point," said Gus.

"They followed the script they'd agreed before they started, guv; then compared notes. That's what we discussed when we later met for a drink in the White Hart. Mark judged Wright as a laid-back character who didn't take life too seriously at first, but he thought him shallow and perhaps too flippant in his replies by the end of their session. Ben remembered Ken Webb being nervous, but he was open and honest with his answers to Ben's questions. Ben and Mark agreed neither driver knew the full details of Clive Palmer's past. They only knew what Tom Angell told them. Ben pointed out that because of the date of the murder, forensic results got delayed by Christmas and the New Year. They were hoping for a break, or the murder weapon would turn up. He spent hours trawling through social media, searching for a positive line of enquiry in the London area. He checked out Marcia Brophy, Palmer's ex-wife and her partner, Adrian Harrold, another teacher. That's who Alex is seeing today. Nothing suggested the couple were connected to Palmer's death. The same went for Palmer's children."

"Perhaps Alex and Lydia will prise a brick from the wall," said Gus.

"Ben and Mark sifted through Palmer's bank details and mobile phone logs. They're in the murder file. We can check them if necessary. Clive Palmer opened an account with the Halifax, in Southside Wandsworth, in August 2012 while on remand. They found nothing remarkable in the details, guv. Palmer's last salary payment from the local authority was there, plus monthly subscriptions to magazines and book clubs. Palmer made small cash withdrawals. After the decree was absolute, he received a cheque from the solicitors. Within days of leaving prison, Palmer bought a second-hand car and the caravan. In the last ten months since his account was active, a monthly sum went to John Oatley for rent. A salary from Rob Dolman came in, and Palmer made a weekly cash withdrawal to cover expenses."

"No significant purchases?" asked Blessing.

"It appeared not," said Neil. "Palmer lived a quiet, simple life. He didn't buy clothes or shoes every other weekend. Mark wondered how he got by without using his debit or credit card. Palmer used cash for the few items he needed. His car spent most of the time in the shed he rented. As for the mobile phone, Palmer had owned the same one since 2013. It contained just three contact numbers - his brother, Oatley, and Dolman. There were no messages or mystery callers to give Ben and Mark a helping hand."

"Another dead end," said Blessing. "Where did they go next?"

"They checked the car and the caravan," said Neil.

"Ben drove the car outside the shed to gain access to the boot."

"The car started the first time," said Gus. "Which suggests Palmer topped it up with petrol and maybe drove it at evenings and weekends. Ken Webb said he was interested in historic sites across Wiltshire. Nobody mentioned hearing about those visits from Palmer. Is that significant?"

"Hardly anybody was talking to him, guv," said Blessing.

"Ben said there was over half a tank of petrol in the car, guv," said Neil. "They checked the interior but found nothing unusual. It was what they found when they opened the boot that stumped them. An old tablecloth, which they believed Palmer must have used to cover something. They thought he didn't want people to see what he had there."

"There was nothing on the bank statements," said Blessing. "What could it be?"

"Ben told me he returned the car to the shed, and then they searched the caravan," said Neil. "The only interesting items were in the living quarters, where Palmer had many books and magazines on Ancient History. He was into the Saxons and the Romans. Mark reckoned the forensics people had removed any official documents. If so, they're still in storage. I asked what led them to Andy Redman, Dolman's brother-in-law. That was Jake Latimer. When they returned to the office that day, Jake asked how the case was going. They said nowhere, and he suggested a career criminal like Andy Redman might be worth a look. We know the rest, guv. The murder file tells us Ben and Mark arrested him, but Redman had an alibi. It didn't fit his usual offences. I think they were desperate."

"Desperate and then re-assigned," said Gus. "What time did you get away from the White Hart?"

"I was home by seven-thirty, guv," said Neil. "Melody was surprised. She hadn't expected me before midnight."

"Thank you, Neil," said Gus. "Give Mark a call to query the difference between Webb and Wright's view on why they stopped drinking in The Volunteer. Then get your report into the Freeman Files."

"On it, guv," said Neil.

"What's next, guv?" asked Blessing.

"I think it's time you and I visited Purton," said Gus.

Chapter Eleven

GUS DROVE them to Purton via the A361. As they passed through the centre of Calne, Blessing queried the bronze artwork of two pigs.

"It commemorates the town's links with Harris's bacon company," said Gus.

"I've not driven this way before," said Blessing.

"We'll pass Lyneham in a few minutes," said Gus. "Flying operations stopped around seven years ago, but the Ministry of Defence still has a school there. Lyneham first opened during WWII and was an essential asset during the Cold War."

"It represents more recent history than the era Clive Palmer was interested in," said Blessing. "When history is above ground, it's easier to see the relevance, but when you've got to dig for it…. I don't know. It can be guesswork, can't it? Sometimes an expert on TV shows you what could be a bracelet, or just a lump of metal, still covered in earth, yet they claim to know what it is. I take it with a pinch of salt."

Gus smiled.

"Royal Wootton Bassett is dead ahead," he said. "Another place in the county that's written its name in the history books. Then we cross the motorway, and Purton lies on the other side."

"Where do we go first, guv?" asked Blessing as they reached the village outskirts.

"The murder site," said Gus. "We're on Restrop Road now, and when we reach the next junction, we'll turn onto High Street. Everything we need is close to hand. We should be able to park at The Volunteer and walk the two hundred yards to Oatley's farmyard."

Five minutes later, they stood in the gateway to the farmyard.

"The farm buildings on our left and straight ahead look the same as in the crime scene photos, guv," said Blessing. "I wonder whether the car is still in the shed?"

"I doubt it, Blessing. The caravan is long gone, too. That patch of ground on the right was where it stood. The trees and dry-stone walling protected it on three sides. Unless you walked past the farm building behind us into the yard itself, you wouldn't know anyone was living here, would you?"

"The youngsters in the village knew, guv," said Blessing, "and so did John Oatley."

A middle-aged man appeared from the far end of the yard.

"Can I help you?"

"Wiltshire Police," said Gus. "Is John Oatley around?"

"He's in the house. It's a mile in that direction. I'm one of his sons, Michael."

Michael pointed across the fields that Gus could see at the far end of the yard.

"What happened to the caravan?" asked Gus.

"Is this to do with Clive Palmer?" asked Michael.

"We're taking a fresh look," said Gus.

"Dad waited six months for Clive's brother to decide what he wanted to do with the car and the van. Then, we took them to the breaker's yard in Gypsy Lane. That's six miles from here, in Swindon."

"What about the contents?" asked Gus.

"The brother collected his belongings," said Michael. "He bagged up Clive's clothes and took them to a charity shop. Dad chased Gablecross and asked what they wanted to do with the books and magazines. He wasn't getting the rent money any longer. A young woman drove over, packed them in a large cardboard box and told Dad she'd make sure they went into storage."

"Was she from Gablecross?" asked Gus.

"Said her name was Louise Arlett," said Michael. "Dad thought she must have been one of the white suits working here for a couple of days."

"How long has this farm been here?" asked Blessing.

"An Oatley has farmed here for five generations," said Michael. "I imagine someone's worked the land for centuries before that. Why?"

"Do you ever dig up buried treasure?" asked Blessing.

Michael laughed.

"Do you think I'd be working sixteen-hour days if I had? No, there *have* been items found near the village over the years. There was a burial ground from Roman times, dating back to 300 AD. The Saxons used it after the Romans left. You'd be more likely to find a skull, or a few bones, than anything valuable."

"Clive Palmer studied History and Ancient History at

Exeter University," said Blessing. "We can't fathom why he chose Purton as a place to live."

"Dad didn't side with those villagers who wanted Clive to move on," said Michael. "Clive never caused him any bother, and Dad needed the monthly rent money. Clive sought a place where nobody knew him. The reason for that came out when he'd been here awhile. After Tom Angell opened his big mouth, there was no way Clive could hope to keep a low profile. Yet he soldiered on without complaining. What happened to him was dreadful. Clive didn't deserve to die that way."

"Did he use the car every weekend?" asked Gus.

"We wouldn't know," said Michael. "The farm keeps us busy every day. I saw Clive in one of Dolman's vans during the week more than I did in his car at weekends. Do you want a lift to the farmhouse? You'd have to ride in the trailer behind the tractor, but Dad's off on a cruise on Monday if you need to speak to him. He'll be gone for three weeks."

"That's okay, Mr Oatley," said Gus. "I don't think there's much more your father can add."

Michael Oatley disappeared behind the farm buildings, and Blessing heard the tractor pull away.

"I wonder if Louise Arlett was the SOCO Ben Moore mentioned," she said.

"We'll check with Gablecross. What made you mention buried treasure?"

"No idea," said Blessing. "I was following your example. You once said you throw in an odd question to mess with a person's head. They might have a series of answers to the questions they expect us to ask. Then, while trying to understand why you asked such a random question, they stop concentrating on their script and give something away they didn't mean to."

"At least someone listens to me," said Gus. "Michael Oatley's answer didn't sound as if you threw him. Did Moore and Harvey check where the two brothers were on the night of the murder?"

"I don't remember reading any mention of them, guv," said Blessing.

"Interesting," said Gus. "Rob Dolman will be in the office until his drivers return to the depot around five. Let's see what he has to say. If we turn right out of the yard, it can't be far."

They soon reached Dolman's depot, and as expected, the yard was empty except for the Portakabin. Gus and Blessing stepped inside and found Rob Dolman studying his computer screen.

"Could you spare us a few minutes, Mr Dolman?" asked Blessing. "I'm DC Umeh from Wiltshire Police. Here's my warrant card. My boss, Mr Freeman, wishes to talk to you about your former employee, Clive Palmer."

"A terrible business," said Rob Dolman. "Please, take a seat. What's brought this on? We have seen no one from Gablecross for eighteen months, at least."

"I head up a Crime Review Team, Mr Dolman," said Gus. "We offer a fresh set of eyes on cases that weren't solved the first time."

"What they call cold cases on television," said Dolman.

"No murder case is ever too cold that we won't have a go at solving it," said Gus.

"I see," said Dolman. "What do you think I can add since I spoke to your colleagues?"

"You could explain why you gave Clive Palmer the

benefit of the doubt when he told you he had just left prison."

"One of my drivers had retired, and I was a man short," said Dolman. "Business was good, and I couldn't cope with two vans on the road. Clive walked in the door behind you and asked if there was any chance of a job. He'd just arrived in the village and lived in his old caravan in John Oatley's farmyard. I could tell he was keen, but I asked where he worked before moving here and if it was the same line of work. That's when Clive told me about the prison sentence. He swore nothing like that would happen again, and I believed him. Clive started straight away, and after a couple of months, I thought I'd fallen on my feet. Clients appreciated how he worked and how polite he was. I enjoyed having him around. Clive was a brainy chap, and he would have helped me grow this firm if Tom Angell hadn't poked his nose in."

"Although you knew about Palmer's past, the turmoil Tom Angell caused did not sway you?" said Blessing. "You continued to support him."

"I thought the storm would blow over," said Dolman. "Storms usually do."

"We know where you were on the Monday night Palmer died," said Gus. "The detectives knew where everyone in the village had been that night; if they thought they were pertinent to the case. The only person whose alibi couldn't be tested was Peter Wright. He lived alone and said he was indoors all evening. Wright said it was too cold to venture outside."

"It certainly was," said Dolman. "I found it hard to get out of bed the next morning. This office was like a walk-in freezer when I arrived. I was still trying to get warm when Peter walked in the door."

"Were you surprised he was the first driver to arrive?" asked Gus. "We got the feeling Wright was a guy who did what he had to, and no more."

"Peter took advantage of my good nature," said Dolman. "I suspected he lingered over the occasional journey, so I needed someone to cover a trip he didn't have time to complete. While Clive worked here, he never complained. Ken Webb had a moan from time to time, but Ken's older, happily married, and Peter's lackadaisical attitude, annoyed him. They used to drink together in the evenings, but that petered out."

"They went to another pub because of Clive Palmer," said Blessing.

"Plenty of customers left The Volunteer," said Dolman. "But it was later, after they switched to the Royal George, that those two drifted apart. Did you know that young Emily Chivers came to me after Clive died? She's still here, but Peter quit. She's a good worker."

"Yes, we heard," said Gus. "She was the barmaid at The Volunteer."

"Trade dropped off after Clive's murder. Country pubs are closing every week. Times have changed, and youngsters don't use the local pub as they did in the old days. Instead, they can get supplies from the supermarket and tanked-up before hitting a Swindon nightclub."

"You sound like you have experience, am I right?" Gus asked.

"Kids are a trial when they're young," said Dolman. "Teenagers are something else."

Blessing glanced at Gus, but her boss's face gave nothing away.

"Why did Peter Wright leave?" asked Gus.

"Peter told me he couldn't face sitting behind the wheel

of a van for the rest of his working life. I've no idea what prompted the sudden move. He was his usual miserable, laid-back self on Friday evening, and then on Monday morning, he dropped into the office to say he'd quit. He left the village within a month, and nobody's heard a word from him since."

"Were you still busy?" asked Blessing. "Did you get a replacement straight away?"

"I coped for a week or two," said Dolman. "I drove the third van myself as I did when I started. Trade always fluctuates in this business, so if I needed a driver for a short period, I got one from an employment agency in Swindon. That proved expensive, so I advertised for a driver in the end. A Polish lad has worked for me for twelve months, but he's considering returning to Poland when the dust settles over Brexit. He's not sure he's as welcome here as when he first came over."

Gus could tell this line of conversation was going nowhere. So he tried another angle.

"What do you know about John Oatley's two sons?"

"Michael and Philip? They're running his farm now. John is semi-retired. I don't think he'll ever stop working altogether. I've heard he's off on holiday soon. The Oatley family is well-respected in the farming community."

"Do they live on the farm?" asked Gus.

"Which one?" asked Dolman. "John took over a couple of failing farms in the 1970s, and the boys ploughed their own furrow, so to speak. Michael is an arable farmer, like his father. Philip raises organic sheep at a farm two miles south of Purton at Lydiard Millicent. Michael's farm is on Cricklade Road, a few miles north of the village. Michael drops in to help his father daily, and Philip drives across at weekends to show his face."

"Do they not get on with one another?" asked Blessing.

"The brothers don't see eye-to-eye," said Dolman. "That's not unusual with families, is it?"

"Did you see much of the brothers while Clive Palmer lived in the farmyard?" asked Gus.

"You know what farmers are, Mr Freeman," said Dolman. "They work long hours. I spent more time with John Oatley the morning after Clive was murdered than I had in all the years I've lived in Purton. So, no, I saw little of Michael or Philip. They must have known their father had allowed Clive to stay there. If they objected, it didn't alter John's stance, and neither of them bothered Clive as far as I know."

"You said Peter Wright left in a rush," said Gus. "I presume he had a house to sell. He would be fortunate to get that sorted in a month."

"Peter rented his property to a young couple from the village," said Dolman. "He might come back when the wanderlust wears off, I suppose."

"Thank you for the chat, Mr Dolman," said Gus. "We'll walk back to The Volunteer now to see whether Dave Awdry and his wife can throw light on matters."

"I hope you discover the person responsible," said Dolman. "I could never understand why anyone from the village wanted Clive dead. Plenty of the villagers didn't want him living here, butchering him as they did makes me think it had to be someone from his past."

When they were outside the Portakabin, Blessing asked Gus whether he intended to talk to either driver.

"The only one we might have spoken to was Ken Webb," said Gus. "He had an alibi, and nothing I've heard or read leads me to believe he was involved. Why? Do you think we should?"

"Oh, no, guv," said Blessing. "Webb didn't kill Clive Palmer."

Gus and Blessing left Rob Dolman to wait for Ken, Emily, and the Polish driver to return to the depot. They walked along High Street and walked up the steps to the front door of The Volunteer. As Blessing scanned the bar area, she saw only two customers. An elderly couple sat in semi-darkness in the far corner of the bar, with a golden retriever on a lead lying at their feet.

"What can I get you?"

"Karen Awdry?" asked Blessing.

"Police?" asked Karen.

"Detectives," said Gus. "Is it that obvious?"

"I was in the kitchen when you parked in our car park. Dave watched you walk into Oatley's yard."

"My name's Freeman," said Gus. "DC Umeh and I need to ask you questions about Clive Palmer."

"We're taking a fresh look into the case," added Blessing.

"Our statements won't change from the ones you've read," said Karen.

Dave Awdry joined her from the other end of the bar.

"What now?" he asked.

"Who did you think was responsible for Palmer's death?" asked Gus.

"We knew the villagers weren't comfortable having a sex offender living on their doorstep," said Dave. "Karen and I had formed our own opinion of the guy's character, which didn't sit well with everyone. That's tough. Our names are over the door. After Clive's murder, our old regulars crept back here, but the pub trade is dying, and we're praying we can hold on until Christmas. The holiday season might give us enough of a boost to survive. I always thought Clive must have upset someone he met while working for Rob Dolman. He drove his van across the county and beyond. Clive also made trips at the weekend, visiting those historical sites that fascinated him so much. So there were plenty of opportunities for his past to have caught up with him. But, despite Tom Angell ranting and raving, nobody in the village hated Clive enough to kill him.

"Let alone do what they said in the Advertiser," said Karen. "That had to be personal."

"Did Clive ever mention his weekend trips?" asked Blessing.

"Not in detail," said Dave. "Any conversation wasn't easy after the others took against him. Clive sat alone, and when he wanted another drink, he chose a quiet time when he didn't have to wait at the bar."

"Clive wouldn't have a problem now," said Karen, "as you can see."

"He was more talkative on a Tuesday night," said Dave, "on a Quiz Night."

"What did he talk about?" asked Blessing.

"The Romans," said Dave. "One night, I asked a question, and Dave told me I'd got the answer wrong. He waited until everyone had left and explained the story to me. He was a clever bloke."

"Can you remember what the story was about?" asked Gus.

"A dowry," said Dave, "but I was checking the till and eager to get upstairs to bed. Karen saw Clive out the front door, locked up, and we did not mention the subject again."

"Was Ken Webb one regular to find their way back?" asked Gus.

"Ken's back, but his mate never returned," said Karen.

"Peter Wright's been gone for eighteen months, though, hasn't he?" said Gus.

"Peter never came here to drink after Clive's murder," said Karen.

"Ken doesn't come out for a drink as often as he did," said Dave.

"What about Tom Angell?" asked Gus.

"He's barred. Not that he's ever tried to set foot in here in the past two-and-a-half years."

"Why did Emily Chivers leave?" asked Blessing.

"We didn't have enough work to keep her on," said Karen. "Dave and I work six days a week now. We don't open on Mondays; nobody has money left after the weekend."

"Thank you for your time," said Gus. "I hope things pick up for you."

"Do you think you'll ever find out who did it?" asked Karen.

"We're closer than we were yesterday," said Blessing.

When they reached the Focus, Gus stood with his keys and stared at Blessing on the passenger side.

"Really, Blessing?" he asked. "Are we closer than we were yesterday?"

"Unless Alex and Lydia come back from London with news that throws everything I've heard today up in the air, then yes, I think we are."

They drove back to the Old Police Station office in silence. Gus was going over what Neil had told them this morning, plus what they'd learned in Purton.

Beside him, Blessing was looking forward to next week and a trip to Gablecross. She was convinced the key to the case lay under lock and key in the evidence store.

Monday, 24 September 2018

"DON'T FORGET, DARLING," said Suzie as they left the bungalow. "Today is Day One."

Gus arrived home on Friday afternoon, looking as if he carried the world's weight on his shoulders.

Suzie knew he would open up eventually but knew better than to force matters. They hadn't made plans for the evening, so she had suggested they drive into Devizes to get the supermarket shopping out of the way. That left Saturday clear if Gus wanted to visit the allotment. When a case was bothering him, as this latest one was, that was where Gus would disappear. Several hours working on the land, or sitting outside his shed, would clear his mind of irrelevant issues, and a solution often appeared.

They drove to the Waggon & Horses for a meal on Saturday evening. Gus had left the bungalow after an early lunch and hadn't returned to the bungalow until well after six.

"A penny for them?" she'd asked as they waited for their main course.

"I'm wondering whether I'm losing it," said Gus.

"What brought this on?" asked Suzie.

"I've spent two days on the Palmer case and can't make head nor tail of it. However, Blessing and I visited Purton on Friday afternoon, and she thinks we're close to cracking it."

"You don't think she's exaggerating?"

"It's not something Blessing's prone to," said Gus.

"In that case, maybe with so many other things on your mind, you've lost focus."

Gus had pondered her comment.

As she drove them home to Urchfont, he'd accepted she was right.

"In the past week, we've closed the Stan Jones file or ended the team's direct involvement in the case. Our efforts have contributed to Ralph Gibbons facing trial for the murder of DI Terry West. Perspiration rather than inspiration got those two tasks over the finishing line. It was the team's hard work rather than anything I contributed. Then Luke dropped the bombshell. Geoff and I had expected it would happen eventually, but it still caught me on the hop. I thought we had time to find something to match his ambition that meant he could stay with the CRT or keep close contact."

"Gablecross isn't the other side of the world," said Suzie as she eased the Golf into the driveway of the bungalow.

They had sat in the lounge with a nightcap. Gus drank another glass of Malbec while she nursed a mug of hot chocolate.

"Even something Rob Dolman said on Friday afternoon had me drifting into matters unrelated to the case."

"He's the haulier Palmer worked for, isn't he?"

"Yes, Dolman's got teenage kids giving him sleepless nights. So I stopped listening to what he was saying and wondered how we would handle that problem when the time comes."

Suzie knew the baby would make a massive difference to both their lives, but worrying over something that might or might not happen in fifteen years or more wasn't productive. Instead, they would handle the problems together, one day at a time.

"I prescribe a day of rest tomorrow. The forecast is for rain, so there's no rush. I want you to relax, listen to music, watch television, and forget work altogether. Then, get to work on Monday and start with a recap on the Palmer case. Listen to what the team has to say. If everyone agrees that Blessing's gut points you in the right direction, then go for it. It's not that you're losing it, Gus. You just haven't been listening because of the background noise."

They had spent a quiet Sunday together. Gus had done as he was told, but as he listened to the Steve Miller Band and watched a David Attenborough documentary, Suzie knew he was dissecting every element of the Palmer case to see what he'd missed.

Gus arrived in the car park as Neil Davis locked his car door. Neil waited for Gus to park the Focus, and they travelled in the lift together.

"Good weekend, guv?" asked Neil.

"Quiet," said Gus.

"I'm looking forward to this morning," said Neil. "We've got Alex and Lydia's report from their day in London, and maybe you'll tell us you uncovered fresh evidence in Purton."

"Are you seeing anything yet, Neil?" asked Gus.

"Well, you know what I learned at Gablecross. There were a couple of small things to check with Ben and Mark."

They heard the lift descend to the ground floor. Alex, Lydia, and Blessing emerged minutes later.

"Any sign of Luke?" asked Gus.

"Sorry, guv, I forgot," said Neil. "He had a call from ACC Gregory on Friday afternoon. Luke's meeting her at Gablecross this morning. He might not be in the office until tomorrow."

"Right, let's take five minutes to recap what we've done so far on the Palmer case," said Gus. He listed the interviews they had undertaken so far on a flip chart.

"Have we missed anyone?" he asked.

Gus caught the look that passed between Alex and Neil.

"We've covered everyone with any connection to the case, guv," said Alex.

"Our source for that list was the murder file, guv," said Lydia.

"Nobody we've interviewed has given us a new name," said Neil.

"Michael and Philip Oatley never appeared in the original investigation," said Blessing.

"They're John Oatley's sons," explained Gus. "We spoke to Michael on Friday, but I didn't get a sense he was involved in the murder. Did you, Blessing?"

"No, guv," said Blessing, "and his brother, Philip, spent even less time at his father's farm."

"What are you driving at, guv?" asked Neil.

"Are you ready to jump in, Blessing?"

"Not until I've heard what Alex and Lydia have to say, guv."

"Over to you then, Alex," said Gus.

Chapter Twelve

"WE SPOKE with James Palmer first, guv, in Tooting Bec. He told us where his brother studied and taught. Gemma Long moved to Clive's Academy in 2012. James knew nothing of Gemma's background at that stage, and his brother didn't tell him she was becoming a nuisance."

"James told us he realised Clive's home life wasn't as happy as it had been, guv," said Lydia. "Their teenage kids were causing him headaches, and Marcia was teaching at a failing inner-city school and finding it tough. Tensions ran high, and Clive must have cracked under pressure. James only learned about the six-month affair with Gemma after the police arrested Clive. Marcia and the children disowned their father. Nevertheless, James stood by him and visited him in prison while he was on remand and throughout his sentence. He accepted the version of events Clive told him; Gemma had stalked him for months, seduced him, and blackmailed him into continuing to sleep with her."

"After Clive left prison and moved to Purton, James continued to keep in touch by phone, guv," said Alex. "The only time he visited the village was to collect a few personal items and take Clive's clothes to a charity shop. James apologised for not getting back to the farmer concerning his brother's car and caravan."

"I asked James why his brother chose Purton to live, guv," said Lydia. "He said Clive told him he had no roots anymore. When he felt the time had come to move on, he'd hitch the caravan to the car and hit the road. Someone didn't give him a chance."

"What about the weekend trips Clive made?" asked Blessing. "Did James know what they entailed?"

"James said it did not surprise him to find so much reading material in the caravan," said Lydia. "The subject didn't interest him, so he left it behind. James said Clive had a passion for his subject. While he was in prison, he was reading and researching. It helped pass the time."

"In the afternoon, we drove to Putney and met with Marcia Brophy and Adrian Harrold, guv," said Alex. "They admitted the affair started before news broke about Clive and Gemma Long. We asked where they were on the fourteenth of December in 2015, and we could confirm they were at a school function until nine-forty-five. Liam Palmer remains in the Far East as a devout Buddhist, while Nicki travels the world with hospitality. They might be a dysfunctional family, guv, but they had no contact with Clive Palmer from the Good Friday when the Metropolitan Police arrested him."

"Alex received your text message, guv," said Lydia. "We drove into Central London later in the afternoon to speak with Steve Long, Gemma's father. He still works in security and acted as a steward at a Premier Division football match on the fourteenth of December. No way was he anywhere near Purton at eleven o'clock that night. Long said the

Monday night match was televised, and he tackled a fan who ran onto the pitch. The national news showed the incident if we wanted to verify his alibi."

"I can't see anything Alex and Lydia learned will help find the killer," said Neil.

"Which leaves our visit to Purton on Friday afternoon," said Blessing.

Gus took the others through their conversations with Michael Oatley and Rob Dolman.

"So, the car and the caravan went to the breaker's yard, guv," said Neil. "I suppose it would be hard to tell something gruesome happened there now."

"A tranquil farmyard scene," said Gus.

"Who asked Louise Arlett to collect the books and magazines, guv?" asked Lydia.

"It depends on who John Oatley pestered at Gablecross," said Gus. "He was fed up with being reminded of the murder. He wanted James to decide what to do with the vehicles. James didn't care what happened to them, nor was he interested in the books. Michael Oatley told us his father asked Gablecross for a decision, and Louise Arlett drove to collect the items. We assume we'll find them in storage."

"Who stopped the direct debit for the rent Clive Palmer paid John Oatley?" asked Blessing.

"His brother would have informed the bank of Clive's death," said Alex. "All transactions would have ceased from that point. Why?"

"I was just wondering," said Blessing.

"What did you make of Emily Chivers filling Palmer's seat in one of Dolman's vans, guv," said Alex.

"She'd lost her job at the pub, Alex," said Gus. "I haven't spoken to the young lady. Dave Awdry said Emily walked in the opposite direction after leaving the pub at eleven o'clock. Emily's parents confirmed she was at home when Clive Palmer was attacked."

"Peter Wright didn't have an alibi, guv," said Neil. "Why did he get an easy ride?"

"Just because Wright didn't have anyone to confirm he spent the evening at home, it doesn't mean he was guilty," said Alex. "Ben Moore and Mark Harvey looked for a motive. Although Wright moved to another pub to drink and didn't speak to Palmer, they'd never argued. So Wright didn't differ from Ken Webb. Why would either of them kill Palmer? It made little sense."

"Which left our conversation with Dave and Karen Awdry," said Blessing.

"Dave Awdry always thought Clive Palmer must have upset someone he met while he worked for Rob Dolman," said Gus. "Clive drove across Wiltshire and into the neighbouring counties. Clive made trips at weekends, visiting historical sites. Those were places where Dave thought his past had caught up with him. However, Dave was adamant nobody in the village hated Clive enough to kill him. His wife insisted the attack had to be personal."

"I asked if Clive ever mentioned his weekend trips," said Blessing. "Dave said on Tuesdays, after a Quiz Night, Clive could be more talkative. He didn't expand on any of his trips, but he talked more about the Romans."

"There was a query on the answer to one question one night," said Gus. "Clive insisted Dave was wrong. So he waited until everyone had left and told them a story about a dowry."

"How does that help us, guv?" asked Neil.

"At this stage, I'm not sure," said Gus.

"We asked whether the people who left The Volunteer had returned after Clive Palmer's murder," said Blessing.

"Quite a few had, Ken Webb among them, but Peter Wright didn't rejoin his colleague.

"Wright quit his job at Dolman's without warning at the beginning of 2017," said Gus. "He rented his house to a young couple and left in search of pastures new."

"Where is he now, guv?" asked Neil.

"Nobody has heard from him since he left, Neil," said Gus. "Maybe it was a gap year he forgot to take when he was younger. Perhaps he's working in a bar in Marbella? According to Rob Dolman, Wright told him he couldn't stand the thought of driving a van for the next twenty-five years."

"Where do we look next, guv?" asked Lydia.

"Are you ready to explain what you meant on Friday now, Blessing?" asked Gus.

"I think so, guv," said Blessing. "We should ignore everything that happened before Clive Palmer arrived in Purton. It had nothing to do with his murder except for the afterthought."

"The mutilation?"

"Yes. Eve Northwood said there was a distinct gap between the stabbing and the mutilation. The killer had to turn the body over for that; they returned it to its original face-down position. Clive Palmer wasn't a small man. So his killer had to have a certain amount of upper-body strength to do that, so they didn't leave DNA from their clothing behind."

"The blood pool wasn't smeared across the carpet," said Alex. "So they grabbed the trouser belt, flipped the body over, made the cuts, and turned the body back again. That reduces the field, guv."

"I believe the key to this case lies in the evidence room at Gablecross," said Blessing. "We must pray that Louise

Arlett added the books and magazines to the material collected by her SOCO colleagues."

"Moore and Harvey searched those books," said Alex. "They found nothing to suggest they were anything other than proof Clive Palmer was a history nut."

"How do we explain the tablecloth in the boot of Clive's car?" asked Blessing. "Why was there no record on his bank account of him having spent a sizeable sum on an item he wanted to keep hidden?"

"Maybe it wasn't valuable," said Lydia. "It was just something he didn't want people to know he had."

"Like what?" asked Neil. "A gun, a sword, a machete? It couldn't be dodgy if we forget everything that went before he arrived in Purton."

"What do you propose we do, Blessing?" asked Gus.

"We retrieve the evidence from Gablecross and recheck it. Ben Moore and Mark Harvey missed something. Perhaps it wasn't what was there that was important. Maybe it was something that wasn't there."

"Alex, can you and Neil arrange the tables so we can check the boxes on different sides of the room? Come on, Blessing, let's drive to Gablecross. Lydia, please call DI Ben Moore, tell him what we need, and ask him to contact Louise Arlett. We'll need to speak to her."

"Got it, guv," said Alex.

Gus and Blessing headed for the lift.

"I didn't understand that last bit you said, Blessing. But I think you're right. The killer was local and had nothing to do with Clive's past. I wish I could see the motive, but I can't yet."

"After listening to Alex and Lydia, I'm more convinced than ever I'm right," said Blessing.

Gus drove them to Shrivenham and parked in the Gablecross visitor's car park.

"Let's hope Ben Moore has given Reception a heads-up," he said. "This place is a rabbit warren. I'd prefer he sent a guide to lead us to the room we want."

A man waiting in Reception stepped forward when they stepped inside the building.

"Good afternoon," said DS Mark Harvey. "Gus Freeman and DC Umeh? We're expecting you. Please follow me."

Blessing tried to keep pace with the tall detective, but it was impossible to do that and make a note of the signage that cluttered the corridors. Gus was right. They could be here for days if they didn't get someone to show them back to Reception.

"Here we are," said Mark Harvey, "My old boss's office."

They entered the office, and DI Ben Moore stood to greet them.

"Gus Freeman? I remember hearing you were back in harness. Who's this with you?"

"Detective Constable Blessing Umeh, sir," said Blessing.

"Have you found something on the Clive Palmer case? We spoke with one of your team the other day. I didn't expect to hear from you again."

"We've come to collect evidence boxes," said Blessing. "Nothing related to the searches outside the caravan. We're concentrating on the bank statements and the books and magazines."

"I see," said Ben. "I can't believe we missed something in the bank details."

"I don't believe you did, sir," said Blessing. "Who asked Louise Arlett to collect the books and magazines after John

Oatley contacted this station? That was six months after the murder, and John Oatley wanted to know why the caravan hadn't been emptied."

"We thought after we contacted James Palmer and informed him of his brother's death that he had cleared everything out months before."

"By 'we', you mean you and DS Harvey?" asked Blessing.

"We weren't on the same team then," said Mark.

Ben Moore looked embarrassed.

"No, I mean, Louise and I thought James Palmer would have wanted to take everything from the caravan. I started dating Louise several weeks after we met in Purton. We've been engaged for over a year. So I suggested Louise bring the stuff here and dump it with the rest of the material from the case. I just wanted John Oatley off our backs."

"Did you take a second look at what she collected?" asked Gus.

"There was no time," said Ben. "If someone resurrected the case to review it, Mark and I would never have handled it, anyway. The Chief Constable chose it from the pile of unsolved crimes and gave it to you."

"Can we retrieve those evidence boxes now?" asked Gus.

"I'll call Louise," said Ben. "She'll know where to put her hand on them straight away."

"I'll take you to the evidence room," Mark said. "Louise can meet us there."

"Thanks, Mark," said Ben. "I hope you find what you're looking for."

"I don't expect to find anything," said Blessing. "Which will prove we're on the right track."

Gus smiled at DI Moore as if he understood what

Blessing meant. They left the office and chased after the long-striding Mark Harvey. After several stairs and corridors, Blessing spotted a sign pointing to the evidence room on the wall. At the end of the corridor stood a pretty young woman.

"Gus Freeman and DC Umeh wish to speak to you, Louise," said Mark.

"Did I do something wrong?" asked Louise Arlett. "Were those books supposed to go to someone else?"

"No," said Blessing. "I'm hoping that by ensuring those books and magazines didn't get lost, you might have helped us find our killer."

"Wow," said Louise. "Let's go inside. I'll sign us in and show you where I stored everything."

"If you don't need me any further, I'll get back to work," said Mark.

"That's fine," said Gus. "I'm sure Louise can help us get the evidence boxes to the car park."

"You get on, Mark," said Louise. "Ben told me Mr Freeman was interested in the statements and those books. We can manage."

Ten minutes later, they were in the car park and had loaded three boxes in the Focus.

"Thanks for getting us out of there, Louise," said Blessing. "My sense of direction is useless, as my boss will tell you."

"No problem. If you're sure you have everything you need, I'll get back," said Louise. "Good luck."

Gus eased the Focus into the busy early afternoon traffic and headed for the office.

"All will be revealed, guv," said Blessing.

"You hope," said Gus.

They unloaded the boxes in the Old Police Station car

park and carried them to the lift. Once the lift doors opened on the first floor, Neil jumped out of his chair.

"Right, let's get these boxes open," he said. "We can't wait to start the search. Does anyone want to tell me what we're looking for?"

Blessing issued instructions, and Alex and the others set to work.

Gus watched as books and magazines separated and arranged in piles on one desk near the fire door. Bank statements were sorted into month and year order and laid on the table at the far end.

"Alex and Lydia," said Blessing. "Can you start with the first date of the first of the three magazines Clive Palmer owned? Then Neil and I will check it's here."

"I've found a direct debit in January 2014," said Lydia. "Three pounds, ninety-nine pence to a publishing firm in Sheffield."

"We've got the January 2014 magazine here," said Neil. "That's Number One of Twenty-four."

"The monthly Direct Debit went out on the first of the month," said Alex, "or the nearest weekday, right through until the first of December 2015. Two weeks before the murder."

"You should have the complete series," said Lydia.

Neil rechecked the pile of magazines.

"Number seventeen is missing," he said.

"We need to contact the publishers and ask what features appeared in that issue," said Blessing.

"Our killer didn't just stand and watch Palmer die," said Gus. "He removed items that could give the detectives vital clues. Which series was that?"

"The Romans in Britain, guv," said Neil. "I looked at the back of the April 2015 issue to see if they advertised what was coming in May. An article on Roman villas rumoured to exist in different parts of the country."

"Can we turn our attention to the next magazine subscription Clive Palmer started?" asked Blessing.

"The Direct Debit for that appeared later in 2014," said Lydia. "The magazine must be quarterly, and the issue numbers suggest it's been running for years. We've got amounts paid to an Edinburgh-based publisher of a Coin Collectors magazine in July and October that year, and then four amounts in 2015."

"Bingo," said Neil. "I've only got five out of the six here."

"Another publisher to chase, Neil," said Blessing. "I wonder which coins were highlighted in that issue of the magazine. My bet is they were Roman and connected to a dowry."

"The quiz question," said Gus.

"Palmer told Dave Awdry the people who supplied his weekly quiz had made an error," said Blessing. "They gave the wrong answer. We don't know the question, but it might not matter. One more magazine to check, and we're done."

"What about these hardback books?" asked Neil.

"Alex and Lydia can check whether anything Clive purchased in the last two years is missing. Several of those Ancient History books will have been in Clive's possession for decades. We can't hope to check his bank accounts before he went to prison. But we can check any missing titles and buy them on Amazon if we need to verify facts these magazines reveal."

"Why didn't Ben and Mark spot this?" asked Neil, holding up a magazine.

"Ben sorted through the stuff he found in the living

space of the caravan," said Alex. "Mark checked the bedroom, kitchen and toilet."

"Ben thumbed through the books a day or so after the murder," said Neil. "He told me it was Thursday, the twenty-third, when they returned to the farmyard and searched the car."

"They drove the car out of the shed, opened the boot, and saw the tablecloth," said Gus.

"They didn't connect the metal detecting magazine and the empty boot," said Lydia.

"If Clive Palmer bought a metal detector after he left prison, there's no record of it in his bank account," said Gus.

"Maybe he bought it second-hand for cash, guv," said Neil.

"I wonder why nobody saw him using it in or around Purton?" asked Lydia.

"Are we saying the killer removed the metal detector from the boot after he'd murdered Palmer?" asked Alex.

"They found the keys in the caravan," said Blessing. "He could have fetched it, returned the keys, and closed the door behind him as he left."

"That's cool, guv," said Neil. "He missed a trick, though, didn't he? Perhaps he didn't realise Palmer had bought this single issue and had tucked it away amongst the hardbacks."

"Well done, Blessing," said Gus. "It was something that wasn't there, as you suggested. So what happens when we find out what was in those two missing magazines? Does it help us prove the identity of our killer?"

"We've got one more trip to make, guv," said Blessing. "Once I decided the killer had to be someone Palmer met after moving to Purton, it was easier. How long will it take you to drive to Chilcompton?"

"Forty-five minutes?"

"We'll contact the two publishers while you're gone, Blessing," said Alex. "I'll get the details of the contents and ask for copies to be sent to us."

"Thank you, Alex," said Blessing. "Neil, can you call Rob Dolman for the address of that injection-moulding firm he has a regular contract with, please?"

"I'll text you the address, Blessing," said Neil.

Gus was holding the lift doors when Blessing trotted inside.

"You know who it was now, guv, don't you?"

"He's well-built, capable of overpowering Clive Palmer and turning over the body. There was no way to disprove his alibi."

As Gus drove them out of town, heading for the A36 and the Somerset town of Radstock, he slotted the last piece into the jigsaw.

"He was the only person to do something different that day," said Gus.

Blessing's phone buzzed. Neil had got the address from Rob Dolman.

"Guess what?" said Blessing. "It's on an industrial estate on the outskirts of Radstock."

Thirty minutes later, Gus turned into the small estate and obeyed the fifteen mph speed limit so they could study the units.

"There it is," said Blessing. "Three units before the place where Dolman made a collection every month. Ken Webb usually made this trip. I wonder how he knew?"

"We'll know when we check the magazines, Blessing," said

Gus. "I bet there was an advert every month, and our man spotted it. Then he chose the most relevant issue to take from the caravan. One that gave the values for the coins he stole from the man who found them. Do you want to visit the unit?"

"The cobbler who occupies it now hasn't had time to replace the original sign, guv," said Blessing. "I doubt she's been here long. Oliver Rogers, the crooked numismatist, is long gone."

A young woman looked up from her workbench when they walked onside.

"Can I help you?"

"We were hoping to find Mr Rogers," said Gus.

"He retired eighteen months ago, Oliver had a shop on the High Street in town for decades, but margins in his business were tight. Although his costs were cheaper out here, he must have had enough."

"He closed the shop in early 2017, I suppose?" asked Gus.

"That's right. The unit was vacant for ages. It's too small for most businesses, but it suited me. So I took it on a couple of months ago. The temporary signage will get replaced from the beginning of October."

"Do you know if he still lives in Radstock?" asked Blessing.

"Oh no, Oliver had family in Wales, somewhere. I've no idea where I'm afraid."

"Not your fault," said Gus. "Good luck with your venture."

They returned to the car, and Gus drove back to the office.

"Do you think we'll find the missing items in Purton?" he asked.

"How would you explain why we needed to look around the house, guv?"

"We could say we were from the Council," said Gus.

"Warrant, guv," said Blessing.

"I'll stop in a lay-by and call Geoff Mercer," said Gus. "He can have someone on the doorstep inside an hour."

Thirty minutes later, Gus parked the Focus beneath the Crime Review Team office, and he and Blessing travelled up in the lift.

"We've got a better picture now of what Clive Palmer was interested in," said Alex. "Our magazine copies are in the post. By the smile on Blessing's face, your trip was successful."

"Uniformed officers will attend an address in Purton in thirty minutes," said Gus. "The young couple who rent the property shouldn't be inconvenienced for too long. The officers are looking for a metal detector and a couple of magazines. I suggested they started in the loft or any outbuilding Peter Wright told them was out-of-bounds."

"Wright must have spotted Clive Palmer with the detector while on one of his weekend trips," said Blessing. "It could have been as early as the time he persuaded Ken Webb to look inside the caravan. Wright monitored Palmer from a distance over the following months. When he and Webb moved to another pub to drink, Webb told us their meetings became less frequent. That was because Wright was more interested in what Clive Palmer was up to. When we've checked the details in that missing 'Romans in Britain' magazine, we'll understand what Palmer found on the Saturday or Sunday before he died."

"Wright waited in the yard for Palmer to get home from The Volunteer," said Gus. "He attacked him as soon as Clive opened the caravan door. We thought Wright spent the next few minutes choosing which items to take with him, but first, he had to find the coins. Clive Palmer wouldn't leave them in plain sight. Then, he sent the police investigation up a blind alley. The mutilation caused the police and the locals to believe it was personal."

"His last job was to open the shed door," said Blessing, "remove the metal detector from the boot and return the keys to the caravan. Wright then shut the door and left it unlocked."

"A specialist coin collector like the one we've just seen in Chilcompton would advertise in a popular magazine," said Gus. "Wright spotted the address and saw his chance. He could get rid of the coins by grabbing the trip from Ken Webb. That's why Wright was in early the following morning. He explained the late return from Chilcompton by saying he stopped on the M4 at Leigh Delamere services for lunch. We suspect negotiations with the coin dealer took longer than he hoped, and he had time for just a sandwich. The coin dealer, Oliver Rogers, closed his business at the same time as Wright quit his job. Either it took Rogers a year to find a collector prepared to break the law, or they waited until they thought the coast was clear."

"Wright was a cool customer, guv," said Neil. "He could have been behind that."

"Maybe," said Gus. "Blessing called Ben Moore while we drove from Radstock. He's already started the ball rolling. Peter Wright hasn't used his passport since he left Purton. Every copper in the UK will know his face by morning. Peter Wright is a wanted man."

"And Rogers, guv," asked Lydia.

"Retired to Wales. He's not our priority. Wright's a murderer."

"What about Clive Palmer, though, guv?" asked Neil.

"What would he have done with the coins he discovered? We'll never know for sure. His brother said Clive planned to tour the country following his passion. I prefer to think as an academic and a teacher; he would have declared them as treasure trove."

"How could Wright be sure the coin dealer wouldn't turn him in to the police?" asked Lydia.

"Wright had killed once," said Gus. "Not just a brutal attack, but a series of cool, calculating moves to divert attention from himself. Police never found the murder weapon. I suspect Wright carried it with him on Tuesday morning to Chilcompton. It might still be hidden at his house. We'll have to wait for news."

"What a day, guv," said Lydia.

"What a girl," said Gus, patting Blessing Umeh on the shoulder.

Epilogue

GUS LEFT the office at five o'clock. The team had spent the past ninety minutes updating their digital files while they awaited news from Purton.

"I suggest you get off home and enjoy the weekend," he'd told them.

His phone rang as he passed the brewery in the centre of Devizes. Whoever it was would have to wait until he reached the bungalow.

The missed call was from Geoff Mercer. Gus returned the call when he was sitting in the kitchen with a cup of coffee.

"Did they find anything on our list, Geoff?"

"And more," said Geoff. "We found two hardback books, two magazines, and an envelope addressed to James Palmer in a small suitcase in the loft. The metal detector was in a shed at the bottom of the garden. It was in plain sight, available for use by the current tenants if they wished. We found a receipt from a firm that last performed a service and repair on the equipment in 2012. Peter

Wright owned the metal detector, and Clive Palmer borrowed it."

"Most of Palmer's research was confined to books and magazines," said Gus. "He must have identified a likely location for this dowry he mentioned. If we questioned Ken Webb again, we might learn Wright discussed owning the detector with him and Palmer when they still socialised in The Volunteer."

"I doubt Palmer would have told anyone he was on the verge of finding a valuable hoard of Roman coins," said Geoff. "I prefer your suggestion that he followed Palmer to see what he was doing with his piece of kit."

"Did they find a knife?" asked Gus. "Something we could prove was the murder weapon?"

"Nothing that matched the wounds Palmer suffered," said Geoff.

"What was in the envelope?" asked Gus. "Can you open it, as it's addressed to Palmer's brother?"

"I called James," said Geoff, "and told him what we'd found. He asked me to send it to him after we'd finished with it."

"I'd like to see that envelope," said Gus.

"Of course," said Geoff. "I'll get the contents copied, and you can collect them on your way to work on Monday morning. I'll give you the gist of the contents now if you wish?"

"Go ahead."

"Clive Palmer prepared an article to submit to a world-famous academic journal that specialises in promoting Roman studies. It concerned a long-lost villa his research led him to believe had existed around thirty miles northwest of Littlecote Manor. If he was right, it was the largest villa ever discovered on mainland Britain. The family that lived there had to be extremely wealthy. They built the villa at the end of the second century, and it was in constant use during the fourth century. After the Romans left Britain, it fell into ruins. Palmer's enthusiasm in the letter accompanying his article springs off the page. He told James the site had been untouched since it collapsed fifteen hundred years ago. Its historical importance was enormous."

"It's easy to imagine Clive saw the discovery of this site as a type of redemption," said Gus. "He would have wanted the article to get published, and whatever he dug up would have been studied by experts for years. But, unfortunately, Peter Wright's greed prevented that."

"There are pages of detail in the article, Gus," said Geoff. "You can read it at your leisure."

"Was there any mention of a dowry?" asked Gus.

"Marriage in Roman times was an agreement between families," said Geoff. "Few Romans married for love, and while a man usually married in their mid-twenties, their brides were often still in their early teens. So instead, the bride's father gave a dowry or *dos*. According to Clive Palmer, the son of the wealthy landowner was called Paullus Gaius Tancinus. His bride-to-be, Antonia Minor, was fourteen years old. Her father, Caius Gratius Marcialis, bestowed a dowry to cover his second daughter's living expenses. Palmer's research showed that included land, jewellery, servants, and a leather pouch containing one hundred and eleven gold coins."

"One of the so-called angel numbers," said Gus, "often associated with luck, love, and spirituality."

"Maybe," said Geoff, "but the number is also a sign of a fresh start or new beginning. Palmer judged this as a warning from the Marcialis family. Paullus wasn't a bad lad, but his family had sailed close to the wind for decades. So much so that the authorities summoned the family back to Rome a week before the wedding. They left the villa at once."

"So, the wedding never took place?"

"Although Marcialis recovered most of the dowry, that leather pouch had been hidden in the villa and was never discovered."

"What might one hundred and eleven gold Roman coins be worth?" asked Gus.

"A conservative estimate would be four hundred thousand pounds today," said Geoff/

"What happened to the Tancinus family?"

"Clive Palmer hadn't followed that trail," said Geoff. "He was only interested in the villa and the historical value of pinpointing where it stood. He'd found the leather pouch among the shards of a stone jar on Sunday afternoon, thirty-six hours before he died."

"Did he say where?" asked Gus.

"Not the exact coordinates. The villa stood on the eastern boundaries of John Oatley's farm."

"Now we can answer the question on everyone's lips," said Gus. "Why Purton?"

"The research Palmer carried out in prison showed him roughly where to search. He asked John Oatley for permission to site his caravan in the farmyard, but we'd need to ask John whether he knew his tenant intended to spend his weekends with a metal detector on his land."

"The letter shows John Oatley was as much in the dark as the other villagers. Palmer knew news of potential treasure would attract the media attention he abhorred. His interest was purely academic."

"We have received no feedback on the hunt for Wright

so far," said Geoff. "Enjoy the weekend, and I'll see you first thing on Monday."

Sunday, 23 September 2018

POLICE ARRESTED Peter Wright in the small town of Montgomery in the Welsh Marches after a high-speed chase along the B4388. Wiltshire Police had sent officers to return him to Gablecross Police Station for questioning. They found a knife in the glove compartment of his BMW.

Gus Freeman was preparing a late breakfast when ACC Rebecca Gregory called him with the news. "That's wonderful," he said.

"While I'm on the phone, Gus," said Rebecca. "I met with Luke Sherman on Friday. He'll be with the team at Portishead next week. Sorry for the short notice. They were keen to get him involved. I hope it doesn't inconvenience your team too much."

"Will I ever get him back?" asked Gus.

"I wouldn't bank on it. Anyway, I must dash. Enjoy the rest of your weekend."

Suzie was standing in the doorway.

"That looks good," she said, eyeing the pan.

"The Lord giveth, and the Lord taketh away," said Gus. "First, Rebecca Gregory tells me they've arrested Wright in Wales. Then she adds that Luke won't be with us next week. We might have seen the last of him in the office. I've lost my appetite now."

Monday, 24 September 2018

GUS AND SUZIE left the bungalow together and drove in convoy to London Road. They trotted up the stairs to the administration area side by side.

"See you tonight, darling," said Suzie as she headed for her office on the left-hand side of the room.

Gus knocked on Geoff Mercer's door, entered the room, and bumped into Amazing Grace.

"DI Packenham, fancy meeting you here."

Grace glared at him and swept from the room. The sound of Geoff's old office door slamming echoed around the mezzanine.

"I was just updating Grace on Luke Sherman's situation," said Geoff. "Here's a copy of everything inside the envelope Clive Palmer left for his brother. Kenneth wants to know when you'll have the Palmer files completed. Of course, he's not expecting you to work miracles. But he hopes you can bring the files here tomorrow at noon. After that, we'll have a working lunch, and he can outline your next case."

"I think we can manage that," said Gus. "Anything else?"

"As Luke is unlikely to return to the CRT office, we need to find a permanent replacement. Kenneth pointed out the budget restrictions we're operating under and suggested I found a temporary solution until the New Year."

"Was there nobody except Amazing Grace?" pleaded Gus.

"It's only for three months," said Geoff.

"The New Year," said Gus. "How sweet the sound."

Next in The Freeman Files series

vinci-books.com/onetruefriend

A cryptic phone call, a mother's disappearance, and a detective's relentless pursuit of justice.

Found lifeless in her car at a scenic location, Katherine's sudden disappearance after an urgent late-night call leaves a trail of unanswered questions. As Freeman and his team dig deeper into the flawed initial investigation, they encounter tight-lipped witnesses that only compound the enigma.

Turn the page for a free preview…

One True Friend: Chapter One

Tuesday, 25 September 2018

"Will everything be ready for me to leave at eleven-thirty?" asked Gus.

"No problem, guv," said Alex. "We've added the finishing touches this morning."

Gus Freeman had been at London Road yesterday when news came through to the Old Police Station office that Oliver Rogers had been arrested at his sister's house in Mold, near Chester. The retired rare coin collector from Stratton-on-the-Fosse had moved to the village in North Wales in February 2017.

Peter Wright had insisted Rogers continue the two-mile commute from home to the lock-up on the industrial estate at Chilcompton until the right buyer could be identified for the one hundred and eleven Roman coins.

Oliver Rogers told police he had feared for his life. He hadn't agreed to broker a deal until Wright threatened him with a knife. His first instinct was to inform the authorities.

All finds of that nature should be reported. Rogers was well aware treasure recovered from underneath the earth belonged to the Crown, where the rightful owner couldn't be determined.

Gus took Rogers's claim with a pinch of salt. DI Gareth Francis contacted the office yesterday afternoon to tell Alex the pair's financials showed they split the money fifty-fifty.

"Rogers had one-hundred and eighty thousand reasons not to complain," Neil Davis had said when Alex told the others the news.

"If Wright could have cut out the middleman, he would have taken the full amount without a second thought," said Lydia. "They both deserve everything they get."

"Oliver Rogers should get five years," said Gus.

"What about Peter Wright, guv?" asked Blessing.

"I would hope for a mandatory life sentence."

"Do we deserve a celebratory drink this Friday, guv?" asked Neil.

"What have we got to celebrate, Neil?" asked Gus.

"We put the lid on our contribution to the Stan Jones case," said Neil. "Then we found evidence to nail Ralph Gibbons for murder. After that, Blessing helped make it a hat trick by unmasking Peter Wright as Clive Palmer's killer. I thought that was a decent return for ten days' work."

"It's what the public expects from us, Neil," said Gus.

"Come on, Neil," said Alex. "Surely you can see why Gus isn't enthusiastic. Its odds on Luke has left us for good, and for the next three months, we've got DI Packenham in the office."

"We don't need to invite her," said Neil. "Let's call it a farewell drink for Luke instead. We can't let him go without marking the occasion."

"I can live with that," said Gus. "Grace doesn't start

until next Monday. DS Mercer told me she had to finish her report on the administration set up at London Road first."

"The Waggon & Horses at nine o'clock," said Neil. "Melody will appreciate a night out. She's looking forward to comparing notes with Suzie Ferris."

"I'll give Luke a call," said Lydia. "He might want to invite a new friend."

"The more, the merrier," said Alex.

Gus hoped there would be other topics of conversation on offer than pregnancies and failed relationships. These social occasions were designed to allow the team to discuss something other than work, but there were limits. For example, sometimes he wished he were interested in sports like Neil.

Forty minutes before his midday meeting with the Chief Constable, Gus collected the relevant file folders and headed for the lift. As he drove towards Devizes, he spotted two council workers. One stood on the fourth step of a six-foot ladder, and the other watched his colleague from the safety of the pavement. Both wore ubiquitous yellow hi-viz jackets and hard hats. Gus couldn't imagine what they did that needed such elaborate precautions.

The usual delays frustrated Gus on his daily trips between home and work and journeys in between. Temporary traffic lights for non-existent road workers, mothers on the school run who couldn't walk their children half a mile to school, and the constant threat of a waste collection vehicle slowing progress to a crawl.

Somehow, he parked the Focus in the visitor's car park at London Road, negotiated Reception, and scaled the stairs to the administration area before the appointed time.

"Good morning, Gus," said Vera Butler. "How's the patient?"

"Suzie, or Bert Penman?" asked Gus.

"Suzie's fine, isn't she?" asked Vera.

"No problems, so far," said Gus. "As for Bert, Irene North is looking after him at home. I've not heard any complaints from Bert about his new walking stick either, so that's good."

"We heard the news about Luke Sherman's temporary replacement," said Vera. "Do you think you'll survive until the New Year?"

"There will be a period of change," said Gus. "but I'm sure Ms Packenham will cope. Geoff keeps insisting she's an excellent officer."

Vera smiled. If Grace thought she would get Gus to change his ways, she had another think coming.

"Kenneth's door's opening," she said. "He's wondering where you are."

"We're getting together at the Waggon & Horses on Friday night," said Gus. "You're welcome to drop in if you're free. It's a farewell drink for Luke."

"We might just do that," said Vera.

"Are you still seeing Rick Chalmers?"

"Heaven's, no. That was a one-off. Divya Yadav's husband, Arjun, has to work nights from time to time, and she hates being alone in the house. So we've started meeting two or three nights a week when Arjun's turn comes around."

"Friday, then," said Gus, crossing the mezzanine to the Chief Constable's office.

Gus tapped on the door and entered. Kenneth Truelove and Geoff Mercer were waiting.

"Time's short, Freeman," said Kenneth. "Is that the Palmer file?"

"Done and dusted, sir," said Gus, handing Kenneth the folder.

"Peter Wright played on Clive Palmer's past," said Geoff, "ably supported by that builder, Tom Angell. But, in the end, the case centred on pure greed. Wright suspected Palmer was searching for something valuable after his work-mate borrowed his metal detector. So he followed Palmer, watched him retrieve something from John Oatley's land on Sunday afternoon, and killed Palmer the following night."

"Ben Moore couldn't see beyond the murder being related to the reason Palmer went to prison," said Gus. "He spent too much time on that facet of the case and ran out of time. Blessing cut to the chase and realised Palmer's killer lived in Purton during the ten months he was there and knew him well."

"That reduced the field of runners to less than ten," said Geoff.

"I don't suppose those rare coins will ever surface again?" asked Kenneth.

"Not a chance, sir," said Gus. "One unscrupulous collector may have them hidden away, but my guess is whoever bought them from Wright and Rogers sold them on, at a profit, to several unsuspecting buyers. Then, when the case gets to court, the odd collector might wonder whether what he purchased was part of the Purton dowry hoard."

"Do you think they would come forward?" asked Geoff.

"Don't hold your breath," said Kenneth.

"Thanks to Blessing's intuitive approach, we wrapped this one up far quicker than I imagined," said Gus.

"Do you know what the PCC complained about the other morning?" said the Chief Constable. "He said if your team was to continue solving these cases in double-quick time, it could reflect badly on other detective teams around the county."

"You must remind the PCC that we have a distinct advantage, sir," said Gus. "First, the original investigating team has covered the groundwork. We don't have to attend a murder scene, identify a victim, and determine the cause of death. We're not waiting days for forensics, identifying potential witnesses, suspects, and so forth because that's laid out in the murder book. Second, apart from last week, when we were tying up loose ends on other cases, we have one unsolved murder to concentrate on at a time and nothing else."

"Exactly, sir," said Geoff Mercer, "The only time I can remember having one case to handle was on my first day as a DC. Then I went for a coffee, and my DS sneaked a couple more into my in-tray while my back was turned. The detective squad at Gablecross runs between ten and fifteen separate investigations per officer at any time. Sometimes they get a good run and reduce the load. Sometimes nothing works, they can't make headway, and the numbers build up. But, unfortunately, the entire squad still has to drop everything for a major incident."

"I haven't forgotten what it was like at the sharp end, Mercer," said Kenneth.

"Sorry, sir," said Geoff.

"Apology accepted," said Kenneth. "Things have changed. We didn't have the PCC whispering in our ears about budgets, targets, diversity, and the role of the police in society."

"The good old days," said Geoff.

"When dinosaurs ruled," said Gus. "Are you suggesting we change our approach, sir?"

"Don't you dare," said Kenneth. "I want these files in

my drawer sorted before I retire. The next case I have for you has been with us for far too long. The murder of Katherine Alford? Does that ring a bell with either of you?"

"Did Trefor Davies run that investigation, sir?" asked Geoff.

"Wayne Barnett was a DI at Marlborough Police Station at the time," said Kenneth. "Trefor had a watching brief because Barnett's first murder was the Alford case. DS Anna Cromwell was Barnett's sidekick."

"She's an ACC in Dorset now, isn't she?" asked Gus.

"Have you crossed swords with her, Freeman?" asked the Chief Constable.

"The Katherine Alford murder was ten years ago, sir. It's one of those that sticks in your memory. A nasty business with no resolution. I found it best to keep out of the way of officers like Anna Cromwell on their fast track to the top. She soon left Wayne Barnett and her superiors at Marlborough in her wake. Rumours started early doors. Anna Cromwell trampled on anyone who disrupted her race to the summit. Therefore, I made a mental note and steered clear."

"It might be an idea to let DI Packenham drive to Dorchester to speak to her, sir," said Geoff. "They'll talk the same language."

"And Freeman can't say something leading to me getting earache from her Chief Constable," said Kenneth. "I like your way of thinking, Mercer."

"I've dealt with DCI Trefor Davies in the past, sir," said Gus. "He's a good sort. I don't foresee any problem with the crew at Marlborough. Can you run me through the details of the case again; to refresh my memory?"

"Katherine was a devoted mother of two, divorced and living in a semi-detached house on the Purlyn Acre estate with her ten-year-old son, Paul. Her twenty-four-year-old daughter, Emily, lived on the other side of town in West Manton. Emily was a single mother with a six-year-old daughter, Sophia. On Saturday, the twenty-eighth of June in 2008, Katherine was at home watching television. Paul was in bed, asleep. Katherine received a phone call at around half-past nine. The identity of the caller was never determined. Whoever it was, and whatever they said to Katherine, it was enough to get her to run next door to her neighbour, Lily Faulkner. Lily, fifty-six, agreed to return to the house and babysit. Katherine told Lily she'd be gone for ten minutes."

"That was the last time anyone saw Katherine Alford alive," said Geoff.

"Apart from whoever she met that night," said Gus. "Where did she go, anyway? How did she get there? Someone must have seen her."

"It was the last confirmed sighting of Katherine," said Kenneth. "She drove off in her red, ten-year-old Peugeot 306 at nine forty-five."

"I remember now," said Geoff. "The Peugeot was spotted the following morning at seven o'clock. A husband and wife from Clench Common, cycling along the A346, turned off past the caravan site and intended to follow the road to join the A4 Bath Road. Instead, they stopped at the West Woods car park. It's an ancient woodland site littered with walking trails to the south of town. There's a carpet of bluebells in springtime that attracts thousands of visitors, but late on Saturday evenings, it was popular with courting couples seeking privacy. As a deterrent, it was a regular occurrence for Marlborough police to send a car to the site. When DI Barnett checked with uniformed officers, he learned a patrol car had cruised the parking lot at

twenty minutes to eleven that night. The place was
empty."

"Who spotted the car?" asked Gus.

"Dominic and Amy Gray," said Kenneth. "Kitted out in
fluorescent lycra and helmets. Unfortunately, their early
Sunday morning ride to Bath and back was scuppered by a
dead body."

"Why did they stop?" asked Gus.

"The husband was annoyed," said Kenneth. "He
thought someone had abandoned the car."

"It was only ten years old," said Gus. "I would argue it
was only just a run-in."

"Katherine Alford was inside the car slumped over the
steering wheel," said Kenneth. "Dominic Gray told police
she showed signs of strangulation."

"He watches cop shows on TV, I suppose?" said Gus.

"Dominic Gray's a doctor at Savernake Hospital, Freeman," said Kenneth. "Katherine was fully clothed, and
although there were signs of a struggle, there were no
apparent signs of robbery or a sexual attack. The post-
mortem confirmed that Doctor Gray's observations had
been correct."

"Was anything found at the scene?" asked Gus.

"Such as?" asked Geoff.

"A ligature, a cord, something of that nature. Or was it
manual strangulation?"

"Police found nothing unexpected inside the car," said
Kenneth. "Katherine left home in a hurry. She took her car
keys and nothing else. There was no weapon, no evidence
left behind by her assailant. Nevertheless, news of the
murder shocked and scared the local community. Neighbours from the Purlyn Acre estate were eager to help in the
police investigation. Nobody enjoys having a savage

murderer on the loose. The residents of Clench Common also expressed concerns."

"Are you having second thoughts over your idyllic country cottage, Geoff?" asked Gus.

"I didn't mention the murder to Christine when she told me she had her heart set on Clench Common. We had looked at over a dozen places that didn't meet her approval. It was ten years ago, and West Woods is two miles from our cottage."

"What progress have you made, Mercer?" asked Kenneth.

"I put our place on the market in early August, sir. We've had several viewings, and the estate agent reckons we'll have no problem getting the price we're asking."

"They always do, Mercer," said Kenneth. "Is the cottage vacant?"

"No, but they are further along with the selling process, and I might go cap in hand to the bank manager for a bridging loan in a few weeks."

"You've got this to come, sir," said Gus.

"Don't remind me, Freeman," said Kenneth. "There's a lot to be said for finding a good place to live and staying put until they carry you out in a box. Moving house has to be one of the most stressful things anyone has to endure."

"Apart from having your mother murdered," said Gus. "How did Emily and Paul Alford handle the following months and years? Did the ex-husband step into the breach?"

"Not a bit," said Kenneth. "Katherine had reverted to her maiden name after the divorce. The ex-husband, Daniel Matravers, was forty-six and lived in Salisbury. He'd moved on. Paul went to live with his sister, Emily, in West Manton."

"Is everyone you've mentioned still alive and at the same address?" asked Gus.

Kenneth checked the murder file.

"There's nothing here to suggest either of the older witnesses has passed. Lily Faulkner hasn't moved from her semi-detached house in Purlyn Acre. She's had the same neighbours since Katherine Alford's murder. Bert Harris was walking home when he saw Katherine's red Peugeot. Harris was sixty-four back then and lived on the same estate."

"What time did Bert Harris say he saw the car?" asked Gus.

"Harris said he left home at half-past ten with the dog. He was halfway home from Coldharbour Lane when the car passed him. He told police it was his usual twenty-minute circuit with the dog."

"So, Katherine left home at nine forty-five in her car and was still driving at around a quarter to eleven," said Gus. "Where had she been? Was she alone in the car? Which direction was she heading?"

"Patience is a virtue, Freeman," said Kenneth. "DI Barnett's enquiries produced one possible sighting of interest. Witnesses came forward to say a woman matching Katherine's description was seen with a man outside The Roebuck public house at around half-past ten that Saturday night."

"That's a five-minute drive from her home," said Geoff, checking the details on his phone. "If that was Katherine, then the man could have been responsible for the phone call that caused her to drop everything to meet him."

"True," said Gus, "but Katherine told Lily Faulkner she'd be gone for ten minutes. Was Katherine with the same man for forty minutes before arriving at the pub? Or was it someone else? Did she meet another person there who persuaded her to extend her stay?"

"DS Cromwell interviewed Belinda Franklin, a barmaid at The Roebuck," said Kenneth. "The twenty-one-year-old told Cromwell she was busy serving drinks all night. Cromwell showed Belinda a victim's photograph, but she wasn't sure she'd seen the woman before. The other witnesses were Charlotte Ovens and Jasmine Park. Both ladies were in their early thirties and engaged to be married."

"Did they describe the man they saw outside the pub?" asked Gus.

"A vague description," said Kenneth. "The man wore casual clothes. He was of a similar height and build to Katherine Alford. Neither girl noticed any distinguishing features, such as rings, tattoos, or glasses. He had his back to them throughout."

"They were on a night out," said Geoff. "No doubt they'd had a few drinks. The last thing they thought of doing was taking note of a random couple in case the police needed to identify a potential killer."

"Yet they remembered that couple talking outside the pub and came forward without being sought out," said Gus. "Why did they remember them? Were they arguing and drawing attention to themselves? Was the man stopping the woman from leaving? Did Barnett and Cromwell get answers to these questions?"

"You know the drill, Freeman," said Kenneth. "Many answers will be in this murder file if you dig deep enough. I'm just giving you the headlines. Then, your team can ask questions not answered to your satisfaction when you speak to the detectives involved."

"From what I've heard so far, I'm struggling to find a

clear motive for Katherine's murder, sir," said Gus. "To add to our woes, police found no forensic evidence from the killer in the Peugeot. The murder took place in June. What do casual clothes suggest at that time of year?"

"Shorts and a t-shirt?" said Geoff. "Although, if her companion was older than Katherine, he might choose a short-sleeved shirt and slacks."

"If he strangled her with his bare hands," said Gus, "surely, he would have left prints somewhere inside the car, showing signs of a struggle."

"Nothing collected by forensics matched anything on record," said Kenneth. "The post-mortem report showed the killer wore light cotton gloves."

"Did those ladies at The Roebuck notice if he was wearing gloves at half-past ten?" asked Gus. "Or perhaps they were tucked into his back pocket, ready for later."

"We don't know whether the killer and this man are connected," said Geoff. "It might not have been Katherine, anyway."

"If I can add another question to the list," said Kenneth. "How did the killer get home from West Woods?"

"We don't know if anyone was in the car with Katherine when Bert Harris saw her drive past," said Geoff.

"We can visit the housing estate and the surrounding roads," said Gus. "I can't visualise the layout. Marlborough isn't a town I know well. But look, if Charlotte and Jasmine got the time right, and the victim was at The Roebuck, then Bert Harris would have seen a passenger in the Peugeot."

"Katherine and her companion must have left within minutes and driven towards her home," said Geoff, consulting the map on his phone.

"They were a fair distance from West Woods at twenty to eleven when the patrol car did its regular check," said

Gus. "I wonder which way the officers approached the car park and which road they took when they left?"

"The patrol wasn't looking for the Peugeot in particular," said Geoff.

"They would have had dashcams fitted a decade ago," said Gus. "I hope DI Barnett checked the footage to see whether the Peugeot appeared. It might give a more accurate time for the car arriving at the West Woods car park."

"Bert Harris's sighting puts them on the road leading back to Purlyn Acre," said Geoff. "Why change direction and head into the country, especially since Katherine had told her neighbour she wouldn't be ten minutes. She was driving, not her companion."

"Which suggests she went with the man willingly," said Gus. "Look, if you had a phone call late at night from a stranger or even a casual acquaintance, would you drop everything and go to meet them?"

"Not likely, so Katherine knew the man well," said Geoff. "But the police questioned her friends and family members, and they had alibis. None of them had a motive."

"Barnett and Cromwell were hunting for a mystery man," said Kenneth. "Someone Katherine trusted but who was unknown to her family and friends."

"No wonder they had trouble finding him," said Geoff.

"So, at around a quarter to eleven, Katherine was driving between Coldharbour Lane and home," said Gus. "How long would it have taken her to drive to West Woods?"

"Fifteen minutes," said Geoff. "Quicker on a Saturday night."

"There couldn't have been an argument at that stage," said Kenneth. "Katherine wouldn't have agreed to drive into the countryside if there had, surely?"

"So, they arrived at West Woods car park at eleven o'clock," said Gus. "Forensics found no signs of sexual activity. Katherine wore whatever clothing she had on when she left the house."

"A short-sleeved, off-white shift dress and a pair of strappy sandals," said Kenneth. "That was Lily Faulkner's description."

"What did the post-mortem report record as the probable time of death?" asked Gus.

"Between midnight and one o'clock," said Kenneth. "West Woods is an isolated spot. The killer could have chosen it because he hoped for something other than a chat."

"They had a lot to chat about if Katherine didn't die until midnight," said Gus. "Something sparked a violent argument which resulted in murder."

"What about the cotton gloves?" asked Geoff. "Are we saying her companion planned to kill her all along?"

"They're not a common item for a chap to carry on a Saturday night out," said Gus, "unless he's a snooker referee."

"Hang on," said Kenneth, "we don't know where this man was before he called Katherine. Perhaps he was at work, and she picked him up and drove him to The Roebuck for a drink and a brief chat. But, on the other hand, maybe they didn't bother with a drink, just stood outside the pub and talked."

"Belinda Franklin couldn't swear either person was ever inside The Roebuck," said Geoff.

"Nobody heard a heated argument lasting for up to sixty minutes in West Woods either," said Gus.

"No witnesses came forward to say they heard screams or sounds of a struggle at the murder scene," said Kenneth.

"The killer chose West Woods because they knew they were unlikely to be disturbed."

"Which adds further evidence that the killer was local," said Gus. "How long had Katherine lived in Marlborough?"

"She was born there," said Kenneth. "Matravers moved to Marlborough from Salisbury to work. They met in 1982, married the following year, and divorced when Paul was two years old in 2000."

"Katherine would have known the area was frequented by courting couples," said Geoff. "Why go there otherwise at that time of night?"

"Forget that for a minute, Geoff," said Gus. "Why did they divorce, sir?"

"Irreconcilable differences," said Kenneth.

"That sounds a cop-out," said Gus. "More likely to be how Katherine explained things to her teenage daughter, Emily. We'll ask Daniel Matravers for the truth."

"As much as I enjoy these get-togethers," said Kenneth, "the PCC demands my presence in his well-appointed office in an hour. So I can rely on you to do your best with the material at your disposal, Freeman; whoever is working with you will help sort out this mystery in short order."

"Has Rick Chalmer's future been determined, sir?" asked Gus.

"I suppose you would have preferred to see Chalmers in your office for the next three months?"

"He's a detective sergeant with bags of experience," said Gus. "Although Geoff keeps telling me what an outstanding officer Ms Packenham is, I haven't seen her track record on murder investigations."

"Grace was involved in the latter stages of the Stan Jones case," said Kenneth.

"I think DS Davis would say her contribution was

minimal at best," said Gus. "Much like a football team introducing a substitute in added time to run down the clock."

"Unlike you to use a sporting analogy, Gus," said Geoff. "You're right about Grace, though; she hasn't worked on a murder investigation."

"We don't get that many in the county, thank goodness," said Kenneth.

Gus looked at the folder on the Chief Constable's desk and thought that if they were all as puzzling as this one, it was just as well.

Grab your copy...
vinci-books.com/onetruefriend

About the Author

Ted Tayler is the international bestselling indie author of The Freeman Files and The Phoenix series. Ted lives in the English west country, where his stories are based. He was born in 1945 and has been married to Lynne since 1971. They have three children and four grandchildren.

His thought-provoking mysteries appeal to readers of Sally Rigby, Joy Ellis, Pauline Rowson, and Faith Martin. His action-packed thrillers are a must for fans of Mark Dawson and J. C. Ryan.

Gus Freeman's cold case investigations are carried out with reasoned deduction rather than bursts of frantic action. In each of the twenty-four books, unsolved murder is accompanied by romance, humor, and country life. The core message in the twelve Phoenix novels is that criminals should pay for their crimes. Unfortunately, the current system fails to deliver the correct punishment, so Phoenix helps redress the balance.

Acknowledgments

The love and support of my family; without them, this would have been impossible.

,